I0620285

HOT GIRLS IN TROUBLE

CHRISTINE GWICK

Copyright © 2015 The Good Word

All rights reserved.

ISBN: 978-1-928076-05-6
ISBN-10: 192807605X

FOR MY OWN
HOT GIRL IN TROUBLE:
T.L.G., #82624-083

MAY IT PASS QUICKLY

THIS IS A WORK OF FICTION. NAMES, PLACES, CHARACTERS, INCIDENTS AND EVENTS ARE WHOLLY THE PRODUCTS OF-13 THE AUTHOR'S IMAGINATION OR USED IN A FICTITIOUS MANNER. ANY RESEMBLANCE TO ACTUAL PERSONS, LIVING OR DEAD, OR ACTUAL EVENTS IS PURELY COINCIDENTAL.

CHAPTER 1

JAYCEE SHEEDY SITS at the wheel of the mauve Lexus, enjoying the quiet hum of its engine and not thinking about anything in particular. She is good at spacing out and going to her special place, and she is good at driving all manner of motor vehicles. *Very* good.

Right now, since she's gone off to her special place, she's not thinking much about the fact that she is two years too young to drive a car legally. She also isn't paying much attention to what her friend Maria meant by, "I'm going to the Apple Store to pick up a few things."

The Apple Store closed three hours ago.

Jaycee is definitely *not* paying much attention to the paunchy older guy running behind her; the guy who's yelling, "Stop! That's my car! I'm calling the cops!"

She steps on the gas and zooms away from the sweating, red-faced guy. Cars are way too much fun, she thinks. No wonder guys love them so much. They're the best toys around, cars. Guys can be fun toys, too.

Soon she reaches the Apple Store. She breathes through her nose and smiles at the new-car smell of fine leather. Once you've driven one of these high-end vehicles, you'll never be happy with anything less.

Jaycee scans the store but can't see Maria or anyone else and the joint is dark. She taps the horn, likes its big, masculine honk, and sees Maria now in the store window, waving her away like a baseball coach urging a runner to try for home. She races around the corner and waits.

Maria—there's someone Jaycee should try hard *not* to think about. The two girls are partners in crime for now, seeing if their association will benefit them both. Maria wants this Lexus to go into a nearby chop shop where the guys will strip it down to nothing and sell off its parts. Jaycee sneers down at the ignition, which has been ripped out, and its wires and dangling like red, white and blue spaghetti. It's a bad deal when you've just stolen a car and already its owner is calling the police on his cell phone. Maria and her friends think they're such clever criminals, but Jaycee thinks they're fools who will soon be busted and locked up.

She drives around and around, loving how this big beautiful car performs. She'd love to win a lottery and buy all the cars and other fancy gadgets she desires.

But now there's trouble. She spots the car's owner, who's freaking out in front of a traffic cop. The cop steps out into the street and holds out his hand for Jaycee to stop, but she doesn't, and the cop jumps out of her way just in time. But she glances in the rearview mirror and sees the cop on his radio: "Stolen Lexus, late-model, mauve, license plate blah, blah, blah."

Jaycee's not smiling as she passes the Apple Store. Maria and two other girls, arms full of iPods and iPads, rush out of the store. The driver stops, the thieves jump in with their loot and the Lexus roars off.

Maria glowers at her. "Jaycee, we were done two minutes ago! Where were you? What's your problem?"

Jaycee says nothing, especially about the traffic cop who's told all the other cops about the stolen Lexus. She drives as fast as possible the wrong way up a one-way street, missing oncoming vehicles by inches. She tries hard not to think about the Lexus she's just ripped off and the big plans Maria has for them. Maria has admired and respected Jaycee's driving ability ever since that day several years ago when they stole a Porsche that was idling while its driver went inside a store for two minutes. Jaycee drove it three or four miles, weaving in and out of traffic the whole time, till they reached big, beautiful Northup University. They left the vehicle there, and ever since, Maria has wanted them to steal Porsches, Beemers, Mercedes and Volvos and Honda Accords because the chop-shop owners pay big bucks for those kinds of cars.

Maria and the two other girls are cutting up the loot, bickering only the way girls can, when Jaycee hears the sirens and sees the flashing lights.

Maria yells, "The pigs, Jaycee! Faster!"

The driver gets it up to seventy-five, dodging other cars, using the sidewalk as a lane and doing just fine. Soon she reaches a public parkade and drives in, snatching a ticket from the dispenser. She zips up past one row of parked cars after another as adeptly as a Hollywood stunt driver. Soon she finds the exit and drives right through the yellow-and-black wooden barricade, reducing it to a thousand shards of wood.

She keeps her foot on the accelerator, unsure of where she's going or if the cops are still following her.

Immediately she's back in city traffic, racing past other cars and ignoring the blasts of horns, and when she spots a corner store she jerks the Lexus onto the side street.

That is the beginning of the end.

A young mother, pushing a baby stroller, steps out onto the street and Jaycee, in a blind panic, steers past her but cannot regain control of the big car. It ends up on the sidewalk, and the passenger's half hits a pile of trash. Jaycee tries to right the big beast but it stays half in the air until it topples over. She hears the sirens again and closes her eyes.

CHAPTER 2

JAYCEE PULLS AT her shoulder-length blonde hair as she opens the clothes dryer and withdraws an armload of orange jumpsuits.

"Yuck," she says, stepping away from the blast of hot air that burns her skin and saps the moisture from her mouth and nose. The jumpsuits feel as dry as sandpaper. She would give anything for an ice-cold Mountain Dew.

The oversized washer and dryer in the Michael Milgrom Juvenile Correction Center hulk over her, showing no mercy or empathy.

"*Orange Is the New Black*" was never like this," she mutters. It has taken all her strength not to cry, and she feels proud to have remained dry-eyed since day one, as horrified as she was when they marched her in for the very first time. She took one look at the tall stone walls with their concertina wire and felt her insides cave in. The only comfort she found was the knowledge that Maria had ended up in some adult facility which was surely far worse than Milgrom.

Don't sweat it, girl. This will be easy time. Maria's doing hard time.

Well, Jaycee assures herself, that's Maria's problem, not mine. That whole day of stealing a car and breaking into the Apple Store? All Maria's idea, and all Maria's fault. Jaycee often flashes back to waking up in the overturned Lexus as the cops or firefighters pulled her out. They kept asking her if she was OK, and once they concluded that she was merely shaken up, they cuffed her and stuffed her into the police car. They charged her with grand theft auto, accessory to a felony and driving without a license.

Even John Gotti was never in so much trouble, she told herself.

Maria's mother was heartbroken, and Jaycee's wasn't altogether thrilled, either. At her hearing, Jaycee was represented by a nerdy young public defender in a rumpled suit. Jaycee blamed everything on Maria, and her lawyer just frowned, as if he had already met his share of Jaycees and Marias and was pleased to know that this particular young female offender would be locked up for a little while.

Jaycee stands in front of the tableful of jumpsuits and thinks of Mountain Dew while the clothing cools off enough for her to begin folding it. Within two minutes, she has to wipe the sweat off her face as she painstakingly matches arm to arm and leg to leg. She reminds herself that laundry duty in this place is considered one of the better jobs. Bathroom duty is infinitely worse. Agriculture duty leaves the girls with sore backs, and kitchen duty fills their nostrils with rancid grease and makes them not want to eat.

They jump her so fast that she literally does not see them coming. They hold her still, pull her jumpsuit down to her ankles, yank her undies down and beat her buttocks with a bar of soap.

"Hey, precious, welcome to Milgrom," one of the

girls says as another whacks Jaycee. The soap feels like a fist. Jaycee, meaning to scream, lets out a tiny whimper instead. She's been dreading this encounter since she got here.

The beating continues, and Jaycee imagines big purple bruises on her heart-shaped, blonde butt. But then the torture stops and she hears the girls run off. Opening her eyes, she sees the formidable figure of Miz Creelman, the boss of this place.

"Sheedy! Why are you standing there with your clothes off? That's an infraction. I'll have to write you up." At Milgrom, if you're stupid enough to let the other girls victimize you, it's nobody's fault but your own.

Jaycee knows better than to explain what's just happened to her. Miz Creelman will want names, and Jaycee, like most other reasonably sophisticated criminals, is no snitch. Report your tormentors to the boss and they'll be back to knock every tooth out of your skull.

"Won't happen again, ma'am," Jaycee says.

"There's someone here to see you."

The big woman escorts Jaycee through one corridor after another as Jaycee tries to figure out who her visitor might be. Also, why is their meeting going to happen in the office rather than the visiting room. After hours, too. This is *not* the way they usually do things at Milgrom. Jaycee doesn't know if she should be thrilled or terrified.

At the security gate, they wait till the guard buzzes them in and searches Jaycee. She has no weapons, so she and Miz Creelman continue on their journey until they come upon an office with an open door.

Inside sits a woman Jaycee does not recognize.

The woman stands and asks, without offering a handshake, "Are you Joanna Christine Sheedy?"

"I go by 'Jaycee.'"

"All right. Sit down."

Jaycee nods and sits, wincing from her badly bruised bottom and not much liking this meeting so far, though she can't say why.

The woman says to Creelman, "Thanks for your help. We'll be fine."

Creelman frowns. "Maybe I should sit in with you."

"We'll be OK," says the woman. "Please close the door behind you."

Creelman shakes her head and stays put. The boss lady is not about to be kicked out of her own office.

Jaycee checks out her visitor. She's about thirty-five, with short dark hair and big, bright eyes. Her lips seem curved into a permanent smile. If this woman is a social workers or something, Jaycee thinks, she must have a reputation for being the biggest softie around.

"My name," the woman says, "is Allison Sullings."

Jaycee nods that she understands. She looks at Allison Sullings, who looks back at her. Several moments of silence pass between them.

"I'm the coordinator of the alternative-living program you've probably heard about." Sullings arches her eyebrows; Jaycee shrugs to indicate she has heard nothing of the kind.

"You are a candidate for our facility," says Sullings.

Jaycee has never paid much attention to jails or other places where they put teenaged girls like Jaycee Sheedy whenever such people get caught. This particular lawbreaker still believes that crime does pay when done properly; she just wants to do her time and start beating the bricks again.

Sullings looks over at Creelman, her face not so happy anymore. "Do you know how much trouble I've gone to in order to get this program happening? And she"—the visitor points at Jaycee—"doesn't even know it exists! She doesn't know she's being considered for a bed!"

Creelman crosses her arms. "I really don't know why she wasn't made aware of it."

Sullings says, "Jaycee, how would you like to leave Milgrom immediately?"

Jaycee thinks this lady with the kind smile really can get her out of this godforsaken place. Once out, Jaycee will ditch her and get back to the busywork of stealing cars and making money. "Right now? With you?"

Sullings nods. "I've gotten a Fresh Start grant from the Johnson Foundation to begin a residential program for girls in the juvenile justice system."

"A halfway house."

Sullings smiles. "Well, yes. Here's the deal: You live with me and two other girls in an apartment. You go to school, receive counseling sessions and do community service. You work hard and stay out of trouble. It's not easy, but nothing worthwhile ever is. Also, it's a way out of Milgrom. You've been here only two months and I can see how much you hate it already. I noticed you sat down gingerly; have the other girls beaten you recently? That's common here." Then, "If you leave with me now and do good time, you'll be free soon. If you do bad time, I'll send you back here to Milgrom."

Jaycee maintains a poker face, but her brain is

speeding along, wondering if this woman is as big a fool as she seems to be. For a kid who has always prided herself on being fearless, Jaycee has been very much afraid of the Milgrom bullies for the past two months. Now this Sullings lady has offered her an escape. Only an idiot would say no.

"What if I refuse?" she says. "Why don't you just choose someone else? What makes *me* so special?"

Sullings actually chuckles. "Do you know what I see? I see a scared teenaged girl who's been intimidated and harassed for the past two months. Your rear end is probably black and blue from that beating, and the other girls are waiting to rough you up again. The reason we're offering you a bed in Fresh Start is that we believe you're more intelligent and sensitive than so many other adolescent female offenders. In other words, there is much more hope for you, and we want to invest our resources in the girls who stand the best chances of becoming decent, law-abiding women. So, how about it?"

CHAPTER 3

AND I THOUGHT Milgrom was bad, Jaycee thinks as she and Sullings drive up to the Abbotsford Correctional Center for Girls, a place that looks as menacing as the footage of San Quentin she's seen online.

"Unreal," says Sullings, shaking her head. "They've got a fifteen-year-old girl in there. Fifteen! I'm here to get her out."

Jaycee, still freaked out by being attacked in the laundry room, rubs her sore backside.

"Don't sweat it," Sullings tells her. "You're not going in, *I* am. You can wait in the car."

"Tell me again why we're here."

"So I can go in there and see if she wants to live with us in Fresh Start," Sullings says as she gets out of the car. "Nothing personal," she says as she handcuffs Jaycee to the steering wheel. "I can just imagine what kind of shape this girl is in after nearly a year and half in this place."

Sullings passes through the series of security checkpoints before ending up in a bare room where she is supposed to meet the inmate. Nearly half an hour later, she looks up to see a woman/child, nearly six feet tall, enter the room in shackles, accompanied by two guards.

Whitney Houston, Allison Sullings thinks. *They've brought me a fifteen-year-old Whitney Houston, only taller.*

The girl is named Santana Perez, and she keeps yawning. Sullings cannot find any trace of fear in the girl's face or posture, even though it is hardly a secret how much Abbotsford inmates fight.

"How about taking off her shackles?" Sullings asks the guard.

"Negative, ma'am. They have to stay on."

"But she's just a fifteen-year-old!"

"She's been convicted of manslaughter."

Sullings looks at Santana. "Is that so? Did you really kill someone?"

Santana gives her a little shrug. "Got in a fight. I hit him. He went down but didn't get back up."

"It happened at Northup University," the guard says.

Santana nods. "Pep rally. Guy was dissin' our school, sayin' it waren't no good. So I hit him."

Sullings says, "Santana, do you know who I am? Why I'm here?"

"You the lady that wants me to come live with her?"

"Yes."

Santana shakes her head. "Wish I could. But I have to stay locked up here till the Man says different."

"Well," Sullings tells her, "I am 'the Man.'"

Santana brightens up a bit. "For real?"

"Yeah. You want to come live with me?"

"Guess so. OK if I bring my guitar?"

"She never stops playing," the guard says. "You get used to it after a while."

"I can deal with that," Sullings says. "Unchain this girl."

The sun shines so hard that it hurts her eyes as she stands and looks around at nothing for the thousandth time. The New England water is full of seals and the woods are full of deer and other animals. It's pure paradise, they've said to her so many times. Wouldn't you just love to stay here forever…?

To Teri Goddard, it's been pure boredom. She's on the ferry, and it can't move fast enough for her. After five months at Brides' Head, the place for troubled girls, she tells herself that her next living situation, no matter what and where, will be an improvement.

"You're a fool to leave here," the counselor had told her. "Brides' Head is one of the most desirable places of its kind in North America. A thousand other girls wanted your bed. Do you have any clue about life in Milgrom and those other juvenile-detention centers? After one hour in those places, you'll be begging to come back to Brides' Head."

Teri said nothing. She'd wanted to say, "It's beautiful and boring, and I can't stand boredom." But she just stayed mute and proceeded with her application for reassignment.

Everyone kept bragging about the Bride's Head's natural beauty. Yeah, right. Milking cows, planting seeds, feeding chickens. Spending every day looking at one tree that looked exactly like a hundred others. People built cities because they got sick of looking at "natural beauty." Teri, a city girl, liked people, especially cute guys. She liked streets and stores, cars and…civilization. She had gone all this time without TV or the Internet. Yuck!

Now she is taking the ferry back to civilization. Yea! Where is she going? Doesn't really matter. When she gets to her new "home," she'll figure it all out.

At her destination, she meets Sandra Mull, the counselor. "Teri, grab your stuff. We've got some driving to do."

Teri nods and gets her gear together. Mull has a truck; Teri hoists her duffel bag into the truck's bed and gets in with it.

"No," says Mull. "You sit in the cab with me."

Teri does as told. "You know what really bums me out?"

"Tell me," Mull says as she pulls out of the parking lot and they begin their journey.

"It's that everything I own fits into that duffel bag and a knapsack."

"That means you have less stuff to worry about." She adds, "The things we own end up owning us."

"I've never expected to live in a mansion and have a hundred outfits. Some girls have those luxuries, but I don't, and I never will. Life has dealt me some bad cards and I figure that's how it will be from now on."

"The first step towards building a new life for yourself is believing that you *can* improve your situation," Mull tells her. "The second thing is to set very realistic goals. You don't need a mansion and hundreds of outfits. Nobody does."

"I'm glad to be out of Brides' Head," Teri says.

"Why? It's one of the best of its kind."

"It's great if you like being in the middle of nowhere. I won't miss them, and they won't miss me."

"I understand that you had racked up some demerit points."

"I couldn't follow their lame rules."

"Couldn't or wouldn't?"

"Don't rag on me, Sandra—"

"Call me Miz Mull."

"Yeah, right. Whatever." Teri doesn't like this woman's tone, so she's going to stay silent for a while. For the first time, she starts thinking of Brides' Head with a trace of affection—the polite (or perhaps merely frightened) girls, the good meals, the smell of fresh air. Teri has been in the juvie-justice system long enough to know that its girls' facilities are sometimes as filthy and dangerous as men's prisons, and now she reminds herself: No one has guaranteed me that I will like wherever they send me.

Teri is a liar, a thief, a pickpocket and a con artist. Mostly, though, she is a shoplifter who supposes she will always live a life of crime. She is eager to steal some more cool stuff, and make some bucks, but of course Sandra Mull doesn't need to know that. She falls asleep in the truck, smiling about her future misadventures.

When she wakes up, she has no idea of how long her nap lasted or where they are. It still looks like some rural area, although the road is much wider. They pass a cluster of trees, and Teri spies the glittering skyline she's seen so many times on TV and in the movies.

"New York City?" she asks, sitting up. "Are you locking me up in Rikers or something?"

"Don't panic," replies Mull. "I'm taking you to an experimental residence here for girls. You and two other girls."

"Do they want me even though I have a long rap sheet?"

Mull smiles. "Miz Sullings asked for you specifically." Then, "Teri, I know you probably think I'm full of crap just like all other adults, but listen to me: If you think you have the worst life of anyone, and you've been dealt the worst cards ever, you're totally wrong. As a young offender, you've had the best breaks possible. You hated Brides' Head, but it was the cushiest 'lockup' any troubled girl could live. Now you're going to Fresh Start, which, in its own way, is every bit as desirable as Brides' Head. Be grateful for this. Don't screw it up."

Teri nods many times, to show that she's listening, but she's already getting her own ideas about her new life in the Big Apple. Maybe she can get day passes and go shoplifting at Macy's and Barneys.

CHAPTER 4

FRESH START IS housed in an old apartment on East Ninety-ninth Street. Its peeling paint looks orange here and teal there. On the fourth floor, in a building with no elevator, it must be the oddest place for a juvenile-justice residential facility.

Inside, it is as cramped as countless other Manhattan apartments: A living room, galley kitchen and two bedrooms. Sullings will have the smaller bedroom, and her three charges will share the larger one. They have already installed bunk beds for the girls.

Jaycee and Santana moved in yesterday. When Teri arrives, Jaycee shows her their room and the two dresser drawers reserved for Teri's exclusive use. Teri, looking around the room, smiles and points at the ancient fire escape that leads to the street below.

"Forget about it," Jaycee says, shaking her head. She walks over and taps on the window sill. "It's locked. Only Sullings has the key."

Teri pouts. "I could get the key from her so fast she would never know it was missing." Adding, "I don't know where you've been doing time, but *I've* been out in the New England boonies, and that sucked. Now I'm here, so I'm gonna see more of this town than just this crappy little apartment. Anyone got a problem with that?"

Santana says, "Yeah, I have a problem with that. Around here, we're sort of in this thing together. If one of us gets out of line, we're all to blame."

Jaycee glowers at Teri. "Didn't Sullings run it down for you? She really had to fight and argue and bargain to get this program started. It's brand-new and Sullings is saying, 'I want to prove to everyone that Fresh Start will work.' Lots of people are saying, 'I hope it fails. Those girls aren't worth saving.' This program hasn't even started and already you're trying to ruin it."

Teri smirks. "Well, maybe we're three chicks who *aren't* worth saving."

Jaycee glowers some more. "Listen, do you where I was before I cam here? I was at Milgrom, which is, like, one of the worst detentions around. Those chicks beat my butt black and blue. I am not going to risk going back there just because you want to go outside and have some fun without getting permission."

Teri throws back her head and laughs. "Wow! I didn't know I had me a Girl Guide for a roommate! Tell me, sweet thing, how long have you been a juvenile offender?"

Santana says, "Oh, are you two gonna compare creds? You take out your rap sheet, and she'll take out hers, and we'll see who's the tougher chick."

"You don't wanna do *that*, girlfriend," Teri says, looking Santana up and down and swallowing a couple of times. "I'm from Chicago, and we lived in Cabrini-Green. You ever heard of it? It was just the most dangerous public housing project ever. I was tight with the Gangster Disciples, the meanest bunch of street hoodlums for a thousand miles in any direction. Now, Jaycee, you wanna tell me how bad *you* are?"

"You win." Jaycee backs off. She isn't ready for confrontations just yet, and her gut feeling is that Teri isn't ready for confrontations with Santana.

As a smallish thirteen-year-old, Jaycee has eluded bullies all her life, or at least tried to ally herself with those able and willing to defend her. But now she's going to be roommates with a bully.

Teri has introduced herself: *Hi, I'm trouble, better be afraid of me.*

Being stupid back home with her bud Maria got Jaycee locked up in Milgrom. Being stupid here with Teri will get her sent right back to Milgrom.

Teri's making a face. To her own amazement, Jaycee eyeballs her right back, fists ready to fly.

Sullings and Mull sit at the dinner table, doing Teri's transfer documentation. Fortunately, they can do the work online, which makes it more convenient. Alas, they must fill out forms for municipal, state and federal agencies.

Sullings stops for a moment to stretch her legs and back. "All these forms for one girl to switch programs. Too bad the system didn't care this much about her before she started acting out."

"Yeah," Mull says. "It's all reactive, not proactive or preventive. These at-risk kids are free to run wild, and when they do get some form of help, it's just too little and too late." Then, "Allison, why are you going to all this trouble for these kids?"

"Because I think these kids are worth it."

"In your case," Mull tells her, "I think it goes deep than that. I work at Brides' Head, which is ridiculously easy compared to what you're doing here with Fresh Start. You've gone to *so* much trouble to get this little apartment so that three girls will get another chance to straighten out their lives. I can just imagine what they neighbors here said when you filed an application for a halfway house. 'Sure, we're all for helping disadvantaged youth—but do it in someone else's neighborhood!' Then you had to get funding for this, and I can imagine how hard it must have been to get enough cash for a two-bedroom apartment here in Manhattan.

"What's the deal, Allison? In what way do you see Fresh Start as being better than, or at different from, all the other group homes and alternative-living situations?"

Sullings thinks for a moment. "There are too many of those places. Kids get lost in the shuffle. With this arrangement, it's intimate enough for me to know I can make a big improvement in these girls' lives."

"And why did you choose these three girls?"

"You wouldn't believe me if I told you."

Mull smiles. "Try me."

Sullings smiles back. "Because they remind me of myself."

"Oh, really? These three characters? In what way?"

"They're good-looking, smart, articulate girls. They've made some bad choices. I believe each of them has huge potential. They just need to hear someone say, 'You have to grow up, and here's how to do it…'"

"So you got into some trouble when you were a

kid?"

"Yeah. No felonies—I didn't kill anyone like Teri did—but I hung out with the wrong people, and when they said, 'Prove you're not a coward; go into that store and steal something our fence can use,' I said, 'OK.' So I got caught, and maybe I wanted to get busted. Who knows?"

"What's the deal with Teri?"

"Teri Goddard," Sullings says, "is a city girl, and the authorities said, 'Let's put her out in the New England woods so she'll become a decent citizen.' Bad idea. Her Brides' Head experience just disoriented her. I'm from Manhattan, and when I first got into trouble, they sent me off to Iowa or Illinois, I can't remember which. They tried to make a farm girl of me, but I just couldn't adapt."

"I guess that's why Teri was so miserable in the New England woods," says Mull.

As the two women finished their computer work and walked to the front door, Sullings said, "So, tell me: How do you think I'll do with Teri?"

"Just fine, I guess," replies Mull.

Sullings eyeballs her. "No, seriously. I want your candid and honest opinion."

Mull sighs. "In that case, here it is: Teri is going to town and have fun, even if she has to push you out of her way or throw you down the fire escape."

The counselor steps around Sullings and hurries out of the apartment. The Fresh Start boss watches her leave, stunned by the Mull's brutal frankness. Then she hears the chaos in the girls' bedroom.

Sullings covers the distance from the front door to the master bedroom in a split second. What she sees is something she will never forget: Santana, like a boxing referee, stands sandwiched between Jaycee and Teri, arms outstretched to keep the two girls apart. Well, almost apart: Jaycee, her nose bloodied, has a fist straining to reach Teri's chin; Teri has a firm grip on Jaycee's small left breast.

Their one nightstand lay knocked over on the floor; a tennis trophy, too, is on its side but intact.

All the girls are pulling in ragged breaths and sweating profusely. Jaycee's nose is bloody; Teri's lips are a bit swollen.

"Break it up!" Sullings shouts. "Someone want to explain this to me?"

The two combatants take their hands off of each other but say nothing. Santana says, "It was nothing. No big deal, ma'am. Won't happen again."

"It better not. Fighting will get you kicked out of here and sent back to Milgrom or another juvie hellhole." Sullings rights the nightstand and replaces the trophy on top of it.

"What's that thing?" asks Teri.

"It's my tennis trophy," replies Sullings. "From when I was your age."

"If it's yours," says Santana, "why did you put it in here?"

"To inspire you to go out and win one of your own."

Sullings leaves the girls' bedroom and goes back out into the living room. She looks out the window and sees Sandra Mull walking down the street towards her truck.

Sandra! Come back! Don't leave me here with these people!

CHAPTER 5

JONATHAN KLINE HIGH School is on Ninety-seventh Street, just a brief walk from the Fresh Start apartment. The school goes as far back as the year 1860, when it was only two stories tall and had a handful of classrooms. For some years it was as big as it needed to be, but by the early 1900s the city tripled the school's size. Many complain that Kline is too old, too musty and in desperate need of a dozen or more major improvements. Of course, no one suggests where the money would come from for such an undertaking.

Allison Sullings walks her girls to Kline the next morning. Due to the miracle of computers and the Internet, the three are already registered, but the principal insists on meeting with them personally and privately. The purpose of their meeting is for him to scold them for all of the heinous things they have done in other schools and may intend to do at Jonathan Kline High.

The three girls sit side by side on plastic seats and, as Principal Cliff Gallant gives them what-for, they let his angry words go into, and out of, their young ears.

Finally, Sullings has heard enough. "Mister Gallant, I mean no disrespect, but I think it's unfair to berate these girls just because they've come to you as young offenders. None of them has done anything wrong here so far."

"Damn straight," says Santana. Sullings shoots her a look that says, *Shut up, kid.*

The principal sighs.

"My point," Sullings tells him, "is that if you have any issues with these girls, remember that they are, in a very real sense, *my* girls. I'm their mom, for all intents and purposes."

Cliff Gallant frowns for a moment or two, then shakes his head. He says to the girls, "As long as you three are here, I'm going to keep a close eye on you. Your attendance here at Kline is a privilege, and if you abuse that privilege, I'll expel you immediately."

Sullings and the girls leave the principal's office and loiter for a moment in the hallway.

"You really stuck up for us in there with that grumpy old fart," Jaycee tells Sullings. "Thanks, Mom."

Sullings starts to smile, but stops as soon as she looks past the girls and sees who's coming—a woman built like a wrestler, with massive shoulders filling out her gray suit.

"Something wrong?" Santana asks.

"Miz Boylan," Sullings mutters. "She's the social worker assigned to us."

"No sweat," says Teri. "I'll just charm—"

"You'll just shut up. She's our worst enemy. She thinks Fresh Start is a joke. She wants to shut us down and send you girls back to Milgrom. She has the power to do it, too."

"Good morning, Miz Sullings." She nods at the girls. "I was going to stop by your apartment yesterday, but I was much too busy with other things. You were my last priority. Another halfway house on my turf? No, thanks." Although she does not smile, she speaks in a polite tone and strikes Sullings as being detached and businesslike. Her hair, rinsed free of gray and styled into a fashionably short, rust-colored do, somehow makes her appear even more menacing. Alas, Boylan's business appears to be making Sullings' life as difficult as possible.

Sullings smiles. "Everything's coming together just great, ma'am. The girls are really eager to begin their new lives. In fact, they were just getting ready for their first class."

"I see…and what is your plan for them at the three-oh-five bell?"

"Definitely. I'll be meeting the three of them at the front entrance."

Boylan nods. "I assume they know that if you are *not* there with all three of them by three-twenty, you are required by law to report any or all of them to the police as fleeing felons."

"Yes—"

"Plus, if they wander, *unaccompanied*, more than one hundred feet from the building, they may be arrested."

"I've covered all that with them."

"Fine. Then let's start school."

The social workers bulls through the crowded hallways, nearly knocking over a few students who are too slow to get out of her way. Her heels go clack-clack-clack on the tile floor as dozens of students check her out with fear and fascination.

Hurrying to keep up, Jaycee thinks, *They all seem to know who this big broad is and what she's about. If she's the social worker, we must be her newest juvie troublemakers.*

They've been at Kline for less than half an hour but are already getting dirty looks from the other students.

Teri whispers to Santana, "I wish we could take this big hag with us to every class. You see how she scares everyone? No one would ever hassle us."

"Quiet," Santana whispers back. "She'll hear you."

Their first stop is a science lab where students sit or stand at rows of tables, cooking pink-colored gunk with Bunsen burners. Miz Boylan steps inside and stays there just long enough for everyone to see her: The Big Lady Is Here to Deliver Another Kid Nobody Else Wants.

The instructor, a thirtyish man wearing a lab coat, says to Jaycee, "May I help you?"

"Freshman chemistry, right?"

He smiles. "Right."

Jaycee hands over her course card.

"Oh, I see," the man says. "A new student."

Jaycee looks around. The classroom is already overpopulated. Where will he put her?

Boylan says to Jaycee, "It looks like you can manage without me." She turns to Sullings and the others. "Come with me."

The science teacher puts away Jaycee's course card and says to the class, "Everyone, we have a new student. Say hello to Joanne."

"I go by 'Jaycee.'" She surveys the room and observes that only half of the students are paying attention to the new pupil. Of those, some are snickering and whispering things; she imagines hearing "juvie," "loser" and "retard." This scene reminds her of her first days at Milgrom, when the other girls were looking her over, checking her out, deciding whether she was hard or soft, tough or weak, dumb or smart.

The instructor smiles and says, as if to himself, "Jaycee." Then, "Why don't you go work with"—he takes a moment to looks around for an available workspace—"Denna? She's over at table five."

Denna, a small black girl, takes a step back as she sees the new girl come closer. Denna's eyes grow wide with terror, as if her experiment were a lump of uranium that has started to burn a hole through the table.

Jaycee grins and says, "Hey, what's our experiment? What's this pink crap?"

Denna opens her mouth but nothing comes out.

The two girls keep the Bunsen burner going till they boil away the pink stuff. They scrape some of the residue onto a slide and insert it under an ancient microscope. Jaycee plays with the knobs for a few minutes, can't focus on anything and gives up with a huge sigh. Reaching for the beaker of goo residue, she knocks it off the table and it breaks into two dozen pieces. Some of the goo ends up on the new Air Jordans of another student.

"My sneakers!" The boy looks down, then up at Jaycee. He glares at her with furious green eyes, then looks away, apparently realizing that she's the new street kid the big lady just brought in. Street kids, man, you don't know about them—what they've been through, what they've done to others. For all he knows, this new blonde chick—Jaycee? what kind of name is that?—has a boyfriend who's a Crip. Look at her the wrong way and those Crips will cut him from A to Z.

"I didn't mean to dirty your shoes," Jaycee says.

"Forget it," replies the boy, who wheels around and peers into his microscope.

Denna blushes purple, as if watching the big green-eyed boy backing down from the medium-sized blonde girl means that the new girl must be truly worthy of everyone's fear and respect.

"I'm harmless," Jaycee tells her in a quiet voice. "I've been in trouble a few times, but I'm trying to get everything worked out."

"I'm very sorry," whispers Denna.

Jaycee wonders if she would have been better off staying at Milgrom. *Even out here, all I'm doing is time.*

Over half a year has passed since Teri Goddard last attended anything that could be called a school. Also, it's been much longer than that since, for an extended period of time, she received an *education*—daily sessions where an instructor taught her things she considered worth learning. To Teri, *school* and *education* are very different things. Throughout her life, she has been perfectly willing to show up in a certain classroom at a certain time. But she invariably daydreams away class time.

In juvie, and prison, they say, "Don't serve time; make time serve you." In school, Teri has become a master at making class time serve her. She can raise her hand for a two-minute bathroom break and return half an hour later. She uses that out-of-class time to wander the hallways and see what's *really* going on.

They've made movies about these infamous New York City schools. Don't make me laugh, Teri thinks.

They have school cops here? So what? The school cops here mainly just eat doughnuts, drink coffee and talk to each other on the radio. In Chicago, those school cops really had to deal with some serious *attitude*.

She hears clop-clop-clop. Police shoes. She can hear them from halfway down the hallway. The cops should get Air Jordans instead. Nice and quiet.

Someone shouts, "Where's your hall pass?"

Teri has fun being chased by a hall monitor, though the kid chasing her is fat and slow, and that's a bummer. She flies down the hallway and down the stairs into a girls' bathroom.

They've removed all the stall doors, and that lack of privacy disturbs Teri. She thinks she might have trouble relaxing enough to relieve herself if nature called during school hours. In one of the stalls, a transaction is happening between two girls; Teri recognizes one of them as her classmate from the previous period. The other girl in the stall has a knapsack from which she has just withdrawn a handful of pills. She hands over the drugs, accepts a wad of cash and slips out of the stall.

The buyer hurries out of the bathroom; the seller goes to the sink and washes her hands.

Teri grins. "You just slangin' pills? What else? Meth? Crack? Weed?"

"Not sellin'," says the seller.

"You got all that product"—Teri points at the girl's knapsack—"you better be careful. Cops in the hallways search your bag and find your stash, they'll bust you for possession. That's a felony."

The girl turns towards Teri, takes out a switchblade and opens it. "Why don't you get out of here while your nose is still intact?"

Teri, still grinning, throws up her hands. "I hear that." She backs out of the bathroom and cackles. After all that time in Brides' Head, also known as the Middle of Nowhere, she is once again among people she can relate to and admire.

"Good times," she says out loud, to nobody in particular.

CHAPTER 6

THE SMALL OFFICE of the Midtown Business Development Association sits above a restaurant, so the office often reeks of stale cooking oil. Despite its smallness, the office has significant ties to City Hall, and in that office Allison Sullings, as part of her Fresh Start project, signed an agreement committing her three charges to a dozen hours of community service each week, cleaning and sweeping.

Their boss, so to speak, is Geri, the most presentable and personable homeless person the three girls have ever met. She has managed to stay off the street for the past couple of years, and she runs the cleanup crew while sleeping in a homeless shelter.

Joining them for that first shift is Troy, a thirtysomething Wall Street wizard who got pulled over after having a few too many martinis. They must all wear orange coveralls supplied by the city.

"Can't wear this," says Jaycee as she stands there with the coveralls around her hips. "It's just like being back at Milgrom."

"Got to wear it," Santana tells her. "Rules are rules are rules. You suit up, get out there, get busy and you'll forget what you're wearing."

Teri puts hers on and giggles. "Just like being

back inside. We're going out to pick up trash and people will be, like, 'Ooh, those nasty folks in orange, they're criminals payin' off their debt to society! I'm scared of them!' I love it when people are ascared of me."

The other girls snarl at her, but Troy the Wall Street guy bursts out laughing. "People are afraid of me every day at work, and I love it too." He tugs at his coveralls. "We all look like convicts, right? I should've brought my iPhone so we could get a picture together. I could put it online with the caption, 'Attica Goes Coed.'" He laughs some more.

"I like this dude," Teri says, clapping him on the back as she follows him out of the room.

Teri feels someone stabbing her in the back with a finger.

"Give it up," says Santana.

Teri turns around and faces her. "Huh?"

"You heard me."

Teri puts her hands on her hips and eyeballs Santana. "Look, girlfriend, don't hassle me. I'm here for the same reason you are: We gotta go out there and make New York beautiful."

"I'll say it again: Give it up."

"Don't know what you mean."

"His wallet. I saw you pick his pocket."

"Keep dreamin', baby," Teri says. "I keep my hands to myself."

"Give me the wallet or—"

"Or *what*, baby?"

"Or when Troy figures out his wallet's gone, I'll tell him where to look. Guess who's going back to the New England woods? Or maybe even Milgrom."

Teri blows out a huge, exasperated breath. "OK,

here's the deal. I'll give you half of what's in his wallet if we keep this to ourselves. In fact"—she shoots a look over at Jaycee—"we can split it three ways. Sound like a plan?"

Santana shakes her head and holds out her hand. "When Sullings interviewed you for Fresh Start, didn't she make it clear to you that kids like us have a rep as hopeless criminals? She wants to help us prove that the world is wrong about us, so why are you ripping Troy off and proving that we *are* hopeless criminals?"

"She's not jiving, Teri," Jaycee puts in. "Hand it over."

Pouting, Teri produces the bulging brown wallet and puts it in Santana's outstretched palm.

"Yo, Troy!" Santana calls out, running after him. "I think you lost something!"

Teri mutters to herself, then says aloud, "All we got here is snitches and bitches."

The three girls and Troy receive dustpans and brooms and instructions to clean up the neighborhood. It's easy enough work, but the job is monotonous and all four soon get backaches and sore feet.

Jaycee sneers at the items she finds on Manhattan sidewalks. "Three used condoms, two hypodermic needles, one crack vial—"

"And a pah-tridge in a pear tree," sings Santana. "Hey, why won't Sullings let me play my guitar and sing out here for the people? That's community service, right?"

"I think," Jaycee tells her, "the purpose of court-ordered community service is punishment. When they make you do community service, it's meant to be something you *won't* enjoy."

"Oh."

"What bugs *me*," Jaycee continues as she sweeps some trash into a pile, "is why so many people out here don't use the trash cans. I mean, maybe the people who leave their condoms and needles out here maybe don't understand what a trash can is all about, but the other people, the ones who buy coffee at Starbucks and drop their empty cups on the sidewalk? They expect us to pick up after them? What's up with that?"

Teri mostly stands around; once in a while she nudges some trash around. When an obese man stuffs a U-No bar into his mouth and drops its wrapper as he waddles past them, she shouts, "Way to go, fatso! How's your diabetes comin' along? Had your first heart attack yet?"

When not berating passersby, she ducks into the nearest Starbucks for a very long time.

Jaycee looks up at what sounds like gunfire. Then she sees two pimped-out cars racing down the street. They disappear immediately, leaving her nearly tearful for her own joyriding, drag-racing days. She hasn't driven a car, or anything else, since she totaled that Lexus during the botched robbery attempt. Jaycee believes that everyone has a special gift, and hers is driving; she's convinced she can drive anything, anywhere, better than just about everyone. It really bugs her that such a gifted young lady should be wasting her time at places like Milgrom and Fresh Start.

After a half-dozen bathroom breaks, Teri comes out of Starbucks and toys with her broom for a bit.

Then, as she pedestrian traffic clears for a few moments, she spots someone she knows—the girl selling drugs in the school bathroom.

Teri smiles and waves, and thinks the girl sort of nods and smiles back. This Fresh Start kid is proud to be seen in these lawbreaker's orange coveralls by a drug-slanging, knife-wielding classmate. *Yeah, baby, I'm street. I'm bad. Just like you.*

When Teri looks again, she can't find the girl.

It's getting late, dark and cold when Geri, their supervisor who sleeps in a shelter, calls it a day. She takes them back to the office so they can change out of their coveralls and get their time sheets stamped.

"They all did terrific," she tells Sullings, who is there to walk them home.

Jaycee rolls her eyes. Geri's compliment sounds to her, and maybe to Sullings, like, *Allison, your three little criminals did what they were supposed to do, and they didn't kill or maim anyone or steal anything for an entire day! Aren't you delighted?*

On the walk home, Sullings says, "I went to the grocery store and got some things for dinner. We're having a lovely vegan meal."

"I'm famished," says Santana, rubbing her stomach. "Hope you can cook fast."

"You're going to help. All of you. I'm not your mama, regardless of what you may think."

"At least in jail, they feed you," Teri tells them. "Half the time, the food's not worth eating, but you just have to stand in line with your tray and they fill it for you."

"One of the things about being an adult in the real world," Sullings tells them, "is that you fend for yourself. You don't wait in line with a plastic tray and expect to have it filled. You work at your job all day, then you go home and cook yourself some dinner. In your case, after you've cooked and eaten, and done the dishes, there's this thing called homework. When report cards come out, Miz Boylan will want to have a look at them, and if they're mediocre or worse, well...we won't talk about that right now.

The four of them traipse up the stairs to their apartment, and they stop for a moment to look around and then at each other. Sullings feels that their expressions say, *I can't believe you went to so much trouble to get this trashy place.* She says nothing, for what is there to say? Fresh Start. A halfway house. It is what it is.

They pass by Missus Berkowitz, their stout, aging neighbor, who at the moment is having trouble managing her two supermarket bags. Santana hustles over, grabs one bag and reaches for the other one.

The old woman screams, "Help! Police!"

Santana hurries back to her group, half hiding behind Sullings.

"It's all right, ma'am," Sullings says. "Santana was just trying to help you."

"Only kind of help I want from you," Missus Berkowitz says between labored breaths, "is to see the moving van come and take you away! I don't have any use for your kind—girls that've been locked up ten times before they're fifteen! They're worse than the boys! You think you can make decent young ladies out of them just by moving into a nice neighborhood like this? Hah!"

Sullings says, "I understand that you had some misgivings about having Fresh Start in your neighborhood. But we're here now, so we all need to have patience and make it work out. You also have to remember that these girls have done nothing to you or this neighborhood since they got here, and they're not about to make any trouble for you."

The old woman makes a face at them and drags herself, and her grocery bags, into her apartment.

CHAPTER 7

JAYCEE, WHO HAS recently served time at Milgrom after stealing and totaling a Lexus, sits in a circle in a fancy office, thinking, *And everyone says* I'm *weird*.

They're all listening as a punked-out boy tells them about the best ways of committing suicide.

"Many people say that freezing to death is the best way to go," says Ira Stein, "but I doubt it. You try putting on a life jacket and jumping into frigid waters, and you're gonna suffer. Hypothermia will freak you out. I always say that the best way is a combination of painkillers and alcohol. Take a handful of Dilaudids, mix them in pudding, eat it so your body doesn't know it's being poisoned, then follow that with a tall screwdriver that's half vodka." He beams. His eyes are the same emerald color as his hair. "Yeah, that would be the way to go."

Doctor Maddux sits up and smooths out the jacket of his power suit. "Thank you, Ira. You have shared a great deal with us today. Now I want to share something with you: Why would a young man like you, in good health and with plenty of intelligence, want to kill himself?"

Ira frowns. "I don't necessarily want to kill myself,

but death is always on my mind. It's on everyone's mind, all the time. Most people just pretend that it isn't."

Jaycee stifles a yawn. Part of Sullings' deal with the Man was that the three Fresh Start kids, in addition to school and chores and the rest of it, would have to see this psychiatrist on every Wednesday afternoon for a fifty-five-minute adolescent-psychotherapy session.

It isn't all bad, though. Jaycee thinks Pete Maddux is as cute as Brad Pitt. This dude even seems to like kids and their problems, which makes him very different from the other shrinks she's met.

"Doctor, I am afraid, too," says Teri. "I'm afraid I'm going to leave therapy without knowing if you're circumcised or not."

The three girls erupt in red-faced laughter. Ira, smirking, makes an obscene finger gesture at her.

"Hey," Teri says, throwing up her hands, "I asked for educational reasons. I know that not all parents have their sons cut." Adding, "If my question was out of bounds, I take it back. I can't help what I say. I'm a wayward girl. That's why I'm here."

"You're here," Ira reminds her, "because that lady who runs your halfway house has to send you here as part of her deal with the Man. We've already talked about that."

"And *you're* here," Teri retorts, "because you like spray-painting your name on everything in Manhattan."

Ira nods. "Guilty as charged. I can't help it. it's a compulsion." Then, "That girl—Santana—hasn't heard a word I've said."

Santana frowns. "Why's he picking on me?"

"Nobody's picking on anybody," Doctor Maddux says. "Ira, sometimes a new member of the group takes a little while to feel comfortable and participate. That's why we have heard very little from Santana and Joanna."

"Jaycee. Call me Jaycee."

"Yes, *Jaycee.* So, what are your thoughts so far on our sessions?"

"I'm not a psycho. I don't really need this. I'm just a kid who got busted."

Doctor Maddux's face darkens. "In here, we don't use words like 'psycho.' You're here, and I'm here, because the judge believed that this therapy would help you."

Teri laughs. "Wrong again, Doc. This 'therapy' is to keep shrinks like you employed. There's no good that can come of this. These rap sessions we do won't help teen criminals like us, because we've already seen how easy and fun it can be to steal whatever we want and need."

"Nice attitude," says Ira.

Teri just shrugs.

"At least I'm not some gangster type," he says, "who's probably already killed a dozen people."

"Well, I guess that makes you better than me." Teri grins. Truth is, she's mostly just a liar and thief; but she's flattered that Ira considers her a killer and gangster.

"Let's take a brief timeout," says the therapist. "We need to be open and honest, but we also need to respect each other's dignity. This has to be a very safe place for everyone."

"I'm not a criminal," says Jules, one of the girls in the circle. "I'm not a hacker. I don't go into Websites and steal people's credit-card numbers. I just download movies and music."

"That so?" Santana asks. "I heard on the news about 'video piracy.' That it was illegal, but I didn't think they ever, you know, *busted* anyone for it. You go on those sites and it says 'one-point-two million users online,' so you think, 'Are they gonna bust all those people?'"

Jules closes her eyes. "The record companies and movie studios hire lawyers to check out the sites. The lawyers can issue subpoenas and get contact information for the people like me who are downloading. The lawyers say, 'We'll sue you for illegal downloading unless you pay us right now.' In my case, they said, 'Either pay us or agree to see a therapist.' So here I am."

Teri hoots. "What a hassle! What did you download? I hope you got something good."

Jules giggles. "I got enough music and movies to keep myself entertained till I'm a hundred years old." She adds, "I took music and movies I didn't even want. I took them just because they were there."

In their fifty-five minutes of continuous blah-blah-blah, Jules' comment is the only thing that really resounds with Jaycee. She couldn't identify with Ira's obsession over the best ways to kill himself—Jaycee, in her young life, has never experienced a suicidal ideation; she couldn't imagine depriving the world of her delightful self—but she knows plenty about stealing things she doesn't want. That day with the girls, when Jaycee stole and trashed the Lexus? She went along, literally, for the ride; she had scarcely any interest in those armloads of Apple gadgets Maria and the others boosted.

Jaycee looks around the circle and thinks that, right now, she would be happy to trade lives with green-haired, suicidal Ira. She would even trade places with homeless Geri, the street-cleaning boss. Or even weird, mean old Missus Boylan, the social worker. Anyone at all.

CHAPTER 8

IN THE EMPTY band room, a teenaged girl sits strumming her acoustic guitar. Whenever she daydreams, as she does very often, she pretends to be Carlos Santana, the rock-music genius for whom she was named. The notes of "Soul Sacrifice," her favorite song, fill the huge, empty space. She knows the song so well, has played it so many times, that she hardly has to look at her instrument's strings and frets.

Santana smiles, thinking, *Did Carlos have to start out this way?* She's seen the movie *Woodstock*, when the man and his band dazzled the half-million hippies sprawled out across the farm. Well, she's no Carlos Santana, at least not yet. But his music has been *so* therapeutic for her, especially during her nightmarish year or so at Abbotsford. She played "Soul Sacrifice" so often that the guards started to ask, "Don't you know any other songs?"

Music has saved my life, she tells herself for the hundredth time. *Without it, I would have killed myself or worse.*

A voice inside her head says, *Your rap sheet says you killed a jock at a pep rally.*

Santana wipes a tear from her cheek. She stops

playing the song.

She remembers things she wants to forget: Hank Adams, Victorville quarterback. His mouth ran even faster than his legs.

Santana's team, the Northup University Thunderbirds, were playing the Victorville Vikings. She loved parties and knew that the pep rally, held on Northup's big, beautiful campus, would be full of cute guys to check out. It was supposed to be the T-Birds' day—everyone showed up in Northup blue and gold, so why did that doofus Hank Adams show up with some teammates in Vikings purple? Adams starting ragging on the crowd, so some of the Northup faithful ragged back, and a fight broke out. Santana, tall and strong and eager to fight whenever the odds were stacked in her favor, sneaked up on Adams as the football hunk punched it out with a couple of T-Birds fans. Just as she was about to jump on him from behind, or do something else to him— she wasn't sure what—he spun around, as if to run away, and she did it.

She hauled off and pounded him right in the face.

He went down and didn't get back up.

The cops arrested her and she confessed immediately. But confessed to what? She went to the rally, the quarterback had been a jerk, provoking everyone, people fought, she hit him and he fell dead. Kid's stuff had got out of hand. These things happen.

But her public defender assured her that it was a very serious matter, indeed. The handful of Vikings players took the stand and spoke of a tall, dark girl, possibly high on PCP, who had roamed the pep rally like a wild animal, practically foaming at the mouth.

A teenaged sociopath, they said, someone who

must be stopped before she kills again.

"You need to take a plea," said her lawyer.

"But why?" she asked.

"So you can avoid a life sentence."

Santana was hardly an honor student or Big Woman on Campus, but she did like to think she had common sense and she *knew* that the death of Hank Adams was an accident, nothing more. So why plead guilty when she considered herself innocent?

"I want," her lawyer told her, "to get this thing kicked down to juvenile court so you won't have to serve time in an adult facility."

Adult facility. She thought of San Quentin, Folsom, Attica. Places so horrible that you need shrinks and meds just to survive. Were the women's prisons any better? Santana was in no hurry to find out.

The guilty verdict came in, and her parents looked almost as bad as Santana felt as the sheriff's deputy led her away to do her time.

Yes, that nice lady Allison Sullings came along and got her out of Abbotsford and into Fresh Start. Still, Santana misses her mom and dad—she's forbidden to email or phone them, so it's like she's still behind bars.

The other day, she went to the post office, bought a pre-stamped postcard of the Statue of Liberty and wrote on the back of it, *Hangin' in there.* But she couldn't bring herself to mail it home. What if the Department of Juvenile Justice found out? She doesn't think she's being paranoid; if she is, well, it's because over a year in Abbotsford did that to her. She has important work to do at Fresh Start and knows she must not screw up in any way.

Santana plays some more, and it takes her a

moment to realize that someone else has entered the room and joined in. The newcomer is playing a different but complementary song, and the two guitarists soon engage in the friendliest of duels that culminates in flailing arms and raucous laughter. Santana wonders for a moment about this alien feeling she's suddenly experiencing. What is it?

It's *fun*. It's *happiness*. That's what has been missing from her life for so long.

The other guitarist gets up and shakes her hand. "I'm Mister Pajala, the music instructor. Are you new here?"

Santana nods, smiling. "Santana Perez."

"Where did you learn to play like that?"

"Here and there," she says, not lying.

"Look, I've got a stage band here at Kline," he tells her. "We play mostly pop and rock—the stuff the kids want to hear. Lately, I've been the band's interim guitarist, but I think you would do fine in that capacity. We practice after school three times each week."

Santana's smile fades. *Nix to that, teach. Right after school, five days per week, my butt belongs to Allison Sullings and Fresh Start. If I'm anywhere else after the bell rings, I'm a fleeing felon.*

Mister Pajala sees her long face. "I'm guessing you already have an after-school commitment."

"Yessir. Big commitment."

"Anything we can sort of work around?"

"No. It's the sort of commitment that I'm not free to quit." The more time she spends here, in the free world, the less willing she is to do anything that might result in her return to Abbotsford.

Mister Pajala tsks. "That's a shame. I don't often

meet students who can play as well as you. If your commitment changes and your afterschool time becomes your own, be sure to sit in with us."

I would if I could. Santana closes her eyes, amazed at how fine it felt to indulge in a simple everyday pleasure like jamming with someone. At Abbotsford, they treated her like a snarling animal, fit to be hosed down and thrown a pound of raw meat. Sitting in the band room, she reflects on how much her time at Abbotsford made her believe she was less than human.

"Thanks, Mister Pajala," she murmurs. "Nice meeting you."

CHAPTER 9

TERI KEEPS GOING back to the girls' bathroom, but the Drugstore Girl is a no-show. *She's run out of product or found somewhere else to do business.* Or, she thinks with a smile, the pusher simply cuts class as often as not. Teri would, too, if she could find a way to ditch without Sullings' knowledge.

Kline has over four thousand students; even Teri's school in Chicago wasn't that big. With such a huge student body, she knows she can't count on finding Drugstore Girl every day, especially if that girl wishes not to be found. Nevertheless, Teri always looks around for her at school and during community service. She wonders: Did that chick get busted? What was her name, anyway? Did some snitch give her away to the cops? Teri can't picture them going through her knapsack and finding her contraband. Drugstore Girl seemed much too streetwise for that.

You've been wrong about people lots of times, she tells herself. *If you think you're hip, you're not. If you were, you wouldn't be living in a halfway house and picking up garbage.*

Drugstore Girl has shoulder-length, dishwater-blonde hair and she's tall. Muscular, too, with a mean face. When Teri spots someone fitting that description, she follows the chick through the sea of humanity in the hallways of Jonathan Kline High.

"Hey! Wait up!" Teri calls out, but the myriad other loud voices drown her out. She sees the chick go to the main foyer and out the front doors.

Out on the sidewalk, she takes a moment to appreciate the miracle of urban pedestrian traffic. All these people, yet no one speaks to anyone. I like that, she thinks. Much better than being stuck out there in the woods of New England.

Teri spots Drugstore Girl, who has just gone into Mickey D.'s for lunch. *One of the bummers of being in the can is that you don't get Big Macs, or anything else that tastes good.*

Hurrying across the street, Teri waits outside the restaurant. Soon the girl comes out, chomping away on something that looks not unlike a burrito.

Drugstore Girl eyeballs her. "You want something with me?"

"Could be I'm looking for some H."

"Go see a doctor and get a prescription."

"Funny." Then, "Is *work*"—the street name for drugs—"your only source of income?"

"Why?"

"Because I may have something better for you."

"Tell me."

"I can show you." Teri takes out her iPod Touch, brand new and gleaming. "You like?"

Drugstore Girl shrugs. "Nice. What of it?"

"I can get more. Lots more. I know people. I have suppliers who can get me as many as I want. You know people who will buy them. We can do business."

Drugstore Girl looks at the gadget, then at Teri, then the gadget again. "You a cop?"

Teri laughs. "No, girlfriend, just a chick. Just a businesswoman." She extends her hand. "Teri Goddard."

"Bounce." Drugstore Girl half-runs away.

Teri beams and waves at the departing girl. Only a potential partner in crime would run away like that.

Teri walks along, following her, hardly surprised when Drugstore Girl slows down and turns around.

"My name is LaDonze," the girl says.

"What kind of name is that?"

LaDonze thrusts out her chin in resentment, and at first Teri fears the girl will pull out her switchblade. But then LaDonze smiles, and Teri can see that they will become friends, or at least shoplifting partners.

"Feature this," Teri says. "You find an Apple Store or other kind of shop, wait till it's closed, then break in—I'll fill you in on the details later. You load up on video games, iPods and iPads, whatever else. You get it to your fence and start counting the money. Sound like a plan?"

"If you're jerking me around—"

"Not me, girlfriend. I'm in business to make money, just like you."

LaDonze frowns and scratches her head, trying to take it all in. Teri smiles some more, because she knows she's found just the right business partner.

Jaycee takes out her digitized student ID card, which doubles as lunch money, and holds it in front of the sensor. After hearing the beep, she looks around the cafeteria and wonders where to sit. Most of the seats are already taken, and if she sits at one of the tables where nobody knows her, they will likely say, "Hey, you—go sit somewhere else."

After a minute or so of standing against the wall, she sees Denna, the timid black girl from freshman chemistry.

Nix to that. She was scared to death of me when we first met, and I was one my best behavior. If I sat with her now, she would have a heart attack and die, and I would be charged with murder and sent back to Milgrom.

Jaycee stands there, checking it all out, when she spies a hand curling around Denna's face. The girl is about to eat some soup when the hand slaps at the spoon, splashing broth into the child's face. The same hand then spills the contents of Denna's tray into her lap. The shocked girl jumps up to face her tormentor, then sees that the bully is a cheerleader half a head taller than herself.

Jaycee takes a few steps in their direction, then stops. *Why get involved in this? That cheerleader could take Denna and me in two minutes.*

While Jaycee stands there contemplating what, if anything, to do, the situation reaches its own resolution. The other cheerleaders cheer and whistle their girl, who smiles, shrugs and rejoins her group.

Jaycee spots an empty seat by the window and plops down to eat. She watches the cheerleaders out of the corner of her eye and snarls. How unfair it is that some bullying cheerleader has many friends while Jaycee has none! As grateful as she is to have been released from Milgrom, she resents the fact that her involvement with Fresh Starts prevents her from having any fun.

Kline's cafeteria food is perfectly edible—she loathed the gruel they served her at Milgrom—but Jaycee most of the time has no appetite. She forces herself to eat her beef stew to conserve her strength; a few times, as an inmate, she missed meals and had to endure excruciating hunger pangs and nights of shivering.

As soon as she finishes lunch, she puts down her plastic fork and looks out the window, checking out the people walking down the streets of Manhattan. Amazingly, she spots Teri Goddard, her Fresh Start bunkie, who's standing across the street talking to some tall, big-shouldered chick with frizzy blonde hair. Jaycee has seen the blonde around school, so Teri's new friend probably isn't some criminal. But Teri is *way* out of bounds right now, being off campus during school hours. Any infraction could get Fresh Start padlocked forever.

Jaycee pushes away her tray. *If Teri gets caught, we're all busted. They'll send me back to Milgrom. Nix to that!*

She rushes out of the cafeteria, dodges a dozen cars and makes a beeline for her roommate.

Teri greets her with an upheld hand. "Bounce, girlfriend. Mind your own business."

"It *is* my business!" Jaycee retorts, her face red. "Remember Fresh Start? Wanna get us all busted?"

LaDonze points at Jaycee with her thumb. "Who's the chick? Your sitter come to check up on you?"

Teri smirks. "She's just some poor psych girl who's gone off her meds." To Jaycee she says, "Bellevue's that way, little one. Better hurry—I hear they're having chocolate pudding tonight for dessert."

Jaycee stands still. She folds her arms. "Say whatever you want to me—or her. But do it *on school grounds.*"

LaDonze looks from one to the other, then back again. "I think you ladies need some private time to get on the same page." She saunters out into the middle of traffic. As cars, trucks and buses honk their horns and drivers scream at her, she pays them no mind.

Teri gets in Jaycee's face. "Are you retarded? Huh? Is that your problem?"

"Are *you* retarded?" Jaycee speaks in a calm not raise her voice. "When you signed on to Fresh Start, the deal was: Go to school, do homework, pick up garbage, see a shrink and stay out of trouble. Which part of that did you fail to understand?"

"You don't tell me what to do!" Teri says through clenched teeth.

"Well, someone has to. As long as you, Santana and I are in that halfway house, what each of us does affects the other two. If you get busted, there are consequences for Santana and me, too. I'll probably have to go back to Milgrom. You may not care, but I sure as hell do."

"Don't see you see what a joke this is? That halfway house is supposed to make working-poor, law-abiding drones out of us. We're supposed to get jobs as fast-food workers and such and say, 'Wow! I have a bad job and my life sucks, but at least I'm not in jail! I'm rehabilitated, and I sure am proud of myself!' I'm not about that crap, and I know I won't go through life breaking my butt and making chump change. I know people, I am connected. I have certain skills. I want a happy, comfortable life."

Jaycee shrugs. "You're a criminal. You have a criminal mentality. You're still a kid, yet you have a long rap sheet. Maybe, just maybe, that means you aren't very good at committing crimes."

Teri, who is much taller and stronger than Jaycee,

has a gleam in her eyes that Jaycee recognizes as the urge to kick some butt. At that moment, the sliding door behind them opens up and out walks Allison Sullings with a bagful of groceries.

Teri darts away, unseen by Sullings, but Jaycee merely loiters. She offers Sullings a small wave.

"Jaycee!" Sullings frowns. "You know you're not supposed to be off campus right now! Better get back to school."

The girl nods repeatedly. "I hear ya." Jaycee, a street kid in so many ways, believes that snitches are the worst of the worst, so she says nothing to Sullings about her conversation with Teri. "Won't happen again."

Jaycee is surprised when Sullings smiles. "I guess you know that when I was a kid I did some juvie time, too. I guess I can overlook this one little infraction."

Jaycee smiles back, but all she can think about is Teri s plans with that muscular blonde girl and how those two troublemakers might end up getting the three Fresh Start girls back to jail.

CHAPTER 10

AT FRESH START, the laundry room is in the basement, just as it is in so many other apartment buildings in Manhattan and beyond. Wednesday night is when they wash their clothes, right after community service.

Santana, sore all over from picking up after other people on the streets of New York, carries her third or fourth basket of soiled clothing down to the laundry room. But her way is blocked by a huge green bag of trash. She looks behind the bag and spots its owner, Missus Berkowitz, straining to move the big, smelly load.

Last time I tried to help you, you ragged on me in front of the others.

As Santana bends and steps around the beach ball of a Hefty bag, she sees that old lady Berkowitz is so staggered by her burden that she may fall over and break some bones.

The girl puts down her own basket and jerks Missus Berkowitz's load out of her arms. When the old woman opens her mouth and points her finger, Santana stops her with a shut-it glower.

The woman says, "You troublemakers—"

She shoots Missus Berkowitz another menacing

face. Santana Perez is scarcely anyone's idea of the world's toughest street chick, but she learned at Abbotsford the necessity of cultivating the Attitude. A yeah-I'm-bad swagger is a vital survival skill when one is locked up with a bunch of other angry, frustrated, horny adolescent females.

Santana's armpits feel flooded as she carries the round mound of garbage to its destination and crams it into the bin. *Thanks ain't necessary, Missus B.,* she thinks as she wipes droplets of perspiration from her chin.

She goes back for her laundry basket and heads for the machines. The room freaks her out with its low ceilings, musty smell and scuffed tile floor. She reminds herself for the zillionth time that this is Manhattan, New York City, the place where people thinks it's a bargain to pay five K per month for crappy places like Fresh Start. But at least in the laundry room she gets to be away from Jaycee and Teri for a while.

"What you want, Jaycee?" she asks.

Her roommate hands her a postcard. "It was in your Levi's. Addressed to your people back home. Wanna talk about this?"

Teri says to Jaycee, "And you're worrying about *my* refusal to follow the rules!"

"Santana," says Jaycee, "don't do this to us. If that social worker Boylan saw this postcard—"

Santana blows out a huge breath. "Well I didn't mail it, did I? No, I don't think so." Then, "Fresh Start sometimes is *such* a bummer. When I was locked up, my folks could visit me. But here, it's like, 'You're trapped in Manhattan and your roommates are your family.' Well, no offense, but you guys are *not* my family."

"No offense taken," Jaycee tells her.

"I don't know much about having visitors when I was locked up," Teri tells them. "First off, you have to assume that when you first get locked up, you have people who *care* about you. And if you do have those people, and they care enough to visit you in jail or juvie or wherever, they will get so freaked out and depressed by the experience of visiting you that they will *stop* visiting you. I've seen that happen many times."

Jaycee nods. "My last lockup was at Milgrom, and I was there for, like, two months. My mom visited me but I could tell it shook her up. She would have stopped coming soon enough."

"The only real friend you have is yourself," Teri says, snarling. "People come and go. I thought I had real friends, even family, when I hung out with the street gangs. They really seemed to care about each other. Trouble was, they kept getting killed or locked up forever."

Jaycee frowns. "My mom has been a real friend to me. She does the best she can. You shouldn't be so bitter, Teri. You're young. Maybe your life will get better if you get your act together."

"You get *your* act together, blondie—"

Santana says, "Well, I'm going *my* act together by doing this." She tears up the postcard into a dozen pieces. "Didn't mail it, crisis over. Right?"

She shakes her head and sighs as she loads the stiff, funky clothing into the washer. Of the three girls, she is the only one with two parents to miss. Teri sees herself as very much alone in the world, and Jaycee feels her mother is the only one who gives a damn about her. But Santana has a mother and father at home. She worries about them and knows how disappointed they are in her.

Tannie Liu is smiling as everyone in the circle admires the gleaming, heavy gold chain around her neck.

"Is that new?" Doctor Maddux asks. "It's the first time I've seen you wear it."

"Yeah. New." The girl smiles. "Nice, huh? From Bloomie's."

Ira sneers. "Tannie, Doc's wondering if you bought it or stole it. Is it hot? 'Fess up!"

Teri rolls her eyes. "If she stole it, what's it to ya? We're all juvie criminals, remember? Anyway, Bloomie's is one of the easier stores to hit. I've been thinking of helping myself to one of their Rolexes."

Santana says, "Maybe this is the wrong place for this conversation."

"It's all good," replies Teri. "It's a shrink's office. We can say whatever we want. You punched out that jock and he died, right? You could tell us about other people you've killed and it's all confidential."

Santana's face darkens. "Be quiet, Teri."

"Back in Cabrini Green, I knew many people who offed many people. I don't mind talking about it."

Sensing Santana's anger, Doctor Maddux says, "Teri, how do you feel about knowing so many killers and victims? Doesn't that bother you?"

"Just a fact of life, Doc. The ones who got killed? In some cases, I think they had it coming."

"But you escaped from Cabrini Green without being killed, shot or raped. Were you just lucky?"

"Lucky, plus I had many friends in the city's most

powerful gang. When you have that, nobody will mess with you."

"Yet you were arrested. You're now at Fresh Start. Before that, you were at Brides' Head. What happened?"

"I got busted for shoplifting. Seems I'm not a very competent thief."

Ira says, "The truant officer caught me ditching. That's all I did. Now I'm in therapy with hardened criminals."

Jaycee says, "I was caught driving without a license."

Teri laughs. "You were caught driving a Lexus you had just stolen and soon crashed. You were using it as a getaway car while your girls broke into an Apple store. You don't get sent to Milgrom just for driving without a license."

Jaycee's eyes narrow. "Who told you all that?"

Teri grins. "We're bunkies, baby. There are no secrets at Fresh Start. Sullings' files are there for all to read."

"My friend Maria put me up to it," Jaycee says. "She got me to steal cars and shoplift. Maria and her girlfriends have this idea about becoming an all-girl theft ring."

"So," Ira asks, "are you blaming Maria for are the trouble you're in now?"

"Who do *you* blame for the trouble you're in?" Jaycee retorts. "I'll be it's your mommy and daddy."

"Let's take a timeout now," says Doctor Maddux.

Jaycee thinks back to all the time she's spent spacing out while committing crimes, and wonders if such lapses are her way of not participating in those activities. Afterwards, she can convince herself that, by zoning out, she wasn't really *there* ad because of that was innocent. Maria, ever since that day the two girls sped off in someone's idling Porsche, had Jaycee fingered for a potential professional car thief, and Jaycee was unable, or at least unwilling, to say, 'No, Maria, I won't do it.'

Why did I always agree to commit crimes with her? Was I afraid of her, or di I just want her approval?

Jaycee glares at Ira, the green-haired boy who hates school. Maybe he's right about one thing: Ira the truant, Tannie the shoplifter and Jules the illegal downloader are in the shrink's office as misguided kids in need of tough love; but the three Fresh Start offenders are considered hardcore throwaways surely fated to live out criminal destinies.

Doctor Maddux, why are you bothering with us? We're just not worth the trouble.

The girls are in a foul mood when Sullings meets them in the waiting room. "What's up with those long faces? We're not leaving till you tell me."

Jaycee stays mute, but Santana says, "Teri has a problem. She doesn't use her brain before opening her mouth."

Teri says, "Santana's problem right now is that she needs to get off the rag."

"The things about therapy," Sullings tells them, "is that it's open, honest and personal. That's why it's effective, and often it's a difficult experience. You're supposed to say what's bugging you or *who's* bugging you, and just deal with it."

"You're not the one who has to sit there and listen to all that crap," Santana says.

"Oh, but I *have* done it. Many times, in fact, and I didn't like it much myself."

"Whatcha got there?" Teri points to the white plastic bag Sullings is holding.

"Glad you asked." She reaches into the white plastic bag she's holding and takes out some oranges. "Check this out."

The girls stand wide-eyed as Sullings begins juggling the shiny orbs. Soon she's got half a dozen airborne, and her charges shout, "Do that! Do that!"

"Think fast!" She tosses the pieces of fruit to them, which they bobble or drop. Then they gather up the oranges and put them back into the bag. Jaycee doesn't know why Sullings entertained them with her juggling act; the young car thief has rarely had bosses who indulged in levity; and Teri, always conscious of the importance of being hip, cool and streetwise, thinks Sullings' clowning is lame. Santana is hungry and wonders when dinner will be and what they will be having.

On their way back the halfway house, Sullings says, "Let's hurry. I have to pee. Bad."

"Why not use a restaurant restroom?" asks Jaycee.

Sullings shakes her head. "No public toilets around here. Besides, I wouldn't sit on one of those filthy things if you paid me."

So she breaks out into a half-run and the three girls keep up with her, making a game of it. They turn the corner and Sullings slams into a large woman.

"So sorry—"

Just then she recognizes the woman. "Missus Boylan!"

The social worker regards Sullings with the consternation the Fresh Start lady has seen entirely too often. "Miz Sullings! Why are you in such a hurry?"

Sullings mops some of the sweat from her brow. She takes a deep breath, trying not to squirm despite a bladder that seems about ready to burst.

"I said, 'Why are you in such a hurry?' Why did you run around the corner like that? You could have really harmed somebody!"

Sullings offers the woman a small, shy smile. "I need to use the ladies'. It's kind of an emergency." She looks past Boylan and sees Missus Berkowitz at the front door, looking and listening.

"There's no 'emergency' that justifies running around like that, bumping into other people," Missus Boylan tells her. "You've got those three girls with you—what kind of example are you setting for them? And they *really* need good examples. This incident will be in my report."

"Wasn't her fault," Santana tells the big woman. "When you gotta go, you gotta go."

Sullings says, "You're right, ma'am. No more running to get home to use the bathroom. These girls are in rehab, so they need to be reminded of what is appropriate behavior. My top priority is their rehabilitation."

Boylan shakes her head. "No, your top priority is protecting the community from these halfway-house offenders. These girls will literally run all over town, knocking people over, if you send them any sort of message saying it's OK to do that. I haven't even gone into your apartment yet, and already I've witnessed unacceptable conduct."

"Hey, lady," Teri says, "if we stay out here two more minutes Miz Sullings is gonna do some 'unacceptable behavior'—like pee her pants!"

Santana slaps a playful hand over Teri's mouth. "Just ignore her, ma'am. When she's gone too long without eating, her brain gets retarded and she says nasty stuff."

The social workers say, "Well, we need to get on with this visit. I have a dozen other things I need to do today—they don't pay me enough to do this job. And I'm sure you know that I'm going to write down every little infraction I find."

Missus Boylan smooths out her suit, turns around and marches towards Fresh Start; Sullings and her girls traipse along behind. Old lady Berkowitz gives them all a sneer; as Sullings opens their door, Berkowitz makes a come-here gesture with her finger to Boylan.

Those old biddies hate us, Jaycee thinks. *I just know I'm going back to Milgrom to get my butt whacked with soap bars again.*

"Do you know how much I worry about having a halfway house in my neighborhood?" the old woman asks the social worker. "Those kids are not fit to live among decent people. You should be concerned with making sure they don't harm the rest of us instead of worrying about 'every little infraction' you find."

The three girls frown at each other. Boylan seems the loveliest lady alive compared to Berkowitz.

Milgrom, here I come, thinks Jaycee.

CHAPTER 11

TERI STARES OUT the window and thinks, *They should call Manhattan the City of Light. You can't get away from it, even in the middle of the night. It's like when you're in lockup—some lights are always on, better get used to it, if you don't like it, too bad for you.*

Fresh Start's windows are barred, and that's one of the reasons Sullings chose this particular apartment. There's also a combination lock of some kind on the front door, and only Sullings knows the numbers. The whole setup says WE DON'T TRUST YOU, and Teri doesn't blame them. She doesn't trust herself.

She smiles in the stillness of the Manhattan night, fingering the key to the grilled window. Sullings doesn't yet know the key is missing, and the woman is so distracted by so many other things that she was totally oblivious of Teri when the girl relieved her of it.

In their cramped bedroom, Santana, who could probably sleep through an earthquake, snorts and farts in blissful slumber. Jaycee, who has restless-legs syndrome, keeps moving and groaning. In the other bedroom, Sullings, ladylike in all other ways, snores like a foghorn.

She checks their digital wall clock and sees that it's

1:41. Time to get busy; she's made plans to hook up with LaDonze in the alley behind the Apple Store at two.

LaDonze. Teri smiles, thinking of the girl who, like Teri herself, has no compunction about breaking the law and taking what she wants. Those chumps back home simply failed to have adequate respect for Teri and her particular talents. But Manhattan, New York, man—it's so full of *abundance* and Teri's decided she and LaDonze are going out there and get theirs. Tonight.

She eases herself out of bed, pulls on sneakers, Levi's and a sweatshirt

The key opens the window just fine, but the grille squeaks and groans. Teri sweats and swallows hard as she pulls open the window, amazed that it hasn't awakened everyone in the neighborhood.

Within a minute or two, the job is done. She breathes late-night Manhattan air as she hoists herself onto the fire escape and takes its narrow steps one at a time. Sneaking around, breaking into places, stealing things—being bad feels pretty good.

She's halfway to street level and thinking about LaDonze and their break-in when she feels someone's arms around her waist.

"Go to bed."

"Jaycee." Teri sighs in frustration. "Bounce. You hear?"

"Back to bed."

"I got a date."

"Not tonight," says a second voice.

"Santana? I said, someone's waiting for me." Teri thinks for a moment about where she is and what she can do now. Get violent? She could take Jaycee in two minutes, but Santana would be a much more difficult opponent.

She grabs Jaycee, who weighs almost nothing, and flings her into Santana. Then Teri tries to take the remaining steps two at a time, but Jaycee descends on her and again wraps two skinny arms around the bigger girl and hangs on for dear life. Santana hurries down, too, but then they hear a voice from above.

"What's goin' *on* down there?" Sullings calls out from the window.

Jaycee slaps at Teri. "Dummy!" she whispers. "You woke her up."

"Not me. You did," Teri whispers back.

Sullings crawls out of the window and gropes her way onto the fire escape. "Nobody move."

Teri tries to free herself from Santana, who's wrestled her into a full Nelson. But Santana's too strong.

"Let's bounce," Teri says.

"Nope," replies Santana. "We do what the boss says."

"She's gonna put us back in lockup," Teri tells her.

"Maybe not."

The Fresh Start honcho is just a few steps away. Teri can't get free of Santana, but Teri knows plenty about dirty fighting. She throws her head back just hard enough to make solid contact with Santana's face, and immediately hears a loud whimper. Santana eases her grip on Teri, and Teri shoves the wounded girl into Sullings, who loses her grip on the fire escape and falls twenty or more feet into a half-dozen garbage cans on the sidewalk.

The girls, as agile as monkeys, climb down to the bottom of the fire escape and drop down onto the street, landing on their feet and jumping to Sullings as she lay on the trash.

"I've killed her!" Santana says with a whimper as she rubs her sore forehead. "She's dead!"

"Not dead," says Jaycee. "Just gone to sleep."

"Looks dead to me," Santana says between ragged breaths. She bursts into tears as the three girls stand over their boss like doctors over a patient.

"Quiet!" Teri says in a loud, hoarse whisper. "You make noise, the neighbors will call the cops, we'll get busted." She bends over the fallen woman and listens. She nods. "Jaycee's right. Just gone to sleep."

Santana peers at the prostrate woman. "Missus Sullings—"

Teri elbows the girl in the ribs. "You wake her, she'll call the cops. Understand?"

Jaycee says, "She's probably got a concussion. Maybe we should take her to the hospital."

Teri rolls her eyes. "Wanna go back to Milgrom?"

"They won't bust us," Jaycee whispers. "It was just an accident."

Teri arches an eyebrow. "Oh? Will anyone believe that?"

The three girls spend a few minutes looking at one another on the late-night Manhattan sidewalk. Finally, Santana asks Teri, "What *were* you doing out here all alone, anyway?"

"Doesn't matter now."

"She had a date," Jaycee says.

"Doesn't matter," Teri repeats.

"A 'date'? You don't look like a prostitute. So I'm guessing you were going to break into a store or someone's house." Santana rubs her forehead again. "Am I right?"

"Doesn't matter. What does matter is Sullings. What are we gonna do about her?"

"Hospital," says Santana.

"Nix," replies Teri.

"I'm telling you, not asking you," Santana says.

"You're not tellin' me nothin.'" But Teri sees that Santana is standing up to her, hands on hips, one chick eyeballing another. Teri very much prefers fights in which the odds are heavily stacked in her favor, and this isn't one of them.

"So we call nine-one-one," Teri says, "and tell them what? Then the ambulance comes by, gets her and takes her away. No questions, no problems. Is that our plan?"

Jaycee says, "We could steal a ride."

Santana smiles. "Drive her there ourselves?"

Jaycee smiles back. "Then dump her at the ER and ditch the ride."

"The pigs," says Teri. "They could follow us."

Jaycee says, "I can drive pretty fast."

CHAPTER 12

SULLINGS REMAINS MUTE and prostrate as Jaycee and Santana prepare to lift her into the nearby Mazda Protégé Teri is stealing. Jaycee is unsure of what is wrong with Sullings; the woman landed on plastic garbage cans, and Jaycee can't find any blood. But she knows that doesn't mean much; sometimes the most severe injuries appear minor.

The two girls look over their shoulders a few times to check on Teri's progress. She uses a simple screwdriver with a locksmith's adeptness and gets into the car with a quickness that amazes Jaycee, who can drive like a pro but has always struggled with breaking into cars. As fast as Teri works, it's not good enough for Jaycee, who feels her shoulders tighten up and sweat run down the crack of her butt.

Santana and Jaycee smile at the sound of the gentle roar of the Protégé's engine. Santana grabs Sullings by the arms and Jaycee by her legs as they hoist her off the garbage cans.

"Hang on, ma'am," Santana says to the woman. "Got your ride waiting."

"You weigh a ton," Jaycee says through clenched teeth. "Better lose a few pounds."

"Don't die on me," Santana says to her boss. "I

couldn't handle doing any more time in Abbotsford."

Teri gets out of the car to help them. The three stuff the limp body in a sitting position into the back seat of the car. Then Teri tries to sprint away, but Santana catches her.

"The job's only half done," Santana tells her.

"But I said I have a date—"

Santana pushes Teri into the back seat. "Keep her company."

Santana plops into the passenger's seat and Jaycee gets behind the wheel.

"Righteous," Jaycee murmurs, caressing the steering wheel as if it were a lover's muscles. "Where to?"

"The hospital," replies Santana.

"Which one?"

"Doesn't matter."

"Where is it?"

"This is the world's most important city. Start driving and I'm sure we'll find one within two minutes."

Jaycee puts the car in drive and flies out onto the street. She heads north for several blocks.

"I think you're going the wrong way," Santana tells her. "We'll end up in Harlem, and we don't want that."

"Don't worry," Jaycee retorts. "We're tough halfway-house kids."

"But the Harlem kids are much tougher."

Jaycee turns right and keeps going till she encounters very heavy traffic for such a late hour. She crosses three lanes of traffic and hears the blare of a hundred horns.

Sullings, in an awkward sitting position, falls over

into Teri's lap.

"She's stiff and cold!" Teri yells. "She's dead! Yuck! Dead people are gross!"

Santana turns around and reaches over to help Teri restore Sullings into a sitting position. "She's not dead till I say she's dead. OK?"

Jaycee wants to kiss this Protégé because she loves it so much. Those Japanese really know how to build cars. This one goes as fast as she wants and doesn't make any weird noises as it flies down Lexington. Jaycee knows that this long island is packed with hospitals…so where are they? Finally she sees a big glass sign saying ALL SAINTS' HOSPITAL and, below it, EMERGENCY to her right.

As they pull up and get ready to do their dump-and-dash, Jaycee says, "Gotta be quick. I'll bet they've had so many people do this that they're keeping an eye out for people like us."

They open the rear door and pull Sullings out.

"Leave her outside, propped against the wall," Teri says. "I'll tell them inside that she's here."

Santana and Jaycee get back into the car as Sullings sits up against the wall and Teri pokes her head inside the ER and calls out, *"Code blue! Code blue!"* Then she scampers over to the car and jumps in just as Jaycee pulls away.

Soon the Protégé is just another car driving through Manhattan in the middle of the night.

"Where to now?" Santana asks.

"Next stop, Fresh Start," replies Jaycee.

"For real?"

"You got a better idea?"

"I missed my date tonight," Teri says. "I'll miss Sullings. She was a good woman."

"Teri," says Santana, "how many times I have to tell you? She's not dead. Now that she's in the ER, she's probably already awake and wondering what happened to her tonight. She'll come back here and it will be business as usual. It will be better for everyone to pretend that this incident never happened."

None of them says anything more, and Jaycee drives them back to Fresh Start.

"Let's go back up the way we got down. Don't touch the door," says Santana.

Jaycee nods. "Nice and quiet. No cop cars, no yellow tape, no nothing."

Making very little sound, they climb the fire escape and crawl back into their little apartment.

"I miss Sullings already," Teri says. "I know she isn't dead, but still—"

"You have a guilty conscience," Santana tells her. "She trusted you and tried to help you, and you tried to run off while she slept."

Teri shrugs. "That's weird. All my life, they've told me, 'Your problem is that you have no conscience. You feel no remorse. You are a sociopath.' Well, maybe I *do* have a conscience after all."

Jaycee says, "All we can do now is chill till Miz Sullings gets fixed up at the hospital and takes a taxi home or something. I'm not sure if she has any money. Maybe she'll call and ask us to come get her."

They sit in the living room and stare at each other. Two in the morning, then three, four.

Teri snaps her fingers. "I have an idea. We're all hungry, right? There's this pizza joint close by that never closes. Wanna chow down?"

"You got money for that?" Santana asks.

Teri reaches into her pocket, takes out a wad of

cash and smiles.

"How'd you get that money?" asks Jaycee.

"I got it."

"How are you going to get up the fire escape with a pizza?" asks Santana.

"Maybe I'll use the front door instead."

"Oh? Do you have the code?"

"Let's find out." Teri goes to the door, punches in four digits and opens it.

"How did you get the code?"

"I didn't. It was a lucky guess."

"Goodbye. Good luck," says Jaycee.

"Oh, I'm comin' back." Teri walks out.

"She's gone forever," Jaycee remarks.

"No, she'll return. She has nowhere else to go."

The Cabrini-Green girl comes back half an hour later with a meat-lover's pie, and her two roommates say, "You surprised us."

"Told you I warn't going no place except the pizza joint. How come folks don't believe me?"

"Because you're a criminal," the other two say in unison.

"I was tempted just to bolt," Teri says.

She puts the pizza on the dining room table, but no one goes near it; as hungry as they are, they're too anxious to eat.

By five o'clock, the girls remain on the living room sofas. Jaycee speaks up: "What if Sullings doesn't call? What if she's in a coma or dead?"

"We agreed," Santana says, "just to keep chill and do our usual thing. We'll keep it up till we have reason to do otherwise."

"Our 'usual thing' this morning would be school," Jaycee says.

Santana nods. "Then that's what we'll do."

Teri grimaces. "School sucks."

"Well," Santana says, "if we don't go, old lady Boylan will know about it in fifteen minutes. Considering all the bad stuff that's happened in the past several hours, Boylan may not seem like such a big deal, but she can still make major trouble for us. She can have us busted and sent back to juvie."

Teri shifts on the sofa. "Do we still have to pick up trash on the sidewalks and see that shrink?"

"Affirmative. Let's hope all this worrying is for nothing. Maybe Sullings is coming back here right this minute. But until that happens, we will continue being the law-abiding little androids the Man wants us to be."

CHAPTER 13

JAYCEE'S SCIENCE CLASSMATES soon get so used to her that they forget she's there. Even Denna, the shy little black girl, can relax as the two do lab experiments together. Jaycee feels sorry for Denna because she seems to have a reputation for being the easiest target at school for all the bullies, and Kline seems to have more than its share of troublemakers. At least Jaycee came here with the status of being a halfway-house criminal, so the bad guys and girls mostly just leave her alone. She supposes that Santana and Teri would have her back if she needed help against the bullies, but then all three girls would be kicked out of Kline for fighting.

Jaycee, as badly as she feels for Denna, at the moment has a crisis of her own. Sullings, her legal custodian, is missing, which makes Jaycee and the other two fugitives. Everything has changed for her; the stability Sullings had provided is no longer there, and Jaycee feels truly alone in the world, orphaned and indigent, going from one boring class to the next, learning nothing.

"Denna," the instructor says, "will you go get me some supplies? I'll make a list."

Denna squirms and sighs. Jaycee knows why. The

science supplies come from a room near the gymnasium, in a section of the school where the male and female bullies hang out and look for kids to pick on.

"I'll go get the stuff," Jaycee says.

Denna smiles at her.

"Fine," says the instructor. "Come up here and I'll give you the list."

Jaycee hurries up to the front of the room, snatches the list from the instructor and, by the time she's out of the classroom, decides that the science supplies will have to be priority number two.

She leaves Kline and heads out to the hospital to find Sullings. That's priority number one.

"I need to see my auntie. Her name is Allison Sullings."

A plump lady with red fingernails enters the name into her computer. "No one here by that name. New York is a big city. Lots of hospitals. Maybe it was Mount Sinai or Midtown?"

"She was definitely here." Jaycee swallows hard. "She came into the ER at about one in the morning."

"Then she wouldn't be in emerg any more. They would have admitted her or sent her home. What was the health problem that was responsible for her visit?"

"She fell and hit her head."

More typing. "Our head trauma unit is upstairs. Maybe they misspelled her name. You can go up right now and check it out."

"Thank you. I'll do that."

Jaycee waits for the elevator, tortured by visions of

brain-dead Sullings in her mind's eye. Men and women in surgical scrubs and white lab coats hurry by. *Doing their best to look important*, Jaycee thinks with a smirk. *Rushin' and rushin' till life's no fun.* She wonders why people would choose to become doctors, nurses and other healthcare workers. You go to a hospital five days per week, surrounded by sick people and their freaked-out family members. Who would want such a job? Does it really pay that well?

The elevator finally arrives. She gets in, along with a dozen other people, and the old car takes its own sweet time in getting to floor number seven. She stands there, reminding herself that she has English in half an hour and her science instructor is still waiting for the supplies he sent her for. *He's probably wondering what happened to me. No—he's not wondering at all. He's thinking that Jaycee, the halfway-house girl, is a good-for-nothing little criminal. Always has been, always will be.*

When she reaches the desired floor, Jaycee rushes from door to door, looking at the patients' names posted. She thinks, *Less than half an hour till English, and when I'm a no-show, they'll use that to expel me.*

She checks out some more rooms, concludes that there must be a mistake, no Sullings here, when she reaches the last room and there's the boss. Jaycee doesn't recognize the soft features at first, but then notices, with relief and amusement, that the woman smiles even while asleep.

She's way unconscious. Is that good or bad?

Jaycee wants to see Sullings' chart, to get some idea of how banged up she really is. Near the bed is the chart, and Jaycee peeks at it.

DOE, JANE.

Jaycee frowns. That's the name they give to the

female stiffs who come in unidentified. Why don't they know who Allison Sullings is?

Then she remembers that the woman had no ID when her three charges, cowards to the marrow, literally dumped her outside and took off. Sullings is still listed as Jane Doe; Jaycee figures the patient has yet to wake up and tell the staff who she is.

"Do you know this lady?" asks a voice from behind.

Jaycee spins around and sees a slender blonde wearing a smock. Her name badge says WENDY WISEMAN.

"Are you a doctor or nurse or something?" asks Jaycee.

"Or something." She smiles. "I'm just a volunteer. Do you know this lady?"

"Yes. No. I sort of, you know…" At this moment, Jaycee, for the very first time, wishes she could be Teri—the smoothest, most convincing liar she has ever met.

Wendy saves Jaycee. "Oh, you must be with the school's volunteer program. You really need a name badge if you're going to enter rooms and participate in patient care. "

Jaycee nods. "Gotcha. Where do I sign in?"

"Right here." She pulls a plastic ID badge out of her pocket. "Laurie Rose signed up for this, but she quit as soon as she figured out she would actually have to *work*."

Jaycee clips the badge to her shirt. She points to Sullings and asks, "So, what happened to this nice lady?"

Wendy shrugs. Her lips become a grim line for a moment. "A mugging victim., I guess. Fortunately, there are no signs of a sexual assault. However, she has a concussion and we have no idea when, or even if, she will wake up." She shakes her head. "No ID, no money, no nothing. Sad."

Jaycee shudders. Never wake up? Does that mean the three girls are murderers? Jaycee stops herself and remembers what Teri had said: "They say I'm a sociopath. I'm all about *me*; nobody else matters." *Well, Teri, here I am, at Sullings' bedside, and my main thought is, 'I hope I don't get in trouble for what's happened to her.' Doesn't say much for me, does it?*

"I don't like that face you're making," Wendy says. "Remember that hospitals are full of very sick people. Many of them die or don't fully recover. If you're going to have trouble coping with that, maybe you should volunteer somewhere else."

Jaycee thinks, *Run*. She doesn't want to stand here and look at Allison Sullings any longer. If Wendy can see what's going inside of Jaycee, the other healthcare providers here will, too—and they'll start asking questions about why this new girl is so preoccupied with Jane Doe. Do this new girl and mystery woman know each other? If so, how?

"Back to school," Jaycee says, hurrying past Wendy.

"Wait! It's not as bad as that!"

Too riled up to wait for the elevator, Jaycee takes the stairs. She doesn't want to go back to school; she just wants to run, flee, escape--off the edge of the world, if possible.

The way back to Kline seems full of pedestrians who glower at her as she sprints past them, as if she's done something awful and is making her getaway. Which, she supposes, is more or less true. Even back at Milgrom, when she was a criminal locked up with so many other juvie offenders, Jaycee did not, even for a moment, believe that she was her crimes. If her deeds were bad, she herself was not; or if she was bad, she was entirely capable of becoming as good as the next person.

At the moment, she's not so sure of any of that.

She darts into English class just as the bell sounds.

"Nice to see that you could make it," says the instructor.

"Yessir." Jaycee wipes some sweat from her forehead as she sits at her desk.

She tries to pay attention, but her mind keeps wandering off to All Saints' Hospital and a comatose patient on the ninth floor.

Teri keeps looking up at the clock, thinking of the movies she's seen in which characters can will objects to move. She would love to make that clock's hands move nice and fast. To her, there's nothing worse than having to sit through fifty-five minutes of classroom boredom. Is this, she wonders, what they mean by "education"? Does a teenager really have to know about intermediate algebra or how to conjugate Spanish verbs in order to have success in adult life?

She looks around at the other androids sharing this classroom with her. But she's there with them, so she supposes she's no better than they are. If she got up and left, she would probably see LaDonze, whom she was supposed to meet last night so they could do a B&E. Last night was a nightmare in many ways, and aside from everything else, Teri left LaDonze waiting in vain all night. LaDonze was lucky the cops didn't pick her up for prostitution.

Teri isn't about to tell LaDonze or anyone else about what happened to Sullings last night. When you tell people things they have no business knowing, they can use it against you, and Teri has spent most of her life being around people who would exploit and manipulate her if she gave them the means to do so. Besides, LaDonze is someone with little interest in excuses or reasons. All *that* girl would say is, "Where *were* you? We made a date to do some business, and you didn't show up!"

Not that Teri is afraid of LaDonze. No way. Teri fears nobody. If LaDonze wanted to persecute or punish Teri, the big blonde girl could put out the word to her friends to harass Teri, and who has Teri's back? Only Jaycee and Santana. Jaycee would be worth less than zero in any sort of confrontation or street fight, and Santana just wants to play guitar and stay out of mischief.

The 3:05 bell rings and Teri scoops up her books and hustles out of the classroom. She's at the main doors when she looks up to find Jaycee and Santana waiting for her.

"Are you here to walk me home?" she asks, scowling. "I don't need an escort. I'm not a baby. I can dress myself. I don't wet the bed."

"We trust you," Santana says.

Jaycee dances and fidgets. Her face is white.

"What's your problem?" Teri asks.

"I saw her today over at All Saints'."

"Sullings?"

Jaycee nods and runs it down for her. "We dumped her there without her ID. They don't know who she is and they've got her as a Jane Doe."

"That's weird." Teri rubs her chin. "I thought with all this DNA testing and stuff, they could just stick a Q-Tip into her mouth and find out who she is." Then, "If they don't know who she is, I guess they don't know who dumped her there. We're not in any trouble yet."

Jaycee blows out a huge breath. "There you go again. Teri the sociopath, always worrying about Number One and nobody else."

"Oh, but I *do* care! But, yeah, I would like to stay out of jail if that's at all possible."

"We'll just keep on keepin' on," Santana tells them. "We'll act as if Sullings will wake up and come back to Fresh Start any day. Business as usual."

Jaycee takes out her volunteer ID badge. "I can use this to gain access to her room. As soon as she wakes up, I'll apologize and take her home."

Santana says, "Let's just hope this plan works out and we can all pretend none of this ever happened."

CHAPTER 14

"WHERE'S ALLISON?" ASKS Sandra Mull in the smelly office above the restaurant.

"She's busy with some stuff," says Santana as she tugs at her coveralls.

Teri doesn't like the question. "Who's gonna be picking up garbage with us today?"

"A couple of priests from one of the local Catholic churches."

"What did they do?"

"Got too friendly with altar boys."

"Oh."

Presently the three girls meet up with the priests to begin picking up trash on the sidewalk. Teri spots condoms here and syringes there, and makes a face as she sweeps the refuse into her garbage bag. She resents how Jaycee and Santana won't look at her or speak to her.

Do those two think I don't know they're copping an attitude with me. They're mad at me because I'm worried about what will happen to me if Sullings dies...but if I don't worry about me, who will?

Teri can't help ruminating over the events of last night, but blames herself very little. *If those two hadn't stopped me on my way out to meet with LaDonze, Sullings wouldn't have come out and none of this bad stuff would have gone down. Plus, LaDonze and I would be flush with cash now from whatever store we'd broken into.*

She sweeps some more crap into her garbage bag and shakes her head with the deepest disgust. *Time to visit the ladies' room. Think I'll make this a nice long one.*

She heads into Starbucks and discovers that its restroom is vacant. Too bad for Teri; a lineup would mean a long wait, and with her empty bowels and bladder, she would be happy to stand in line for a while, even make small talk with the others waiting to use the can. As she opens the door, she feels herself pushed from behind and she goes stumbling inside. She puts out her hands to cushion her impact into the wall and spins around to see LaDonze, practically shaking with rage, reaching into her jacket pocket.

"LaDonze, let's talk about this."

When LaDonze says nothing, Teri rushes at her; but LaDonze steps aside and ducks, and Teri slams into the door. Teri switches on the hand dryer, which fills the small room with a roar as loud as a jet engine.

"No violence, OK? I stood you up, but some things happened—"

Bam! LaDonze with a mighty push sends Teri into the dryer. Teri feels a sharp pain between her shoulder blades and wonders if she's broken something.

"We'll try again, LaDonze! We can work it out!"

"Really? How?" The girl asks with a big mocking smile.

Teri resents condescension as much as the next person, but at least now she isn't being shoved against walls. "You know I'm a criminal. I've been in jail, I'm living in a halfway house. I'm surrounded by snitches.

94

I tried to get out to meet you, but these other chicks got in my way. Nothin' I could do about it."

LaDonze puts her hands on her hips. "So what are you gonna do for me now?"

"We try it again. We hit the Apple Store or wherever else you want. You get seventy-five, I get twenty-five."

LaDonze shakes her head. "Wrong. I get a hundred, you get zero."

Teri shrugs. "Whatever." This moment reminds her of how alone she is in New York. Back in Chicago, she lived in America's most notorious housing project and had friendships with many powerful, dangerous people. No small-timer like LaDonze would have dared to shove her around or talk tough to her.

"If you goof this up," LaDonze tells her, "you better go back to Chi-town."

"Whatever," she repeats.

The girls' new plan is to act as though it's business as usual at Fresh Start. They do all the normal things at the appropriate times; they have conversations with their absent leader, in case anyone is listening. They see old lady Berkowitz nearby, and when they peek inside their apartment and say, "Yeah, Missus Sullings, I'll meet you downtown," their old neighbor never seems to notice that Sullings is never around.

"Old hag." Teri sighs. "She's always, like, 'I'm watching you, in case you do something wrong,' but she doesn't seem to notice that Sullings is gone."

"Let's keep it that way," says Jaycee.

Santana laughs. "Berkowitz is starting to lighten

up. Now she lets me carry her heavy stuff up and down the stairs. She doesn't thank me, but she accepts my help. I would say that represents real progress on her part."

Jaycee visits Sullings at All Saints' Hospital as often as she can. The news is seldom good or bad. Wendy Wiseman tells her, "The coma isn't getting worse, and her brain activity is encouraging."

"You spend so much time here," Jaycee says. "Do you want to become a doctor or nurse?"

"Nothing like that. I volunteer for its own sake. My father works on Wall Street. Actually, he doesn't really work; he just sort of shakes people down all day. He makes zillions of dollars and pays minimal taxes. He said, 'I used to wonder what I could do for my fellow man. But I couldn't think of anything that wouldn't have put me to considerable inconvenience.' So I sort of volunteer on his behalf."

"How unselfish of you."

Jaycee doesn't know much about Wendy's father and his zillions of dollars, but every time she goes to visit Sullings, Wendy is there somewhere on the ward. Wendy cares about Sullings because she cares about every patient, period. She tells Jaycee about Professor Packham from Columbia University, who lectured on, and wrote books about, numerical heat transfer and fluid flow until a bus broadsided the taxi he was riding in and caused a head injury that erased many years of learning from the man's brain. Or Missus Studnicki, who has motor-skill problems since taking an A-Rod foul ball in the kisser at a Yankees game.

Jaycee learns fast enough that spending so much time with Wendy sends the message that Jaycee can move out on the ward without being asked who she is or why she's there. Her All Saints' Hospital badge, which now reads Jaycee Jones, gets her past all security checkpoints and instant access to the storage closets. When in her young life has she ever moved so freely among so many people—so many *adults*? She wishes she could use this hospital time as community service instead of having to sweep up condoms and syringes near Time Square. This hospital work stimulates her mind and gladdens her heart—except, of course, when she's thinking of Sullings and what she and the two others did to that poor woman.

"You," Wendy tells her, "are a compassionate person. You have empathy. Those are admirable qualities. Just remember: Keep your distance. You can't help them if you suffer along with them."

Oh, I keep my distance just fine—except when the patient is named Allison Sullings As for empathy and compassion. I'm a car thief and shoplifter who recently destroyed a brand-new Lexus. I'm also one of the people responsible for knocking Sullings off that fire escape, and I drove us away after Teri dumped the woman's body at the emergency room. If you only knew the real me.

The fake volunteer leans into her boss's face and looks for signs of awareness. Negative.

"Come *on*, Miz Sullings," Jaycee whispers. "You've got to get it together. Wake *up*."

Santana really wants to learn to play the electric guitar, so Mister Pajala hands her one. She's sitting in the Kline cafeteria, devouring a crap sandwich because she's so hungry and dinner is probably going to be less substantial than she would like, when the music instructor shows her the instrument and invites her into the music room to give it a try.

Santana, unplugged, plucks a few chords. The guitar is a Les Paul, scarcely new but in great condition, and the girl can imagine herself onstage at a vast arena, playing for hundreds of thousands. She plays some of this and that, at once impressed by how much she's already learned and humbled by how far she has yet to go.

"You're the next Chrissie Hynde," he says.

"I doubt it."

"You've done all right with the acoustic guitar, so this electric one should be easy and fun."

"It sure feels good." Santana strokes the Les Paul as if it were her pet dog.

"It's like everything else. Once you've had the best, you'll never want anything less." Then, "Once you've had some practice with this guitar, you'll be ready to play with the school band."

Santana smiles. "I would if I could."

"Look." Mister Pajala sits across from her. "That 'afterschool commitment' you mentioned? I know why you're here. You've been through the system and have seen some of the country in different girls' facilities and such. Right now you're in a halfway house, but I'm sure we can work something out if I talk to your group-mother—"

"Missus Sullings?" Santana swallows hard. "No can do."

"Don't worry about a thing. I've worked for years with kids who've been in and out of the system, and they always benefit from things like playing music and working with a band. She'll just have to alter your schedule a little bit to accommodate us two or three times per week."

"No," is all she can say.

"As you wish." Mister Pajala's mouth is grim.

Santana gets up and, with great care, hands over the guitar. "Thanks anyway. I appreciate the offer."

"What if we met here every day at lunch?"

"Still can't do it."

"Santana," he says, "let me tell you where I'm coming from. I am a music instructor. As such, I have an obligation to foster the development of 'gifted students'—and that would be you. Wanna play some rock 'n' roll?"

Santana smiles. "That's what I live for."

When the three girls walk into Doctor Maddux's office on Thursday afternoon, Jaycee feels sure that he will sense their unease. But no; the handsome shrink pays little attention to them and spends most of the session with Ira, the boy whose greatest wish in life is to eat painkiller-laced pudding, wash it down with vodka and go to sleep forever.

"I like your punctuality," Doctor Maddux tells the Fresh Start girls. They smirk at each other; Sullings always seemed unable to make it on time. They are so concerned with remaining at the halfway house—and out of juvie—that they are doing everything Sullings told them to do and none of the things she warned them about.

"Maybe that's how the Man is going to put us back in jail," Teri says. "We're being too good, too straight. People are going to say, 'Why are those kids so squared away? Something's wrong at Fresh Start.'"

"Well," says Jaycee, "we *are* the most conscientious, cooperative students in the history of

Jonathan Kline High."

"Except when it comes to homework." Santana snarls at Teri. "It's hard enough for Jaycee and me to do ours, then we have to bully *you* into doing yours."

Teri puts down her textbook and crosses her arms. "I don't see why I have to learn Spanish. Last time I checked, this was America and we speak English. I have no use for Spanish."

"Learn it anyway," says Jaycee. "We have to show up, do our work and get good grades. We also have to keep this household running and pretend that Sullings is running it. If we fail, they'll close Fresh Start and put us back in juvie."

"Could be we were better off in juvie," says Teri. She points at her textbook, *Basic Conversational Spanish*. "That book is so boring. When I was locked up, all I had to do was time. Nobody expected me to learn anything or improve myself. Many of the other inmates spoke perfect Spanish, but they still ended up being locked up. Spanish, algebra, geography…who needs any of it?"

"We were *not* better off in juvie," Santana tells her, "and we are *not* going back just because you refuse to do homework."

"It's not that I'm refusing. It's just that book learning is not my thing. I can spend all night trying to learn Spanish and by the next morning I can't remember any of it. All the learning I've ever done was on the streets—learning things I *needed* to know so I would survive."

Reading is the worst part—Spanish, history, whatever; it's all so lame and boring! The teachers really think this will help her at some point in life? Plus, now she's got Satan—Santana—always watching her. Inevitably, Teri will tell her off and they'll start screaming, or even punching it out, unless Jaycee can get in there and cool them off.

"Now I know why you hate homework," Santana says after ducking a slap from Teri. "You can't even read!"

"Oh? And are you some kind of genius?" Teri retorts, red faced. "You're at Fresh Start, too. When Sullings first met you in Abbotsford, you were in shackles. Don't think you're any better than I am."

"We're just trying to help you," says Jaycee.

Teri gives her a mirthless smile. "Great. The thirteen-year-old car thief wants to help me. You crashed that Lexus, didn't you? Sounds like you couldn't even do *that* right." She pauses and says, "For the time being, we have no Sullings, so maybe that means we can have some fun. Instead, we're being harder on ourselves than Sullings ever was on us. We're even dusting and vacuuming in case old lady Boylan knocks on the door saying, 'I want to inspect the premises.' What a drag. You guys suck."

"Teri," Jaycee says to her, "forget that noise about how 'we'd be better off back in juvie.' Are you kidding? You've told us lots about how much you hated Brides' Head, and Santana's made no secret of what a nightmare Abbotsford was, and I've said what I thought of Milgrom. You're thinking that maybe juvie wasn't so bad because now you've been out of juvie for a little while and your bad memories are starting to fade. But we can't go back there. We need to move forward and keep on with rehab. Fresh Start is so much better than anything else we've ever had, and we can't let old lady Boylan come by and say, 'Here are three convicted felons without supervision at Fresh Start. Let's send them back to where they came from and close this halfway house.' No way."

Teri always pays the closest attention to Jaycee's reports on Sullings' condition. Teri hopes that Sullings will get better and come back to Fresh Start. But what she wants most of all is for Sullings to get these other two girls to stop ragging on her.

On Wednesday morning, the girls arrive at the office to change into their coveralls and do community service. On their way, they see crime-scene tape across the door of Kwan's Discount Electronics Store on Times Square.

Not even when they took her out of Cabrini-Green for the very first time and put her in juvenile lockup has Teri felt so alone and lonely. Sure, she remembered saying to LaDonze, "Kwan's is the easiest target, much easier than Apple." Then she explained why. But now she sees, and cannot believe, that they've gone ahead and done the job *without her*. It seems to be the ultimate betrayal.

Teri spends most of her cleanup shift sweeping up around Kwan's and peering into its cracked window. Finally, Jaycee says, "I really, really hope you don't know anything about that break-in."

"Shut up and get back to work," Teri shoots back.

At school the next morning, LaDonze loiters by the front doors. When Teri approaches, LaDonze looks past her and says nothing. But LaDonze murmurs, "Thanks, girlfriend," and shoves something into Teri's pocket before walking away. Teri reaches into her pocket and pulls out a latest-generation, brand-new iPod Touch.

CHAPTER 15

JAYCEE PUSHES THE tray along the hallway, and Wendy plucks off single-serving fruit juice cups and cookies in envelopes before disappearing into each room and doing her usual *shtick* with the patients.

"Hey, guys! Me again. I'm taking drink orders now. Do you want martinis or Manhattans? Maybe Jack Daniels on the rocks? Oh, sorry! I forgot that this is my hospital job, not my bartending job. All I have for you is cookies and juice."

Jaycee leans on the cart and laughs. Wendy is such a saint, just too devoted to serving others. Jaycee's shifts here are now as much about spending time with Wendy as getting progress reports on Sullings. Jaycee hates running from Kline to All Saints' at the noontime bell, then rushing back to school for her afternoon classes. Wendy, like Jaycee, has no life of her own; she spends most of her weekends at the hospital, so Jaycee does likewise, simply to be near Wendy. Also, Jaycee has little desire to be at Fresh Start, where Santana is "tutoring" Teri in Spanish and helping the struggling student write a paper for English on the novel *Seize the Day*. For Santana, the only experience more exasperating than making Teri read is making her write. The Chicago gangsta girl's penmanship is atrocious, so Santana borrows Sullings' MacBook Pro and types as Teri talks. As long as they use the computer, it is unlikely that they will try to kill each other.

Wendy returns to the cart and says, "Next."

They take their time going from room to room, saying nothing as they pass 909, where Sullings lay in a very deep sleep, getting *her* juice and cookies through a needle in her left arm.

Later on, Wendy says, "We're all done for now, Jaycee. You should go sit with Jane Doe. I can tell you're thinking about her all the time."

In that room, the golden glow of a sunny Manhattan day brings Jaycee no comfort. All she can see is the tiniest suggestion of a smile on Allison Sullings' naturally curved pink lips. Jaycee keeps waiting for her eyes to open and her mouth to speak. It does not happen.

"Then *you* should speak to *her*," says Wendy. "Just because she doesn't respond doesn't mean she can't hear you."

So Jaycee does as Wendy says.

"The science teacher gave me a B on my paper," she tells Sullings. "I think it's going better now that Denna doesn't think I'm a criminal who's going to slit her throat. I'm just another chick, same as all the others. The schoolwork is going well. It's really not very hard. I think there's a lot of pressure on the teachers to give us all passing grades even if we can't read, write or do arithmetic very well."

Jaycee, sitting at Sullings' bedside, thinks it's odd how she, always the most indifferent of students, now takes her studies so seriously. Before now, she saw little difference between As and Fs, and public education was one big joke. But she knows that Fresh Start is the best thing that's happened to her in quite a while, and one bad test or quiz may result in a poor grade that Missus Boylan will learn about. The old woman will knock on their door, figure out soon enough that Sullings is absent, and that will be the end of Fresh Start.

This challenge is making me more intelligent.

Or maybe she's had intelligence all along; she's just never needed to use it. Plus, all her life, people have said to her, "You're stupid and useless," and entirely too often she's believed them.

"I'm doing better in school now than I did last year or the year before. Back then, my friend Maria used to make me get up before dawn so we could go steal a Beemer or Mercedes and drive it to a chop-shop. So when I did get to school., I would fall asleep and end up flunking everything. It got to the point where lots of times I would just steal cars at night and stay in bed all day and miss school."

Jaycee feels like an actor in a movie, spilling her guts to a comatose person. She pretends that key, back and fill lights, huge and hot, burn down on her, and she's wearing half an inch of makeup. She gets up and walks around as she continues with her monolog. At the windowsill, she opens the blinds and looks out at the Manhattan skyline, wondering what's she's doing in the world's most powerful and important city. Suddenly she sneezes.

"God bless you."

Jaycee wheels around so fast that she feels dizzy. No one has entered the room, so who just spoke to her? Then she looks down and sees Sullings eyeballing her.

The girl jumps so far and fast that she nearly ends up in bed with the woman.

"Miz Sullings! You're awake! I'm so sorry about what happened! Can you ever forgive us? Say something!"

Sullings looks at her, then around her. Surveying the room, she asks, "Who are you? Who am I? Where are we?"

"You're kidding," Jaycee mutters.

Just then Wendy comes breezing in. "Jaycee—" She looks down at Sullings, who's checking her out. "Jane Doe! You're awake!" To Jaycee, she says, "When did this happen?"

"Just now."

"I better go get the nurse." Wendy, breathless, spins out of the room.

Sullings sits up and swings her legs around to the side of the bed. "Where's the bathroom? I want to have a look in the mirror."

Jaycee goes to take her arm, but Sullings says, "I can walk just fine. It's not my body that's the problem."

Sullings leaves the door open as she stares into the mirror. "I don't even recognize myself," she mutters, her face white with panic.

Presently the room fills with nurses, orderlies and a doctor.

"I'm Doctor McKenzie," says a youngish man. "Glad to have you here at All Saints' Hospital, madam. Do you have any memory of what happened to you?"

Some color returns to Sullings' face. "You're a doctor? *You* tell *me* what happened!"

"We're here to help…"

Jaycee tunes them out. She has some of the information Sullings and the doctor need. She should speak up now. But she doesn't, because she knows that she, Santana and Teri would end up back in Milgrom, Brides' Head, Abbotsford or wherever, and Sullings, due to her memory loss, could do nothing more for them.

Letting out a big, silent sigh, Jaycee decides she can't put up with this drama even more another moment. She slinks out of the room, scarcely noticed by the others, and pads down the hallway till she finds an empty wheelchair folded against the wall. She pulls it open and collapses into it, wiping cold sweat from her brow and wondering if she's coming down with something. Rocking back and forth, hugging herself, she hears the excitement in Sullings' room but can't get excited herself.

The boss has amnesia! Jaycee has seen enough TV dramas about such a condition to assume that Sullings will spend the rest of her days trying to put back together that huge, shattered jigsaw puzzle of her life.

I'd love to pin this on Teri, but Santana and I are also at fault. We did this to Sullings. When everyone else was calling us riff raff, she actually cared about us and wanted to give us new lives. So we destroyed her life. Maybe the system is right about us—we are riff raff.

She closes her eyes and maybe nods off for a moment or two when she feels a small but firm hand on her shoulder. Then another one on the other shoulder. Looking up, she sees Wendy, smiling down at her.

"I thought *I* was the only one," Wendy says, sounding choked up. "The only one who cared more about these people than I cared about myself. But after seeing you with Jane Doe…"

She begins massaging Jaycee's shoulders. The halfway-house girl says, "You were right—I need to keep my distance."

An orderly calls out, "Wendy, some help please?"

"Right away." To Jaycee she says, "Same time tomorrow?"

She gulps. "OK." Ever since Sullings' fall and hospitalization, Jaycee doesn't feel she has any normalcy left in her own life. She isn't sure there will *be* a tomorrow, for anyone, much less one in which All Saints' Hospital will still be there when Jaycee arrives.

Hurrying off the ward, Jaycee strips off her smock and dumps it into the laundry bin. She takes the stairs all the way down to the main floor, not stopping once even to catch her breath. She's grateful at this moment to be a lifelong nonsmoker with unlimited physical stamina. At Milgrom, many of the girls smoked, but Jaycee couldn't stand the smell of the stuff. She's surprised that Santana and Teri don't light up, either.

Exiting the huge hospital, Jaycee hears the blare of honking horns and raised voices of New York City. To her, it's vastly preferable to the chaos raging inside her own head.

A Federal Express truck pulls up at the curb and its driver, sweating and chomping on gum, flies out of the vehicle and into the hospital with a half-dozen small packages in the crook of his arm.

Jaycee hops into the truck before she even realizes what she's doing. She wants to flee, both in time and space, to escape this mess and go back to that day when she and Maria jacked that car and drove it out to the U. just because it seemed like a fun thing to do and that's what life was about: Finding fun things to do and doing them.

The truck, with no mind of its own, is ready to do as Jaycee pleases. She is about to step on the gas and drive it to—where? Suddenly, she throws it back into park and takes her hands off the steering wheel.

She can't do it. She thinks back to that night with Maria and the girls at the Apple Store. The cops and the Lexus and flipping the car. They pulled her out, asked if she was OK and cuffed her. The judge sent her to Milgrom, where the other girls literally beat her butt black and blue.

Now she's in a courier truck full of other people's property.

Which part of "crime doesn't pay" has she failed to understand?

"Hey! Little girl!" A man stands ten feet away, pointing at her. "You're not the driver! Get out before I come in and drag you out!"

Jaycee jumps out just as the driver returns.

"You see that little blonde girl?" The man points in her direction as she jogs away. "She tried to steal your truck, man. Glad I was there. I was just about to take her over my knee and spank her."

CHAPTER 16

SOMETIMES, SANTANA TELLS herself, running out of options can be a good thing.

The girl walks down Times Square, remembering Jaycee's report on Sullings. "She doesn't even remember her own name." Santana thought at first that such news was disastrous.

But then Teri said, "Well, she's a nice lady, but she's our *boss*. If she's not coming back, it means we don't have a boss anymore. I'm OK with that. I don't like bosses, period."

The three convicted felons maintain their normal routine—school, community service and group therapy—with the difference being that they have no idea when, if ever, their routine will end.

"Better get used to it," says Jaycee.

At some point, of course, someone of importance and authority will come by and check them out. That day may tomorrow or next week or in three months. As long as the liaison from Kline High tells Social Services that the girls are passing everything; as long as Sandra Mull and Doctor Maddux file no complaints, and Pearl Boylan's two zillion other clients keep her too busy to scrutinize Fresh Start, its three residents may be able to keep playing house indefinitely.

"Maybe," Santana says, "something will come along and fix this problem for us."

"I can't imagine what," says Jaycee.

"Me neither. But it won't happen if we're back in jail." She adds, "I've been locked up for so many years already, I don't know what to do with all this free time. in lockup, they tell you what to do and when to do it."

Sometimes she walks Jaycee to All Saints' Hospital, and the little blonde keeps on about her special new friend Wendy.

"Who's Wendy?" Santana asks, grabbing Jaycee by the arm.

Jaycee babbles for another few moments, but her blush and twinkling eyes tell the older girl all she needs to know.

"You're supposed to go there to see Sullings, not find yourself a girlfriend."

"It's not like that." Actually, Jaycee doesn't know what it is or isn't. As a cute little blonde in this or that all-female lockup, she's been kissed or felt up many times by bigger, older girls. She likes it, too—the kisses on her lips, the tongues in her mouth, the hands on her breasts or between her legs. She likes boys, too, she thinks, but hasn't done much with them...yet.

"At least that hospital thing is keeping you out of trouble," Santana says. "Teri is, like, 'Now that Sullings isn't here, I'm going to check out this town and see what's happening.'"

"I guess she'll get busted and sent back to juvie."

"Yeah. I think she's got this idea that this LaDonze chick she's hanging out with is some kind

112

of great criminal who can help her get rich. Which she is not."

Santana gets off the subway alone and takes in the city in her own way. Walking along a street lined with nightclubs, she hears the pounding dance beats beckoning her to go in and boogie. She's heard many things about this section of town and its vibrant nightlife but did not believe that she, a convicted felon staying in a halfway house, would ever have the liberty to head down here and check it out *in person*.

She walks a couple more blocks and there it is— the center of Lower East Side nightlife. It looks like nothing more than a series of dilapidated brownstones. Yet each door opens and a blast of something—rock, funk, jazz, blues, hip-hop, punk, grunge—assaults the neighborhood.

The clubs' names seem hidden somewhere; Santana guesses that the hip people who frequent such places know their monikers. She enters a place whose name seems to be the Worm in the Apple simply because its sign says *NO COVER.* That is the only kind of place Santana Perez can afford right now. The money they found in Sullings' wallet will be spent soon enough, and the threesome will need to cope with a cash shortage. Teri started flashing a small wad that came from "doing a job with LaDonze." Santana didn't want to hear about it.

Inside the club, the music is so loud that Santana instantly thinks of the time she stood near a runway and watched a jumbo jet take off. Her ears took two days to stop ringing. The bouncer here doesn't even ask for ID—this girl could pass for twenty-five, and with her Whitney Houston face and better-than-average breasts, she's the kind of chick he wants in his establishment; he doesn't want to scare her off.

Santana nods and smiles. Then she enters the nightclub itself, which is smaller than many apartments she's been in. The band, called Pap Smear—what genius thought of *that* name? she asks herself—is loud and amateurish, but the dozens of people filling the minuscule dance floor don't seem to mind the bad music. They bounce up and down and against each other. Santana retreats to the back, where the bar is located.

"Like a beer?" asks the bartender.

She rubs two fingers against her thumb, the universal gesture for "I'm tapped out."

"Girls drink free," he tells her. "Like a beer?"

She nods and accepts the can of Pabst Blue Ribbon. Pap Smear is pretty incompetent, but Santana leans back and drinks it all in, happy to be here, by herself, just another cute chick in the big city. Nobody in this joint knows, or needs to learn, that she is a convicted felon who lives in a halfway house where they want to know every time she drops a deuce. She watches the band and pays close attention to the guitarist, whose fingers slip up and down the frets and plucks the strings as if he'd been doing it all his life. He's better than the rest of his band, she thinks. As an inmate at Abbotsford, she lost touch with emotions such as *desire*, because what point was there in wanting something when the Man would never let you try to get it?

I have seen the future of music in America, and its name is Santana Perez.

The band finishes its set, followed by another band, and then one more. Santana loves it—this puny nightclub with three bands! It's one nightclub in a neighborhood with a dozen other, in a city with a dozen other neighborhoods, in a country with a few dozen other cities full of nightclubs. These bands play for chump change, hoping that in the audience, *someone* of significance in the audience will say to them afterwards, "I'm with artists and repertoire at such-and-such records, and I'd like to sign you on."

At just after three in the morning, the nightclub turns on its house lights and says goodnight to its patrons, who, like the customers at the other music joints, stumble out the door and into the night. Few, if any, are ready to go home just yet. Santana stands up against the building, watching them with amusement. She remembers a nightspot in Chicago where, night after night, the partygoers hung out in the parking lot, mingling, sometimes fighting and always making plenty of noise. The nearby residents lost so much sleep that they implored city hall to close the club. The mayor's office, instead of padlocking the place, simply canceled its pouring license, compelling the nightclub to close because it could no longer sell alcoholic beverages on the premises.

Santana looks at a nearby fence covered with bills and posters. One of them says:

GUITARIST WANTED. MUST PLAY ORGINAL MUSIC. SERIOUS INQUIRIES ONLY

She tears off a strip with the contact phone number and puts it into her pocket.

"Santana? Is that you?"

She turns around and sees Ira Stein, the green-haired boy who wants to die. In this milieu, he fits right in—studded leathers, half-dozen earrings, nihilistic attitude. When the bands take their breaks, he probably tries to make suicide pacts with them.

"Do you come out here often?" Ira jumps and fidgets, from exhilaration, or drugs, or both. "It's more fun when the cops come out to clear the neighborhood. We outnumber them, we refuse to leave, there's this big confrontation. It's as exciting as dancing."

"You must have great fake ID. You look nowhere else to twenty-one."

"Nobody ever cards me. I come down here with tons of cash. I drink like a fish. I tip well."

"I would never have expected to see you down here," Santana says.

"Why?"

"Because you're not...*hip*."

"Oh? And you are?" Then, "You know what I like so much about this neighborhood and these nightclubs? They're real."

"Real as opposed to fake?" Santana asks.

"Real as opposed to pretentious. These are people who come down here to drink, dance and have fun. They don't care what anyone else thinks, and I totally respect that." He pauses. "So, Santana, what's the deal with you? You said in the shrink's office that you live in that halfway house with those other chicks and it's into bed at nine o'clock or something. Does that boss lady know you're down here at this hour?"

"Do *your* parents know that you're here now?"

"Nope. They're so full of guilt over having a suicidal maniac for a son that they give me whatever I want and they let me go my own way. I know it's different with you. You've been locked up a lot. You killed someone once, right?"

Santana feels her blood turn into ice water. "I thought the shrink told us, 'What's said in this room stays in this room.' Neither of us is supposed to be out here at this hour, talking about these things. So let's pretend that this conversation didn't happen, all right?"

"I hear ya. But I'm wondering about this halfway house you live in. What's it like? I've never met anyone in that kind of situation."

Santana shrugs. "As you New Yorkers would put it, 'It is what it is.'" She looks Ira up and down and decides he's no threat to anyone. He might even be handsome if he let his hair grow out to its natural color, took off some of his earrings and put on a few pounds of muscle. The problem is, what if Ira told someone that Santana, Jaycee and Teri were out gallivanting at insane hours while Sullings was supposed to be supervising them? Breaking curfew is not the end of the world, but if old lady Boylan shows up and finds out what is actually happening, the three girls may as well be selling pounds of crystal meth and molesting children in Central Park.

"Ira," she says. "I need your help. I've got two roommates at that halfway house, and we're all kind of acting out right now. But I need to you keep this a secret. Can you do that for me?"

"Damn straight."

They shake hands. Santana doesn't like the idea of sharing secrets with Ira, who sees Doctor Maddux twice a week, who in turn speaks to old lady Boylan on a regular basis. But then, Santana reminds herself, she has few options in life right now.

CHAPTER 17

JANE DOE, THE woman thinks. That's what they're calling me. I don't like it. I wish I could have my name back, whatever it is.

The doctors have told her she is between thirty-five and forty. They have been candid enough to inform her that someone propped her up against the wall at the emergency entrance before taking off. So here she is—in All Saints' Hospital? is that what they call it?—with no clear idea of anything.

Concussion, said the doctors. Amnesia. The woman believes them; she feels as if she's been conked on the head with a crowbar.

"It could be worse," Doctor Wozny tells her. "I'm glad you can read your chart and understand what's being said to you. In some cases of amnesia, the patient forgets the English language and has to learn it all over again. Once you start learning about yourself and your life again, the things you've forgotten will come back very quickly."

"But I still don't know my own name!"

"No, but we can correct that soon enough. But you do know you're in this hospital, in New York City. In America."

"Yeah, but only because you people have told me

those things." She groans. "Now I'm going to have to learn all that stuff I've forgotten."

"Look, you were in a coma for about a week. That is a very serious matter. Don't start beating up on yourself. Your memory will return; it will just take some time."

"Easy for you to say, Doc. You want to know how I feel? It's like I've walked into a movie theater halfway through the picture. The plot and characters are a mystery to me. I'm just guessing about the facts of my life. Do you know how that makes me feel?"

"I empathize with your frustration—"

"Do you really? How do I know that I don't have a husband and children somewhere who are trying to find me?"

"We've been busy with that," says Lieutenant Jerry Lankford. "Thus far, nobody has stepped forward to claim you."

"Oh, that makes me feel so much better. So maybe I have a family somewhere but they don't care enough to look for me."

"We expect to get some results soon."

"But I've been here a week. Isn't this the computer age? Can't you just take a hair off my head and get my DNA markers and figure out who I am?"

"Doesn't work quite that way, ma'am. If we could do that, we would have done so by now." He adds, "I'm pretty sure you're fairly new to New York because you speak with a regional accent from out west. The people back there figure they'll hear from you when they hear from you, and your contacts here figure everything is OK because you haven't called them in the past week. We live in a very mobile culture, with people moving around all the time. Give it a little longer, and the people who know you here will start calling us and saying, 'Where is she? I'm getting worried.' And we'll say, 'Please give us a physical description of her.' Then we'll be able to tell you who you are and a hundred other things."

"In the meantime, I just wait and ask myself, 'Do I have any health insurance? What do I do for a living? Do I like my job? do I have an apartment here in town?' Am I homeless?' Well, if I was a drunk or dope addict, I'm cured. I have no desire for a drink or a fix."

When Wendy, the bubbly cutie who never seems to go home, bops in and says, "Do you still like your coffee black?" Jane Doe nods. She thinks she's been drinking the stuff for years but isn't sure. She thinks Wendy is a sweet kid, but the girl's nonstop smiling, twinkling and giggling are starting to annoy her.

That small blonde girl—the Jodie Foster lookalike—who goes by the name Jaycee, says, "Try your coffee with cream. That'll smooth it out."

Jane Doe does, and the coffee tastes better. That Jaycee, she's a shifty, sly kid. If she didn't know better, Jane Doe would guess that Jaycee and Wendy were going steady. She's never liked girls that way, but who is she to judge? Whatever turns you on.

Wanting to have a woman-to-girl talk, Jane Doe is about to say, "When I was your age…" but then can't remember a single thing about what she thought or how she felt about being Jaycee's age. It might help, she thinks, if she knew at least what her name was, assuming she has one and it's not Jane Doe.

Jaycee Sheedy is sitting on a sofa somewhere in the

staff-only lounge of All Saints' Hospital, making out with Wendy and not caring if the whole world looks. She spaces out a lot, and that's a good thing, because it allows her not to think about Allison Sullings' amnesia and the fact that she is close, very close, to being sent back to Milgrom. She also remains wonderfully oblivious to the knowledge that this predicament is largely her own fault—hers and Santana's and Teri's.

"Quit spacing out," Wendy whispers into her ear. "You're on Planet Fringus. I need you here with me."

"It's good where I'm at. I like Fringus."

They see each other exclusively at the hospital. So far as Jaycee know, Wendy is just a figment of her imagination; the girl doesn't exist outside of All Saints' Hospital. But the person who *always* exists here is Allison Sullings, and Jaycee can't run very far from the fact that Sullings' prognosis is a huge question mark. Wendy, too, figures out that, for Jaycee, Sullings is a special patient—did Jaycee and Jane Doe know each other before Jane Doe's admission?

Jaycee fears being unable to forgive herself for what's happened to Allison Sullings. She also discovers that this is probably the first time she's ever given a damn about anyone except Number One.

Santana finishes screwing together the parts of Missus Berkowitz's do-it-yourself kitchen cupboard.

"All done," the girl says. "Should last you a while."

"Where did you learn to do this?"

"Here and there." There was nothing "do it yourself" about this project; the old woman would never have managed it herself, and Santana needed every bit of her juvie cabinetmaking training to do the job.

"Santana?"

"Yes, ma'am?"

"How's Missus Sullings these days? Don't see her around much."

"Oh, she's as busy as the rest of us. She has to go out for meetings and deliver progress reports on Fresh Start."

Teri calls out, "Santana, you got a phone call."

"Who is it?"

"Dunno. Come here and find out."

Santana does.

"Santana Perez?" asks the voice.

"Speaking." It must be the guy who's looking for a guitarist! She's amped.

"Where do you come from with that funny accent?"

"Out West." She's lived in a half-dozen states for all the wrong reasons, but this guy doesn't need to know that.

"We need you here in half an hour." He gives her the address.

"I'm already there."

Santana feels winded as she reaches her destination. She thinks maybe she's stumbled into a Grateful Dead documentary: A bunch of row houses, windows open, music loud enough to be heard from Ellis Island. It's a wonder the cops don't show up and tell them to turn it down.

She opens the unlocked door and climbs the cracked, scarred floor. Santana can feel the music in every cell; it fills her up like protein, making her strong. It's one thing to stand there and listen, even dance; it's quite another to *jam*.

She reaches her destination and stands before the band. They look at her; she looks at them. Nobody can think of anything to say.

"Well," one of the guys says at last, "I didn't know Whitney Houston would be sitting in with us today."

These boys are all pallid and emaciated. Santana doesn't know their band's name but thinks they should be called *Boys of Auschwitz*.

"Where did you get that guitar?" the boy guitarist asks her.

"In jail. That's where I learned." She's taller than they are, and now they know she's been locked up. They probably respect her now, or maybe just fear her. If she can't be respected, she'll settle for being feared.

The guitarist takes off his electric instrument and hands it to her. She takes off her acoustic guitar and lays it on the floor.

"Try it," he says.

She lets her fingers explore the strings and frets. It feels much like the guitars she's used at school.

"You don't have to play air guitar," one of the boys says. "You're strapped into the real deal."

Santana plucks a B chord and smiles at how the music comes through the speaker. "Too yummy."

"School's out," the guitarist tells her. "We're not here to teach, we're here to play. So, *can* you play?"

"Yeah."

"How good?"

"I can play good. Real good." Santana says.

CHAPTER 18

IT'S GETTING ON close to two in the morning, and Teri's doing her thing in the streets of Manhattan. She loves the city because it's full of options— snoozin' or cruisin', whatever's your choosin'.

At the moment, she's checking out a specific building just south of Harlem. It's a highrise that's hardly the best but far from the worst in Manhattan, definitely not Trump Tower. The main thing she's noticed is that its front door is warped and often doesn't lock securely—the management or maintenance people are too stingy or lazy to repair it. So she waits behind a bush until there's nobody around, and when she gives the door a good hard tug it opens without much resistance.

Presently she's in the lobby, standing at the elevators, relieved that the place doesn't reek of feces and urine. Back at Cabrini-Green, there just weren't enough restrooms to go around, and things got a little bit funky sometimes. In the elevator, she punches floor 25 and likes how nice and smooth the ride is.

Apartment 25C has only one lock, and Teri's just fine with that. She takes out Sullings' driver's license and slides it right in there; the door opens with the tiniest *click*.

Inside, Teri frowns. Despite the darkness, she can tell that the place is clean, comfortable, tastefully furnished. No Cabrini booty smell in here. Don't mean a thing—she's not here to steal anything, just say hi in her own way.

She takes baby steps, trying to figure out which bedroom is which...

The lights come on so fast that she has only a moment to see the aluminum baseball bat flying towards her. Young and agile, she does a dance around it, hearing the bat slice through the air with a *whoosh!*

Teri takes a moment to figure out that the bat is being swung by someone—an older woman in a blue terrycloth bathrobe. The woman has Teri trapped in a corner.

"Come up here to rob me, young thing?" she asks, her eyes blazing with rage. "You're better off slangin' dope. I got nothin' here worth stealin'."

"I didn't come here for that," Teri says.

"Oh? You come up just to say hi? Funny, I didn't hear you knock. Maybe I oughta knock some sense into you." She raises the bat, but Teri can see that the old woman is tired and weak; dodging her next swing will be easy.

At that moment, the door opens and Teri sees a familiar face.

"LaDonze!"

The other girl sneers. "Teri? What you doin' here? I don't recall invitin' you to my mama's place."

"Came by to say hi. Your mama's been tryin' to hit me with that bat."

"She broke in. Didn't buzz from downstairs or knock on the door," said the old lady.

"She shouldn't have broke in," LaDonze says, "but I *know* this fool, Mama. No need to be beatin' on her."

"If she yo' friend, how come she don't buzz or knock? Listen, chile, I warned you about makin' friends with everythin' you meet at school. Half them kids at school? They already been in and out of jail, and that's probably where they headin' soon as school's out." Mama looks up at the wall clock for a moment. "And how come *you* be boppin' in here after decent people's gone to bed?"

"I got *business* to do, Mama. You need that money I bring home, right? It puts meat and potatoes on the kitchen table, don't it? Well, I got to do what I got to do." LaDonze snatches the white slip of paper from Teri's hand. It says: THINKING OF YOU. TERI.

"Want to tell me what this is about?" LaDonze asks, looking more confused than angry.

"Let's take this out into the hallway," Teri says.

"You ain't got nothin' to say to her you can't say in front of me." Mama shakes the bat a little bit, to show them who's the boss.

"Outside," says LaDonze, pushing Teri towards the front door. Then, "Mama, you git back to sleep, OK? This stressin' out ain't doin' your diabetes any good."

In the hallway, LaDonze says, "First off, don't never come by unless I invite you. Hear me? Now, tell me what's so important that you had to come here in the middle of the night."

"That note is what's important. My goal was to come here, put that note on your pillow while you slept and leave without making any noise. I think you underestimate my abilities."

127

"Like how?"

"Well, your last score was at Kwan's. Nice, huh? I put you on to that. You and your girls need my help. I can do that for you. But you need to trust me and have confidence in me."

"You got another score in mind, or are you just talkin' because you're in love with the sound of your own voice?"

Teri chuckles. "Oh, I got a few things in mind."

CHAPTER 19

JANE DOE'S HEAD feels better every day. They keep giving her painkillers and sleeping pills until she falls asleep naturally every night and wakes up well rested. She thinks, *I'd be fine if only I could remember my name and a hundred other things...*

Doctor Wozny says, "Wendy, I want you and Jaycee to help with her rehabilitation. Use those cards to quiz her on common objects."

Jane Doe gets a perfect score. "I know what houses, cars, bottles and footballs are. What I *don't* know is my name."

"Don't be in such a hurry," the doctor tells her. "It will all come back to you. It will just take some time."

Sullings just sighs and nods. Jaycee, too, takes little comfort in the doctor's words; her conscience tortures her each day over Sullings' ordeal and Jaycee's culpability in it.

Two dozen times each day, it's all Jaycee can do to keep herself from blurting, "Your name is Allison Sullings, you're thirty-four years old and you run Fresh Start." Maybe that's just the woman needs to bring it all home.

But Jaycee has to keep her yap shut until Sullings

is able to come back to the three girls and Fresh Start. They will need her to keep up the fight against Pearl Boylan, the evil social worker.

She's done all she could so far to get us off the streets or out of jail and into Fresh Start. We need to assume that she wants us to continue whatever progress we've made.

The girls just have to wait until Sullings' memory comes back, however long that takes.

At Fresh Start, Teri does her homework sometimes. Santana has stopped ragging on her about it, mostly because the music girl is too busy trying to learn all of her new band's songs. The band, Doomsday, has a gig coming up at some Lower East Side joint called the Hole. Santana has a fantasy of being a young, female Bob Dylan who's going to get up onstage and blow everyone away.

"Your band," Teri says, "needs a new name. 'Doomsday'? I've heard lots of other bands go by that name. Find something new. How about 'Santana'?"

"I think that's already been used, too. I thought of 'Fresh Start,' but that sounds too goody-two-shoes. Anyway, it's not my band. The lead singer, Prisoner, is the boss. He thinks our name suits the band perfectly."

Jaycee is sitting at the desk as she writes Sullings' report to Social Services on their leader's MacBook Pro. She will then hit SEND and the report will travel electronically. No one will know Jaycee wrote it. "Maybe call the band Headache. Its music is sure giving me one."

"Quiet," says Teri. "I got to read this thing for English." She holds up a Harry Potter novel.

Jaycee cackles. "Pretty challenging stuff. Sure you can handle it?"

Teri ignores her. "I liked *The Onion Field.* That was about real people, real life. School is a vacation from reality."

"Yeah, Teri. If you were getting good grades, you would say, 'School is a great thing. I look forward to it five days a week.'"

"Hey, show me some respect. Santana's onto a good thing with that band, and you're at the top of your class at Kline. I have talents, too."

"What are your talents?"

"Guess."

Jaycee shrugs. "Tell me."

Teri sits up. "I am an accomplished criminal."

"Not so accomplished. You got busted. That's why you're here."

"You should put that into your report to Social Services: 'Teri Goddard is an accomplished criminal.'"

"Boylan would love to read that. It would motivate her to shut us down."

Santana caresses the Gibson guitar she's holding. "Got to play it real cool right now, Teri. Don't get anyone mad at us. Jaycee has to be careful about what that report says before she sends it in."

"You two should cut me some slack," Teri tells them. "After all, who's bringing in all the jack right now? Who's feeding us?"

"What 'jack' are you talking about?" Jaycee asks. "That hundred you brought in? Well, it didn't last very long. We're three growing girls who need their three meals per day, and that means a regular supply of money. Do you know what we're having for dinner tonight? A bowl of air."

"So I'll go out and shoplift some bread and butter," Teri tells her.

"You'd get caught," Santana says, "and Boylan would find out, and that would be the end of Fresh Start." She sighs. "I definitely don't want to go back to Abbotsford, ever."

Jaycee nods. "I feel the same way about Milgrom. Let's try getting through this crisis in a lawful way."

"Well, I'm working, sort of," Santana says. "This gig coming up? I'll get paid something. That should help a little bit."

"A little bit," Teri mutters. "I'm just totally overwhelmed."

Santana snarls. "At least I'm kicking in *something*."

"I have something going on," Teri says. "When it happens, we'll have so much scratch that we'll be able to eat steak eight nights per week."

"I hope," Jaycee tells her, "that your 'something going on' has nothing to do with that chick you're always hanging with. Donna? LaDonna? Madonna?"

"Her name is LaDonze."

"LaDonze the gangbanger. I'll bet you hung out with lots of LaDonzes back in Cabrini-Green, huh? Lots of good they did you, too."

"If you want to make a score," Teri says, "you need to have connections. LaDonze and I have already worked together and it went well. If you have a problem with that, too freakin' bad."

"We have a problem with losing our freedom because of you," Santana tells her.

Teri takes off a Nike and throws it at Santana's head. "Don't start raggin' on me, OK? You just joined a band that has zero talent and has a great shot at making no money, and this *chick*"—she points at Jaycee—"found herself a *girlfriend*. At least *I* have some money-making goals and I'm no dyke, which is

132

more than I can say for her."

"My love life is none of your business." Jaycee spins away from the laptop. "Her name is Wendy. She doesn't know about Fresh Start or how I know Sullings. Wendy goes to a different school. She's Jewish and her family is rich."

"A rich Jewish girl in New York," mutters Teri. "Imagine that." Then, "Wendy is going to find out all about us soon enough. She's a chick; we're chicks. Chicks ask lots of questions and they listen to the answers. She probably remembers everything you've said to her."

Jaycee looks down at the floor. "Yeah, she does that. She wants to know all about me."

Jaycee, who spaces out so often, doesn't know why Wendy wants to spend all that time with her. Does Wendy, rich and Jewish and pretty, somehow get turned on by the idea of having a same-sex fling with someone her parents would surely dislike? Jaycee, an only child, spent most of her time from age nine getting into trouble with Maria without getting caught very much at first, and carrying on that way because her mother was too exhausted to do anything about it. Nights of roaming around with Maria and stealing cars, then driving them into chop-shops seemed the normal thing to do.

Consider Santana. Every day she must restrain herself from phoning home and yapping away with her family.

I never get homesick. Why not?

Jaycee knows that Wendy's people are rolling in money, but the street kid doesn't much care about that. What Jaycee envies is that when Wendy talks about her family and what they do, the girl speaks with a sense of familiarity and affection that Jaycee has never known.

Most of the time, Maria seemed to be the only family I had.

"I want you to meet my family," Wendy tells her.

"Why?"

"Because you're so much different from the other friends I've had. Rich people are weird. They seek out each other, and then try to figure out who's richer. You don't have any money, yet you have this 'I'm OK, you're OK' vibe that really resonates with me. You're not after money, and my dad thinks everybody is after it—or at least everyone is after *his* money."

"And I'm not?"

"Not at all. All you want is to love and be loved."

"Do I love? Am I loved?"

"Oh, yes. *Yes.*"

"Nice for me."

Jaycee promises to be Wendy's date for a yacht party in a week or so. She has nothing to wear, but doesn't care, because she's Wendy's charity-case friend and those on the yacht will scarcely expect her to be their kind of people.

"Sure, Wendy," she says. "I would love to be your date."

Wendy beams, and Jaycee feels warm all the way to her soul.

The late morning is very clear but breezier than Jaycee would like. A magnificent sun makes the harbor sparkle, and the girl thinks that even the ugliest city looks good in fine weather. Not that she thinks New York is ugly; she's driven through worse places.

Her only problem is that she doesn't know where to meet Wendy. She's already late due to mechanical problems in the subway system.

Jaycee looks up and down, then around. Finally, she sees Wendy—the young lady with the crew members and fashionably arrayed high-society types. They're all about to board a yacht big enough for *Lifestyles of the Rich and Famous*. A small helicopter hovers overhead.

Wendy shades her eyes with her hand and uses the other one to wave at Jaycee. "Over here!"

The street girl waves back and walks in Wendy's direction. In this world, Jaycee thinks, there's *affluent, rich, very rich* and *don't even ask rich*. Guess which category Wendy's people fall into?

Jaycee keeps walking, and Wendy meets her halfway. The two embrace. Wendy whispers, "Do you love? Are you loved?"

"Yes."

"Then let's party."

Wendy takes her by the arm. Jaycee feels giddy, staring at the gleaming behemoth they're about to board. She pictures Wendy's father "shaking down" people on Wall Street every day.

Nice work if you can get it.

Wendy introduces her to the crew; Jaycee shakes hands, smiles, lets the people's names fly in one ear and out the other. The crew members offer Wendy big, loving smiles—who doesn't?—but give Jaycee small, tight ones that ask, *So, little waif, has Wendy made you her latest charity project? Is that why you're here with us today?*

They board the yacht, and Jaycee thinks it looks like a Las Vegas resort, if such places could float and sail around the world. Everything is immaculate and impeccable. She's getting hungry and wonders what kind of chow they'll be serving. Probably lots of everything—caviar, lobster, all that yummy stuff that rich folks love to eat. She's never tried any of it.

Wendy pulls her closer and says, "Once we're done with my parents and their boring friends, we'll have the rest of the party to ourselves. There are a hundred places we can sneak off to in this tub."

Jaycee giggles. "When you said your dad had a boat, I didn't think you meant *this*."

Wendy giggles back. "He always says bigger is better. Maybe he has this sexual-inadequacy thing so he has to compensate by buying a huge yacht. I think he's bored with my mom but for whatever reason he never cheats on her. In business, he's so greedy for money and power that he practically says to people, 'Give me the best deal possible or I'll ruin you.' So he makes tons of money and spends it on the biggest, splashiest, most expensive things. Middle age may have something to do with it. He knows he's in the second half of his life. Maybe it freaks him out."

They sneaked up to the helipad and sat pressed up together. Jaycee looked out at the glittering skyline and sparkling water. She turned her head and gazed at the charming, sweet-smelling young thing who just couldn't seem to get enough of Jaycee Sheedy. *And just last month, the chicks at Milgrom were pulling down my panties and smacking my butt with a bar of soap. Go figure.*

Just then, a crew member pokes his head up in front of them and says into his radio, "Made them. End search." To them he says, "Wendy—"

She nods. "I know—I'm out of bounds."

"If you know it, how come you're up here?"

"Because I like it up here," she says with a laugh.

"Well, we couldn't find you and we were getting worried. So how about coming down with me and saying hi to the guests? I think that's what your dad wants."

"And what my dad wants," she mutters, "is all that matters. Right?"

"He also wants to meet Jaycee."

Jaycee gulps. "Do we have to do that?"

"Yep," says the man. "This way, ladies."

They follow him down to the main part of the yacht, where all the guests stand, sipping cocktails and nibbling on *hors d'oeuvres*. "Be cool," Wendy whispers. "My dad likes everyone who has good manners, and that's you."

Jaycee sees that she has nothing to sweat: Mark Wiseman is just another Wall Street guy whose waistline looks as if he's had a few too many *hors d'oeuvres* over the years.

"So your name is Jaycee?" he asks. "I've never met a Jaycee."

"My name is actually Joanna Christine. Jaycee is my nickname."

One of the men smiles. "Nicknames are fun. When I was a brand-new cop, they called me 'Bones' because I was so skinny." He pats his paunch and adds, "Success has spoiled me a little bit."

Jaycee's heart skips a beat. The man said *cop*.

"Do you ever watch the TV news?" Wendy's father asks Jaycee. "If so, you probably have seen my friend here, Lieutenant Jerry Lankford. He's the department's unofficial spokesman."

So Jaycee stands there, a teenaged convicted felon and unsupervised halfway-house resident, shaking hands with one of New York's finest.

What would Santana or Teri do in such a predicament?

CHAPTER 20

THE COVER CHARGE at the Dungeon is ten dollars, but Teri just points to the party of six ahead of her and says, "I'm with them." The bouncer shrugs and lets her in. Maybe the guy isn't worried about entrance fees; most of these young women, once they're in, will get guys to buy them a dozen drinks.

Teri nearly laughs out loud when she sees Jaycee get carded and refused admission. Teri herself thinks the Dungeon is one very lame dump, but Jaycee said, "We have to go see Santana play so we can give her moral support." Teri didn't have the heart to say, "Jaycee, have you looked in the mirror lately? The drinking age in this country is twenty-one, and you don't look old enough to buy a Tampax."

I should leave now. It's so dark in here, and there are so many people that Santana couldn't spot me in the audience anyway.

She pushes past other club patrons and ends up at the emergency door. She throws it open and is unsurprised when no alarm sounds. *This joint is so ready to fall apart that I'm amazed the fire department hasn't closed it down yet.*

Teri looks into the darkened alleyway. "Jaycee! Get your buns in here!"

The tender young blonde runs in, and Teri closes the door.

"Jaycee, I told you they weren't gonna let you in."

The girl nods. "I guess you're right—I don't look old enough to have my first period."

Teri understands why Jaycee respects a mature, adult, assertive woman such as Allison Sullings so much. This little blondie is a wuss. No wonder the chicks at Milgrom had so much fun picking on her.

The music starts. Teri puts her hands over her ears, thinking at first that it's just feedback. But no— that's what passes for music at the Dungeon.

On the dance floor, the kids flail their limbs and don't seem to care much if they hit each other. When the band stops playing, they hurry over to the bar or bathroom.

"Santana is on next," says Teri. "Let's get up close so she can see us." She pulls Jaycee along with her.

"Teri—it's him! From therapy!"

"Who?"

"Ira. The kid who wants to die. Can't let him see us." Jaycee thinks it's weird to see Ira at the Dungeon, then decides it makes perfect sense—it's his milieu, with its crazy studded-leather freaks, loud and bad music. It's Disneyland for the overprivileged suicidal crowd.

Teri smirks. "Fine. We won't go over and say hi. But what happens when Santana's on and they put the spotlight on her? I think Ira will recognize her."

"Maybe we should go warn Santana."

Teri smirks some more. When, not if, old lady Boylan figures out that Fresh Start has become a lie, Teri will just bail on it and maybe head on back to Chi, maybe look up some old friends and get

140

reconnected in the community. If Santana and Jaycee don't do likewise, well, too bad for them. "Chill, girlfriend," she tells Jaycee. "Santana is realizing her dream tonight—to get up and play crappy music for nut jobs like Ira. Let's not break her heart."

Presently the house lights go out and Doomsday begins. The first thing everyone hears is a guitar riff so loud and murderous that Teri feels her bones vibrate. She loathes this kind of music—to her, it's just so much noise—but she can see that the kids surrounding her like it just fine. They're jumping every which way; their sweat flying onto Teri and Jaycee.

The lead singer is darting about the stage as if he's been freebasing for hours. The other boys are pounding away at their instruments.

But everyone is watching Santana Perez, the girl guitarist, still as a statue, staring at her guitar as she plays it—she knows she's beautiful, she knows she's good. Now it's time for the rest of the world to begin digging on her.

People stop dancing and point at her. "Who is she?" they begin to shout.

"She's my roommate!" Teri shouts back.

As Doomsday's performance continues, Santana loosens up and smiles. She knows her band's songs but decides they're boring, so she tweaks them here and there, doing unexpected little things on her Gibson. Jaycee loves how the long, lean guitarist confuses the others with her little tricks; the little blonde wishes the boys up there would quit playing and just let the girl guitarist show off for a while.

Finally they stop playing because they've run out of songs. The audience, jumping up and down and pounding the walls, has jarred loose some of the plaster from the ceiling, which has snowed down upon them. As the musicians nod and bow before exiting the stage, the fans fling ice and beer at them in appreciation.

"She was outrageous!" Jaycee shouts into Teri's ear. "Just unreal!"

"Let's go and congratulate her."

In the crush of people backstage, they end up nose to nose with Ira Stein.

"You two! I had no idea you were here! What a great surprise!"

Teri shrugs. "We came to see Santana play."

"She killed it! She absolutely killed it!" Ira has to stop for a moment to catch his breath. "I come down here every weekend, and we hope, just hope, that we'll see something special. And tonight, do you know what we saw? We saw history happen! Just freakin' history!" Then, "I can't believe she's a criminal."

"Not so loud," says Jaycee.

"I just mean that you're living in a halfway house, and that lady keeps you on a short leash. You've all done time and have had hard lives, right? So I wonder how Santana managed to develop such musical talent."

"She developed her talent *because* she was locked up," Teri tells her. "She had all day, every day, to sit in her cell and teach herself the guitar. We're about to go in and see her. We'll tell her you said hi."

The girls push past Ira and keep going till they get to Doomsday. A guy all in black, with short hair and a handful of business cards, is talking to Santana and her bandmates.

"Now is the time for you to start thinking of yourselves as professional musicians rather than just as hobbyists," he tells them. "If you sign with me, I can get you into the studio to make a CD—"

"Santana!" Teri yells.

Santana smiles and waves. "I saw you two in the audience. Shoulda told me you were coming. I woulda asked them to waive the cover charge."

"It's all good. We got in for free anyway."

"Santana," interjects the lead singer, "we have this man here and we're talking business. Get with the program."

"I played my first gig with you just now," Santana replies. "We're not U2 quite yet, so chill."

Teri and Jaycee give her grim little smiles. They know that, for legal reasons, Santana cannot sign a recording contract any more than she can go on a music tour.

The manager continues with his pitch to Doomsday, and Santana drifts off with her roommates.

"A star is born," Jaycee says.

Santana smiles. "Not yet, but maybe soon. Thanks for coming to see me tonight. I liked seeing that I had friends in the audience. Don't mind that manager guy. In this business, a lot of people do a lot of talking and it never goes anywhere. I'm not really taking that guy seriously."

"You know that Ira from therapy is here tonight?" asks Jaycee.

"Yeah. This is sort of his home away from home. There are quite a few people like him—mentally ill club kids with rich parents. Ira probably comes down here to buy crack and meth."

"Ira is a one-person Santana Perez fan club," Jaycee says. "Problem is, I'm not sure if we can count on him to shut up about all this when he's in Maddux's office."

"I'll threaten him in a very polite way. I'll make it clear that he must say nothing about seeing us outside of the shrink's office. The penalty will be death blows to the brain. Come on, let's go home."

As they exit the Dungeon through the side entrance, they encounter Ira in the alley. He rushes up to Santana and says, "You were magnificent tonight!"

"Over here." Santana takes him by the shoulder to a darker part of the alley.

"I'm not sure what kind of deal you have at that halfway house, Santana. They let you join a band and come down here at this hour? For real? What's that all about?"

Santana sees that Teri is right—Ira needs to shut up. She could easily kick every tooth out of his head, but that's not her style. She has another idea: She grabs the boy and gives him her longest, juiciest kiss.

At first, Ira can't seem to believe it's happening. But then he warms up and leans into it, and Santana thinks he's a half-decent busser, considering that the poor boy is probably quite new to this sort of thing.

When their kiss finally ends, Ira lets his lips fall limp.

"I can't believe it," he says. "I've just been kissed by Whitney Houston."

CHAPTER 21

JAYCEE IS SITTING at her desk, minding her own business, when she looks up and sees Missus Brader standing in the doorway. Missus Brader, the office manager, comes to the classroom only when there's some very big, important reason for her to do so.

"Jaycee Sheedy? Please come with me."

Jaycee does as told. She even gathers up her books and follows the woman until she's led into a conference room and told to sit down. Waiting for her there is Lieutenant Jerry Lankford of the NYPD. Jaycee can't imagine why a big-shot cop has such a keen interest in a little nobody such as herself. Actually, she understands it fairly well.

"How did you manage to find me?" she asks.

"It was easy enough. I know you're Joanna Christina Sheedy; that was enough. Part of my job is finding people, even if those people would rather not be found."

Jaycee nods, having no idea of what to say.

"Frankly, Jaycee, I like you a great deal. We met on that huge yacht, and I thought you were the only person there who was a total phoney-baloney. You were just being yourself, and if the others didn't like it, well, too bad. I could tell right away that you were poor, a kid who's getting her first taste of the good life. The problem, you see is Mark Wiseman—*he* doesn't particularly like you. Or maybe he does like you, but he doesn't like how chummy you are with his daughter—maybe he thinks you and she like each other *the wrong way*. Now, at your age, girls can be affectionate with each other…but to him, it may have looked like you two were romantically involved, and Mark Wiseman isn't eager to have any gossip about whether his daughter likes boys or girls.

"So, Jaycee, here's the deal: It would be a terrific idea if you and Wendy just never saw each other again. Do you think you could agree to that?"

Jaycee nods, grateful that all Lankford wants is to break up her little fling with Wendy.

"Furthermore, I know about your history as a car thief and shoplifter. I'm glad you're willing to stop running around with Wendy, but if you change your mind, I can call this lady Sullings and have you back at Milgrom within twenty-four hours."

Lankford doesn't know about Sullings! He really doesn't know!

Relief washes over Jaycee like a warm bath. The big deal here is that Mark Wiseman thinks his daughter is getting much too friendly with the girl who helps out at the hospital and lives at some halfway house. Those people don't know that Jaycee's halfway house is in total chaos, its boss stricken with amnesia and her three girls looking after themselves.

Jaycee shifts in her chair, feeling a sudden sense of loss. Since that night with Maria when Jaycee lost control of the Lexus and had to be pulled out of it by firefighters, exactly two great things have happened to her: Allison Sullings and Wendy Wiseman. She feels as if she's helped destroy the first one, and now this cop is taking away the second.

Since she stole her first car at age nine, Jaycee has stolen many, many things from countless people and slept like a baby afterwards because her whole attitude towards life was ME ME ME ME ME. She simply didn't care about how her actions affected her victims. Now *she's* losing Sullings and Wendy and feeling the pain of those losses.

"So I have to stop seeing Wendy?" she asks Lankford. "How do I do that? What will I say?"

He shrugs. "Pick your moment and be gentle. Do it in a very polite way, but do it as soon as possible."

Lankford leaves, and Jaycee sits there alone for the longest time, zoning out. When she finally returns to class, the room is empty.

"Jaycee?" the teacher asks. "Is everything all right?"

The girl shakes her head and runs away. *All right?* No, nothing is ever *all right* with Jaycee Sheedy. She is fourteen years old and lives in a halfway house. The last time she felt that things were *all right* was when she spent her nights on the prowl with Maria, looking for cars to steal. Things back then were nowhere near *all right*, but Jaycee felt happy and wanted and valued, so to her things were as *all right* as they could be.

This is now lunchtime. Normally she would run over to the hospital to help Wendy, but that relationship is now over, and Jaycee doesn't want to go to All Saints' Hospital ever again, for any reason.

Since meeting Wendy, she doesn't eat much, so she keeps herself going by grabbing something—a piece of fruit, a candy bar, a cup of noodles— whenever her hunger pangs become too painful to ignore. Today, however, she gets a full meal: A cheeseburger, side of fries and pint of chocolate milk. A similar meal at Mickey D's would make her slather, but this one looks as if it's been sitting there all day, which it probably has.

While carrying her tray and looking for somewhere to sit, she spots Denna, her lab partner, being dumped into a trash bin by a jock and his buddies.

Jaycee has witnessed such persecution since her first day at Kline. But today is different; she's just been picked on Lieutenant Jerry Lankford of the New York Police Department and is fed up with bullying. Eyes blazing with rage, she rushes up to the jock and throws her chocolate milk into his face.

"What the—"

The jock wipes the splash of muddy beverage from his eyes and scowls as a half-dozen of his pals gather behind him. Jaycee wishes at least one teacher would come along and break up this confrontation, but the three staff members in the cafeteria are standing together, chatting.

Jaycee shows no fear. Those girls at Milgrom pulled down her panties and whipped her bare bottom with a bar of soap; she doubts that these brainless wonders standing in front of her now could humiliate her any more than what happened to her in juvie.

She swallows hard, ready for the first punch. But then she senses that she is not alone; looking over her shoulder, she sees Teri standing behind her, a Cabrini-Green kid who grew up surrounded by boys ten times meaner and tougher than these Kline jocks. *You want to fight, big boys? Bring it on.*

"What's your problem?" Teri Goddard asks the

bully.

"No problem here." The jock steps back a bit. "Your little girlfriend has the problem. She's gonna die." He throws a halfhearted slap at Jaycee just as his pals pull him away. The slap misses her by nearly a foot.

"Why are you steppin' in?" he asks his friends.

"Let's bounce, dude. Fight's over."

"No chance. Nobody throws milk in *my* face and gets away with it!"

The jocks practically roll their eyes as, in this noisy cafeteria, they lean in and, as discreetly as possible, try to explain why fighting these two girls may not be the wisest course of action. Teri and Jaycee overhear "criminals," "jail," "armed and dangerous" and, finally, "guys don't fight chicks."

Jaycee thinks it's funny that these musclebound fools know so much about Teri and her. Even better, they're afraid of the two girls. Or, more accurately, they fear the bad girl from the badlands of Chicago.

Teri says, "Hey, guy, you look ridiculous with that milk on your face. Better go clean yourself up."

The bully looks away, his face red. He storms out of the cafeteria, his friends following just a step or two away.

Denna lets out a huge breath. "Thanks for that."

Jaycee, too rattled to do more than nod at Teri, manages to say, "We're not street kids."

Denna smiles. "Doesn't matter—you're true friends to me."

"Forget this happened," Teri mutters. "If I let those chumps thrash one of mine, that would make me look like I wasn't lookin' out for my own."

Jaycee wants to say, *I'm not one of yours, OK?*

Instead, she says, "Well, I'm glad you were here when we needed you."

She believes that if she had gone to All Saints' Hospital to see Wendy instead of being here at Kline, this ugliness would not have happened. She stayed here to have lunch, and what happened? Her meal ended up in a jock's face, and she avoided a beating only because Teri intervened.

I must hook up with Wendy and do what I gotta do.

The hike to All Saints' Hospital, which Jaycee by now knows so well, seems long and boring now. Normally, she's so eager to get there that she sprints the distance. But that was then and this is now.

She gets out at the ninth floor and makes a beeline for Jane Doe's room, hoping for good news and a long visit. But the doctor is with the patient and their eyes are glued to a MacBook Pro, so Jaycee stands in the doorway. Presently she feels a finger travel down the crease of her spine.

"Hey you," Wendy murmurs from behind.

"What are they up to?" Jaycee points at the doctor and patient.

"They're going through old YouTube videos to see if any of them will jog her memory."

Bonita, one of the nurses, comes up and says, "Wendy, we're running out of linens. Would you go to the laundry room and get an armload more?"

Wendy and Jaycee have discovered that the laundry room is their best place for quality time together. They're the only people who actually enjoy going in there, with the roar of machines and the stink of chemicals.

As soon as Wendy starts making plans for their next liaison, Jaycee says, "No can do."

"Then how about if we—"

"No more. Never again."

"Because…?"

Jaycee shrugs. "I…I've met someone else."

"Have you? What's her name?"

"Doesn't matter. You and I are through."

Wendy stares at Jaycee for a moment and sees that she's serious. "Are you dumping me? What's the problem? My father's yacht? His money?"

Jaycee tries to zone out but can't. This isn't one of her old joyriding misadventures with Maria. She cares about Wendy, cares about her a great deal, and feels enraged at Mark Wiseman for saying to Jerry Lankford, 'I don't like this relationship, so I want you to bust it up. But make sure my daughter doesn't know it was my idea.'

"OK," says Wendy, squaring her shoulders, "if this is how it has to be, I can accept it."

"Aw, come on, Wendy—"

She gives Jaycee a hard shove across the laundry room. "Don't speak to me that way! Don't speak to me ever again! And don't come into my hospital again!"

Jaycee leaves, tempted to remind Wendy that she does not own All Saints' Hospital. Or maybe she does. Maybe her daddy bought it for her.

CHAPTER 22

TERI STANDS NEAR the support by the East River, hugging herself as the icy wind blows off the water. Her coat just isn't heavy enough; she knows that Sullings, if she were back, would buy them all parkas. *Well, if this goes all right, I'll have enough cash to buy the best parka in town.*

She stops hugging herself and stands there nice and still, pretending she's perfectly comfortable. That's the key to doing business with LaDonze and her girls—looking confident and composed. If you show weakness, LaDonze will sense it right away and use it against you.

LaDonze arrives nearly an hour late; she knows that if you're important enough, they'll wait. She's flanked by four of her girls whom Teri recognizes from Kline. Nobody is smiling—it's all about attitude.

Teri speaks first. "So, what's the deal? Are we going to do some business together?"

LaDonze frowns. "Don't know about that. I only do business with my own. Last time I checked, your name warn't on the list."

"That so?" Teri frowns back. "You seemed to think I was cool when I said, 'There's Kwan's. Go hit it. Easy score.' You did, and you didn't invite me, and all I got was an iPod. I'm thinking that next time, we work together."

"Sounds like you've been doin' a lot of thinkin'. It also sounds like you're tellin' me what to do." The other girls titter, but LaDonze shoots them the briefest glance to shut them up. To Teri she says, "If you think this is just some kind of girls' social club where all you got to do is give me a kiss and a smile, you got it wrong."

Teri smirks a bit. She's heard this rap before. LaDonze has every intention of doing business with her. The only thing left is what LaDonze wants from Teri as the price of admission.

"What can I do for you?" Teri asks her.

"I'll show you."

The bunch of them walk a few blocks north to a desolate neighborhood of crumbling tenements. They reach a tiny park that has a couple of benches and the remnants of a swing.

"Nothin' here," Teri says.

"Look closer," LaDonze tells her.

On one bench, a homeless woman is stretched out. By her side, a supermarket cart is filled with many items.

Teri shrugs. "Bag lady's asleep. So what?"

LaDonze chuckles. "That's Esther. She's so wiggy, even the other crazies won't hassle her."

"Like I said, 'So what?'"

Just then, one of LaDonze's girls hands her a bottle of vodka. "See this?"

"Vodka," says Teri. "We gonna drink a toast to Esther?"

"No vodka in here. Just gasoline."

"What for?" Teri asks, not wanting to know.

"Here's what I want you to do: Pour the gas on Esther, light her on fire, then put her out and load her into her cart. Then push the cart into the river."

Teri says nothing. She just lets out a big nervous laugh.

"You think I'm playin' with you?" LaDonze's face hardens. Her eyes sparkle with anger. "I am *not* playin' with you. That old woman has a bracelet on her wrist from school or somethin'. It's been there so long, it won't come off. I want you to bring me that bracelet to prove you did what I said."

Teri shakes her head. "LaDonze, why would you want to set a crazy old woman on fire and dump her in the river?"

"Oh, now you're not so tough," LaDonze retorts. "All this time, I'm thinkin', 'Here's Teri, she grew up in Cabrini-Green, she's seen and done it all.' Now maybe I'm thinkin' you're wrong for our crew."

"And *I* thought you and your crew were about money, money, money. I'm a thief who's after big bucks. I'm not about burning people alive and stealing their bracelets. That's nowhere."

"We want you to burn that old woman," Teri says, "to prove you're not a cop."

Teri laughs. "If you don't know me by now—"

"Meaning?"

"I accepted that iPod from you. Stolen goods. You *know* I'm as criminal as you are."

Teri gets an ill feeling in the pit of her stomach. From early childhood, she has known that the most crucial relationships in her life would be with her peers: Make friends with the toughest kids around, and take whatever you need from whichever person has it. In New York, she thought she had found such

155

a friend in LaDonze, the girl selling drugs out of her knapsack in the girls' bathroom.

I thought she and I were on the same page. Looks like I was wrong. Real wrong.

Teri looks over at Esther as the old woman sleeps on the bench.

"I'm not setting her on fire."

"Either she gets lit up," LaDonze says, "or *you* do."

Teri steps back. LaDonze nods at her girls, and they move in on the Fresh Start kid.

Just then they hear the wail of a siren. They all look around and spot a police car, its lights flashing, LaDonze's girls run, but before their leader departs, she says to Teri, "I didn't come all this way for nothing. If you want to do business with us, you make sure you do ol' Esther! Hear me?"

CHAPTER 23

THE CAKE SAYS 'CONGRATULATIONS, TANNIE.' It's her graduation day. Doctor Maddux cuts one pieces after another and they pass it around the room.

"I think you've made terrific progress," the doctor tells the girl. "I'll miss you in these sessions."

"I'll miss all of you." Tannie wipes a tear from her cheek. "Especially you, Doc. I've brought you a little something."

The doctor swallows hard. His face turns pink as he accepts the meticulously gift-wrapped box. "Oh…this wasn't necessary." He puts it aside.

"No," Tannie says. "Open it now."

He does as told. Inside the box if a Hermes necktie, blue and green in a sort of geometrical pattern. Such an item would cost at least a few hundred dollars in a Park Avenue boutique.

"Great," mutters Jules, who's in big trouble for illegal downloading. "I'm glad she's been cured of her klepto issues."

"Jules," Doctor Maddux says, "we must assume that Tannie legitimately bought this tie. Anyway, in group we must never say or do anything to hurt anyone's feelings."

"Did you buy that tie or steal it?" Jules asks Tannie.

"Enough," says the shrink. "Does anyone else have anything they need to say to the group right now?"

"Yes," says Ira Stein. He points at Santana. "You didn't call me."

Santana shrugs. "Didn't have your number."

"You could have looked it up. It's easy to find."

"Look," the doctor says. "At your age, people are going to have feelings for each other. The thing is, you must not act on those feelings when they are inappropriate."

"Tell that to Santana," Ira says.

Doctor Maddux's eyes narrow. "Are you saying that you two have become a couple while attending group?"

"No," says Santana.

"There's no room her in life for anyone," says Ira. "She's into this 'I'm gonna be a rock star' trip."

"What do you mean by 'rock star trip'?" the doctor asks.

"She's in a band called Doomsday," Ira says.

The therapist turns to the guitarist. "Santana, is Miz Sullings OK with that?"

"She hasn't objected to it."

Doctor Maddux says, "Please have her call me as soon as she can. I need to check this out with her."

It's dinnertime as the three girls walk home after therapy. They are all full of anxiety.

"The shrink needs to 'check this out,'" Jaycee says. "Translation: 'How can a kid living in a halfway

158

house, who's going to school, doing community service and group therapy, put aside time to play rock music in nightclubs? And why is her live-in supervisor letting her do it?'"

"I should have thrashed Ira," mutters Teri.

"What would that have accomplished?" asks Santana.

"Would have made *me* feel better," replies Teri. "Anyway, you shouldn't have kissed him outside the Dungeon. You gave him the wrong idea—that you liked him or something." Then, "I hope at least he was a good kisser."

Santana shrugs. "I've had better."

"You don't have to worry about my relationship with Wendy," Jaycee tells them. "Her daddy wants me to stay out of her life."

"Why?" asks Santana.

"Because I'm not their kind."

"And what kind is that?"

"Rich and Jewish, I guess. Plus, I think her old man knows a few things about my checkered past." She turns to Teri and says, "Something bugging you? You look even more troubled than usual."

Teri nods. "I've got stuff going on."

"Then spill it. We're in this together. Your beefs are ours, too."

"Well, it's like this. There's this bag lady up near Harlem, and I have to torch her and then dump her into the East River."

"Huh?" The other two girls eyeball her.

"It's all LaDonze's fault. She's, like, 'If you want to do crimes with us, you have to prove you're not working for the Man. And the way to prove that is by pouring gas on this old woman and lighting her up, then putting her out in the river.' So I said, 'Not gonna happen,' and LaDonze said, 'If you don't do her like that, we'll do *you*.'"

Santana rolls her eyes. "I thought the whole idea with Fresh Start was for us to put criminal ways behind us and to start living right. But you've been trying to get tight with that LaDonze since our first day at school. You hang out with her long enough, she's going to do some serious time—and she'll drag you down with her."

Teri nods. "You remember that Kwan's store in Times Square that got broken into? I advised her to do it, and all I got for my trouble was an iPod."

"Maybe," says Santana, "you should just forget about just forget about being a career criminal. Getting away with ripping people off is a combination of skill and luck—and I don't think you have much of either one. Jaycee was a much better criminal than you are, and she got busted anyway. You should just stay away from LaDonze for a while and just work with us while we pretend that Sullings is still with us."

By now they're at their front door. Santana lets them in with her key, then goes to help Missus Berkowitz with some sweeping.

"Where's your boss?" the old lady asks.

"She's been in meetings. Always keeping busy."

"She doesn't mind that you're unsupervised so much of the time?"

"No, ma'am. She says that as long as we mind our manners, we'll be OK."

"I see. You seem like a nice enough girl, Santana, and the other one, the little blonde, she seems nice enough, too. But that Teri? I don't know about her."

Santana smiles. "Teri's been a good friend to us.

She's just trying to make her way in life, like everyone else."

The old woman nods and sighs. "I suppose."

Once they're back inside the apartment, Santana says, "Old lady Berkowitz keeps asking about Sullings. We can't keep on like this forever."

"We just need to stay cool and work together," says Jaycee. "If we do it right, we can keep on going for a while longer." Noticing that their answering machine's red light is flashing, she hits the PLAY button.

"Hello, Miz Sullings? This is Pearl Boylan. I'm sorry for being unable to speak to you personally in the past little while, but I've just been too busy with my other clients. However, I will be at Fresh Start on Wednesday at nine for a personal evaluation. I have contacted the school and told them that the girls won't be there that morning. The electronic reports you have sent me have been highly encouraging, and I hope my visit will go just as well.

The girls stand there and stare at each other. They have six days left to get Sullings back.

CHAPTER 24

JAYCEE HAS BEEN to All Saints' Hospital many, many times, but this is Teri and Santana's first visit since they dumped Sullings there on that dreadful night.

On the elevator ride up, Teri notices that Jaycee's volunteer badge reads JAYCEE JONES.

"For real? That sounds like a black girl's name."

"I thought of Teri Goddard, but that name was already taken."

"Don't use my name, blondie. It's too good for you."

"Both of you," Santana says, "shut up. We already have enough things to get uptight about. You know what? Those guys at Doomsday are ragging on me about giving them my Social so we can sign up with that manager. I don't even have a Social Security Number!"

"The top guy at the NYPD has taken an interest in my relationship with Wendy," says Jaycee. "If he does a little digging, he'll have enough on me to send me back to Milgrom."

"LaDonze is still mad at me," Teri tells them. "I'm afraid to take a leak because she's selling meth and stuff in the girls' can. I don't want her girls to jump me."

"Let's hope Sullings knows who we are and is glad to see us," Jaycee says, changing the subject.

"And let's hope that my Powerball ticket wins me fifty million dollars," Santana retorts.

The three exit the elevator had head for Sullings' room. Jaycee thinks of Wendy and their time together. Somehow she just doesn't care if they take her out of Fresh Start; without Wendy and Sullings in her life, New York seems empty and cruel. Still, she hopes they don't send her back to Milgrom.

When they reach Sullings' room, their mouths drop open. In Jane Doe's bed is now an old black woman.

"That's not her," says Santana. "Is it?"

"No," replies Teri. "Definitely not. What's the deal, Jaycee?"

"I'm gonna ask."

Just then Bonita the nurse comes in and says, "Hey, Jaycee! I guess you've come in to see your Jane Doe. We transferred her yesterday."

"Do you mean she's cured and you've discharged her?"

Bonita shakes her head. "I wish. No, since she's physically healthy, we couldn't justify keeping her here, and she had no money or insurance, so we did the only thing we could do. We sent her to New York State Hospital."

"Psychiatric?" Jaycee's voice is little more than a croak.

"Yes."

Jaycee chokes back a sob.

"Chill, girlfriend," Santana murmurs. "Got to keep it together and think this through."

"I'm terribly sorry, Jaycee. We knew you'd be really upset about Jane Doe, and we wanted to tell you what was happening, but we had no way of contacting you. Jane Doe asked about you, but we didn't know what to tell her. Wendy said you weren't volunteering anymore. That so?"

"Yes."

"Well, it's just till her memory returns. Hope it happens soon. State Hospital is kind of creepy."

Jaycee mutters to her roommates, "Time for a meeting." They hustle down into the stairwell. Jaycee feels so disoriented that she leans against a wall. Of all the bad stuff that has gone down, Sullings' transfer to the puzzle factory is the worst. *Will I wake tomorrow from this nightmare?*

"So, smart chick," Teri says to Jaycee, "what's the move?"

"Do you know where State Hospital is?"

"No. Do you?"

"Yep. It's in Queens."

"I don't know where Queens is."

"Well, Teri, you're going to find out soon enough, because the three of us are going to visit Sullings there and bust her out of that place."

Teri laughs. "Simple as that, huh?"

"Yep."

Santana says, "I think they have, like, security people there. What if they won't let us take her?"

"Then we'll say, 'This is our boss, Allison Sullings, and we're here to collect her.'"

Teri says, "Uh, we could get in big trouble for pulling such a stunt."

Jaycee makes a face. "Uh, we're already in big trouble."

Teri nods. "OK, so where's the nearest subway station?"

CHAPTER 25

THE FRESH START three make it to Queens in spite of themselves. They depart the subway station and immediately see the immense gray box that is New York State Hospital.

"Yuck," says Teri. "I've been in juvies that looked more invitin' than this."

"It looks like what it is," mutters Jaycee. "A big gray place for excess populations that are unemployable."

"But Sullings is in there, and she's not unemployable," Santana says.

"She's in there because she's *temporarily* unemployable," Jaycee says. "Time to get her out."

Entering the building is simple, but the interior seems to Jaycee entirely another matter. An armed guard sits on a stool behind the receptionist, a glum-faced woman who sits behind six inches of Plexiglas. The doors are electronically secured—everyone must be buzzed in or out.

This is nothing like All Saints' Hospital. It's more like Milgrom. How are we going to get her out of here?

"May I help you?" asked the receptionist.

"Um, we're here to see a friend," says Jaycee. "They transferred her from All Saints' Hospital yesterday. We'd like to come in and see how she is."

"What is her name?"

"You have her as Jane Doe."

"What's her real name?"

"Don't know."

"You said she was your friend."

"I knew her at All Saints' Hospital as Jane Doe," Jaycee says. "I'm trying to help her get her memory back." She holds out her Jaycee Jones ID badge. "See?"

The receptionist hands her some printed forms through the narrow opening in the Plexiglas. "Fill these out and return them to me."

"Then what? Do we get to go and see her right away?" Jaycee's hands start sweating as she squeezes the forms.

The receptionist says, "Return them to me and I pass them along to the appropriate department. They run you through the computer and if everything checks out, you'll be permitted to visit starting next week."

Wonderful. Just freakin' wonderful.

They stand out on the sidewalk, looking at one another as if ready to ask, "So, what are we going to do?"

"We definitely have a problem that we can't solve," Jaycee says. "I guess we just keep on keepin' on till next week, then tell old lady Boylan exactly what the deal is. Maybe she can make a call or two and get Sullings out of there."

As she speaks, the hospital's doors slide open and out steps a familiar face.

"*Wendy!*"

Jaycee beams and waves; Wendy scowls.

"Go away."

Jaycee steps in front of her, and Wendy stops, apparently ready to speak and be spoken to. Jaycee assumes that's a good thing.

"You refused to give me your phone number, Jaycee. I guess you just didn't want to have me in your life."

"Oh, but I did—I do—"

"I thought you were so wonderful with Jane Doe back at All Saints' Hospital. Now she's in *this* place, with all *these* people! She shouldn't be here. It's awful."

"I don't believe you've met my roommates," says Jaycee. "Wendy, meet Teri and Santana. Teri and Santana, meet Wendy."

Santana asks, "Wendy, did you say you've seen Jane Doe? How did you get authorized?"

"That was easy. My dad knows everyone worth knowing in New York. He made a phone call or two. I'm sure he can do the same for you." She takes out her iPhone.

"Bad idea," says Jaycee.

"Are you kidding? You're the best friend Jane Doe has. She really needs to see you now."

"Nix!"

"Because…?"

"Because of your father," Jaycee says.

"What's he got to do with anything?"

Jaycee lets out a nervous little laugh. "Oh, just about everything. He's sent down the message: 'No more hanging out with Wendy.'"

"Did he say that to you personally?"

"No, he sent his pal Lankford to Kline High to tell me to bounce."

"Why would my father do such a thing?"

"Because he doesn't much cotton to the idea that his daughter would be friends with someone like me."

"I don't believe that. I'm going to call him and see what's happening." She starts scrolling through numbers on her iPhone, and Jaycee plucks the gadget out of her hand.

"Hey! What's the big idea? Give it back!"

"You can't tell your old man about any of this. He was, like, 'Stop seeing Wendy, and make sure she has no idea that I had anything to do with it.' He would go ballistic if you called him and said, 'Did you order Jaycee to stop being my friend?'"

Wendy thrusts out her chin. "Are you really that afraid of him?"

"Uh, yeah. Him and Lankford. They can push me around all they want." Then, "Look, Wendy, I'm not exactly who you think I am. I think it's time I told you the truth." He gives her back her iPhone.

"You're freaking me out, Jaycee. Tell me what's going on."

"That Jane Doe in there? She's actually Allison Sullings, the leader of Fresh Start, the halfway house where Santana, Teri and I live…"

Wendy listens with utter fascination as Jaycee runs it down for her: Three young criminals selected by Sullings to move to New York with her; the awful accident on the fire escape and Jaycee's ruse as a volunteer to check on Sullings' progress.

Wendy shakes her head. "So you've known her identity all along? And you said nothing? What kind of an idiot are you?"

170

"Not an idiot," says Jaycee. "Just a coward. Anyway, the doctors at All Saints' Hospital were, like, 'Her memory will return very soon and she'll be fine.' We kept thinking that would happen."

"Well," Wendy says through gritted teeth, "it *might have happened* if you had said, 'Your name is Allison Sullings and I'm Jaycee and we live together at Fresh Start.' *That's* the kind of help those docs were looking for, and you had it all along."

Santana says, "Yeah, Wendy, but what if we had said that to Sullings and she still didn't make any progress?"

"Well, gee, Santana, you could have *tried*, right?"

"Sullings' life work was in keeping us out of jail," Teri puts in. "If we had ended up back in jail, Sullings' work would have been for nothing. So, if you look at it that way, we've handled everything the right way."

Wendy cackles. "You three crack me up. You know what you are? You're con artists. You stand here, after all the screwing up you've done and all the totally selfish behavior you've indulged in, and now you're rationalizing and justifying all of it. You'll make great lawyers if you can stay out of prison."

Jaycee says, "Wendy, we're not here to visit Sullings. We're here to smuggle her out. We've got the social worker coming for a visit, and our plan is to get Sullings out of here and back to Fresh Start so we can help her ourselves."

"New York State Hospital has major security. I don't see how you can get her out without their consent."

"Hey, if we get caught, we spill it: Sullings' name, occupation, Social Security Number. She gets the triggers she needs, we go back to juvie."

171

"Our options are almost nothing at this point," adds Teri.

Wendy nods. "I can help."

"Negative," Jaycee says. "You could get in big trouble."

"No, I'm golden. I'll just have my dad call some people and get me a transfer here. I can check out the place and figure out how you can get her out of there."

Jaycee beams. "For real? Would you help us like that?"

She nods. "Especially after what you've told me about how my father has mistreated you. Plus, we need to do this for Miz Sullings."

Santana says, "Jaycee, I have to say this: You choose your friends very well."

CHAPTER 26

WHEN JANE DOE woke up in All Saints' Hospital with amnesia, she thought things were about as bad as they could be.

They have just gotten worse.

She has just been transferred to New York State Hospital in Queens, the most notorious psychiatric facility in the Northeast. As a sane person locked up with a bunch of psychotics, she now knows how Jack Nicholson must have felt in *One Flew Over the Cuckoo's Nest*.

"This is just temporary," Doctor Silverman tells her. "Till your memory returns."

"But why *here*?"

The good doctor shrugs. "It's just the way the healthcare system operates sometimes. But, again, you are not what we call a 'formal' patient. You have not been committed here."

"So I can leave whenever I want?"

"You can leave as soon as we believe your memory has returned."

"So I *have* been committed."

Just then a tall, corpulent man in a hospital gown yells at another patient, "You owe me money! Pay up or die!"

A couple of orderlies grab the big man by his arms and lead him away. "Time for your shot, Bubba."

"It's a shame that someone like you sees such things in here," the doctor says to Jane Doe.

She lets out a small, bitter laugh. "I see that every day in this place. As soon as his heavy meds start wearing off, Bubba gets nasty and convinces himself that someone owes him money."

"Bubba has been here quite a while. Like so many psych patients, he takes meds that slow down his metabolism and stimulate his appetite. He gains weight, so maybe his dosage should be increased. I'll check into it."

"I'll say it again: I should not be in this place. It's for people with severe mental illnesses. I'm just someone who had a concussion. My head doesn't even ache anymore. Let me out of here. This place is full of crazy folks and it smells bad."

"It's just for now. Till your memory returns."

"What if that doesn't happen?"

"Oh, I'm sure it will." Then, "If we discharged you, where would you go? If you think this place is bad, just try staying at a homeless shelter. While I agree with you that this hospital is full of, um, *characters* wandering around and it doesn't smell so good much of the time, you *are* getting 'three hots and a cot,' and the best thing for you right now is to stay cool and hang out till your memory returns, *which it will.*"

"So I don't get to leave until you sign my discharge order."

She feels alone and lonely here. The only bright spot was finding Wendy Wiseman in the common room. Wendy from All Saints' Hospital!

"What brings you all the way out here?" Jane Doe asks, hugging the girl and nearly weeping with joy.

"It's all part of my healthcare education. I was doing that thing at All Saints', now I'm doing psychiatric here." Her face darkens. "I guess this isn't exactly what you had in mind, huh?"

"I'm hoping it will be a brief stay." She feels delighted at first at the prospect of seeing this wonderful, vivacious kid several days per week, but then notices that Wendy has a dozen balls to juggle at the hospital—becoming oriented to her new workplace, learning different procedures and helping restrain unruly patients if the orderlies are busy with other difficult patients.

Jane Doe notices that Jaycee isn't with Wendy but doesn't ask about her. They've probably gone their separate ways, and that's a shame. Jaycee is a great kid, too, but she has some kind of hunted, hungry look about her, as if she's had to fend for herself since birth.

People come and go, and that's life. But you wish a few more of them would stick around for a while.

Jane Doe closes her eyes and wishes it would all go away.

CHAPTER 27

THEY ARRANGE TO have the meeting at Empire State Pizza, Sullings' favorite place to eat. The girls agree: They serve a good pie at that joint.

"They make a pretty decent pie in Chicago, too," Teri says. "In Philly, well, that's cheesesteak town. You won't find a better one in the world." Then, "Wendy better like meat-lovers' pizza. I refuse to eat veggie pizza."

"I don't know what kind of pizza she likes," Jaycee tells her. "We didn't have enough money to go out for pizza. For a chick from a rich family, she sure had empty pockets."

Santana moans as she stuffs a long slice into her mouth. After swallowing, she says, "We have enough jack till Wednesday or Thursday. After that, Sullings starts paying our bills again or we go back to juvie and eat whatever they serve us."

Teri wipes some of the grease from her lips and looks up at the wall clock. "Where's Wendy, Jaycee? hope she won't be standing us up."

"I guess she's taken the long way, in case her old man has sent someone to spy on her. If he had that chump Lankford tell me to leave Wendy alone, maybe he's got someone making sure I'm not seeing her any longer."

Just then the door opens and Wendy breezes in. Jaycee almost weeps at the sight of her. It's a new thing for the street kid, having such deep feelings for someone. "What a cutie," Teri mutters. "She could have anyone and everyone she wanted." The volunteer spots them and takes a seat next to Jaycee.

"Having to commute from Queens is a hassle," she tells them. "My life has always been in Manhattan. Oh, well." She looks down at the pie. "Meat, meat, meat. Too yummy."

"Dig in," says Jaycee.

"Don't mind if I do." She helps herself to a big slice and chews it with her eyes closed.

"So," Teri says, "let's get down to business. How much of the nuthouse have you seen so far?"

"Too much. It's run like a prison—once you're in as a patient, their top priority is making sure you stay in until you get a discharge—if that ever happens.

Teri shakes her head. "Security at those places? It's a joke. There are lots of ways to get in and out— skylights, windows, whatever."

Wendy swallows a bite of pizza and washes it down with a mouthful of Coke Zero. "Negative. No skylights in that place. The police station is nearby, and the fire marshal comes by every day or so. Even the door leading to the roof is locked and chained."

"Sound more like a prison than most prisons," Jaycee remarks.

"Come *on*," Teri says. "Place like the looney bin? It's gotta have weak spots. They have to feed people, medicate them, clothe them. They must have delivery trucks coming in and going out. That's where we should be looking."

Wendy frowns. "Could be. I noticed that there's a lane leading up to the loading docks. All the deliveries happen there, and that's where they dump their garbage. But they have a guard there to keep track of everyone, and you have to be authorized by the hospital to get in."

"I wonder if the guard is there all day and night, every night." Teri says.

"No, they're too stingy for that. After hours, they pull the guard but padlock the door."

Teri laughs. "Just a padlock? We're in!"

Jaycee says, "OK, so let's pretend Teri has picked the padlock and we get into the alley. Do we just choose any door, go inside and say, 'Hey, Miz Sullings! We're come to take you home!'?"

Wendy shakes her head. "It's much harder than that. All the doors in that alley have no keyholes or even knobs. If you're in the alleyway, you have to knock so that someone inside can open it for you. However—"

"Yes?" the Fresh Start girls ask in unison.

"A popular visiting place there is the cafeteria, and I've noticed that at one end of the cafeteria is the kitchen, and in the back of the kitchen is a hallway. At the end of hallway is a door that opens out into the loading dock. I can visit with Miz Sullings and very casually take her through the kitchen and to that door, where you girls be waiting after Teri has picked that padlock."

"What if the kitchen workers wonder what you're up to?" Teri asks.

"They won't. Those people are mostly immigrants who just go to work and keep their mouths shut."

The three say goodnight to Wendy and walk back to Fresh Start, none of them saying anything—for what is there to say? They will sleep poorly or not at all, then travel back to Queens to attempt a feat that none of them believes will work. Jaycee wonders if, in a few days' time, she will end up back in Milgrom, where there will be no Wendy to come by and visit her.

They reach their front door when they hear the one syllable.

"Hey."

The three girls look into the shadows and see four or five girls emerge. Teri recognizes the voice right away.

"LaDonze. Wassup?"

"Just came by to say hi, girlfriend."

Santana eyeballs her. "You want somethin' with us."

LaDonze seems to falter a bit. "Not you. Just her."

"Not gonna happen," Teri says. "I'm not gonna torch that old lady and dump her into the East River. If that's your thing, go find someone else."

"Wrong. You'll do her or we'll do you."

"Bounce," says Teri.

LaDonze crosses her arms. "You came to us, like, 'I wanna do business with you.' Well, this is part of doing business. I'm not asking you to do that old woman, I'm *telling* you."

"And I'm saying no."

Santana and Jaycee step alongside Teri, to make it clear to LaDonze and her girls that Teri's friends are ready to fight if necessary. Jaycee thinks any of these

180

girls could take her in two minutes, but LaDonze versus Teri? That would be a pretty fair matchup. Nobody in LaDonze's crew wants to take on Santana, who is so tall and menacing. But of course, Jaycee does not want to fight anyone; a person could get hurt that way.

A gallon of water comes splashing down on LaDonze and her friends. The girl first tugs on her Yankees satin jacket, now drenched. Then she scowls at Teri, and finally looks up to see Missus Berkowitz looking down upon them from a window.

"You gangbangers! I see you giving those nice girls a hard time!" the old woman shouts. "You get out of here and don't come back or I'll call the police. You hear me? Git!"

After wiping some water from her forehead, the girl gangbanger points at Teri. "You better go do ol' Esther or I'm comin' back here tomorrow night."

LaDonze and her crew take off down the street.

"Same time tomorrow night," Teri says, sighing.

"They're harmless," says Santana. "That old lady scared them off with a little water and a threat to call the cops. What a bunch of wimps."

"Could be, but now they know just where to find me."

CHAPTER 28

WENDY WISEMAN FINISHES her paperwork and takes off her white coat. Although her shift is now over, her other volunteer gig—the really demanding one—is about to begin. She almost feels too afraid to do what she has promised she would do as she walks down the hallway.

"Hey, Wendy, how do you like it so far?" asks one of the orderlies. Here at New York State Hospital, unlike All Saints' Hospital, she has made no effort to learn anyone's name.

"Too much fun," she replies with a big smile. The orderly, while not a security guard, is tall and prodigiously muscular, with no compunction about intervening whenever patients become uncooperative. He knows what his job is, as does everyone else here. Wendy, probably like so many others at this institution, keeps thinking of *One Flew Over the Cuckoo's Nest*. She also thinks of *Titicut Follies*. Occasionally she wishes she was back at All Saints' Hospital.

New York State Hospital is composed of four wings. North Wing is where the criminally insane are housed, and those people never leave their rooms; they even eat their meals while sitting at their desks. A few of them were on trial for well-publicized crimes, and their attorneys boasted to reporters that their clients would be spending the rest of their lives at New York State Hospital instead of Attica or Sing Sing. Wendy wasn't sure that any of those defendants got such a good deal.

Fortunately, Jane Doe, also known as Allison Sullings, is on one of the mellower, cleaner-smelling wards, where many of the patients are more or less mentally together.

Wendy hurries over to Sullings' section of the hospital, and there sits the Fresh Start leader, staring at the TV set. The woman sitting next to her is mumbling to herself, but Sullings seems not to mind.

"Hey, Jane," she says.

Sullings looks up at her and smiles. "Wendy! How did you like orientation?"

"Now I own this place. I'm the boss."

Sullings laughs. "Terrific! Now maybe you can discharge me. I'm so sick of this place."

"I'll bet. Come on, let's go get a cup of coffee in the cafeteria."

"They only have decaf in this place. 'Decaffeinated coffee' is a contradiction in terms."

"Well, I'm sure we can find *something* you like."

She nods. "Yeah, I need to get back to Planet Earth for a while."

The cafeteria, on the main floor, is big and painted white. It has every kind of vending machine Wendy has ever seen. "What can I get you?" she asks Sullings.

"Whatever you're having."

Wendy buys two cups of hot chocolate and puts one in front of Sullings, who seems more relaxed in this new setting. The woman sits back and takes a sip of the beverage. "Well, it's much better than their coffee."

I wish I could sit back and take it easy right now. Wendy can't recall feeling so full of anxiety. She has work to do tonight, a task that could get her into the deepest trouble of her life. But she must not let Sullings know about it. She keeps glancing at the doorway that leads into the kitchen, and at the other end of the kitchen is the doorway that leads into the alley—and freedom. The girls will be waiting in that alley within minutes.

The sign says ABE'S LINENS, and the truck is small but big enough. Jaycee drives it, muttering about its bum clutch. "Abe needs to find a new mechanic."

"How much longer to Queens?" asks Teri.

"We'll get there when we get there," Santana tells her. "The truck is good enough. At least the price was right."

"And I thought my days of stealing rides were over," Jaycee says with a chuckle.

"Well, don't get too cocky till we have Sullings back in Fresh Start," Santana says. "Getting the truck was the easy part. Getting the boss into the truck and not getting caught on the way back to Manhattan? That's the hard part."

"Don't forget that Wendy is going to help us," says Jaycee.

"Whatever," retorts Santana.

So far, there's been very light traffic, and Jaycee

drives as fast as she can. Then, suddenly, it's bumper to bumper and nobody's going anywhere.

"What's up with that?" Santana stares out the windshield. "Why don't you take a sidestreet and ditch all this traffic?"

"Can't do it. We're stuck."

"How come?"

"I think it's called New York City traffic. It'll start moving again when it starts moving again."

"When?" Teri asks, her voice rising. "We're running out of time."

"No kiddin'," Jaycee says. "There's probably an accident up ahead. There usually is in a city this size where so many people have cars they don't fix often enough. Everyone's in a hurry, too."

"Including us," Santana says.

"We're in a bigger hurry than everyone else," Teri adds.

"At nine-thirty," Jaycee reminds them, "Wendy is going to take Sullings to that door at the back of the kitchen. If we aren't there—"

"You're going back to Milgrom and I'm going back to Abbotsford," Santana says.

"We'll get the job done," Jaycee mutters.

Fifteen or twenty minutes later, they have moved maybe a dozen feet. "At least no one has to go to the can," Santana says.

"Be grateful for small miracles." Jaycee grins.

"This accident up ahead?" Teri says. "It better not be something minor. If we're going to sit here and wait all this time, I want to see some blood and broken bones on the road!"

Soon the dashboard's digital clock reads 9:00.

"We'll never get there now." Jaycee whimpers. "I

wonder what will happen to us now."

"Like I said, Milgrom and Abbotsford," Santana tells her. "I don't know about Teri."

"I'll just go back to Chicago and look up my old friends." Then, "Check it out!"

The traffic begins moving. Within moments the vehicles are zooming along.

"Faster! Faster!" shouts Teri.

Jaycee increases her speed, weaving in and out of traffic. "Take a shortcut," she mutters as she goes down one side street and up another one, ignores red lights and stop signs and finally drives onto the sidewalk to save a few seconds.

At 9:28, they pull into the access lane behind New York State Hospital. "Wendy was right," Jaycee says. "Guardhouse empty, big fat padlock keepin' us out." To Teri she says, "Can you help us with that?"

"Nothin' to it."

Then a silhouetted figure appears before them.

"Nobody move," Jaycee mutters.

They watch as the figure walks out to the middle of the access lane, shines a flashlight around and walks away.

"She didn't say nothin' about no security guard," Teri says.

"He's gone now. Probably headin' for his donuts and coffee," replies Jaycee.

"Do it," Santana says.

Teri hops out of the truck and ambles over to the gate. She works on the padlock like a dentist fixing a patient's tooth.

At 9:29, the gate opens and the truck drives in. Teri shuts the gate and gets back in. The girls peer around but find only barred windows and dark walls.

Jaycee, wiping sweat from her chin, finds a row of Dumpsters and, next to it, a big steel door with no knob on the outside.

"Let's do it."

CHAPTER 29

Sarah Wiseman holds up the document and says to her husband, "Mark, Wendy's left her homework here and it's due tomorrow. She said she was staying the night with Gillian."

She picks up the telephone. Two minutes later, she hangs up. Mark by now is standing.

"Gillian says she's not there, and the two had no plans to see each other tonight. Did Wendy lie to us? That is *so* not like her!"

Mark Wiseman nods. "I can find her."

Lieutenant Jerry Lankford often works late, and he doesn't mind. But when his bosses are out of town, he, in many ways, becomes the boss. He likes that just fine.

Lankford is thinking of going home for the night when he gets a call from Mark Wiseman, one of the people whose calls he will always take.

"Geary," Lankford calls out to his sergeant, "where is that file on the Jaycee kid—the one who's always running around with Wiseman's daughter till I told her to knock it off?"

The sergeant gives him the file, and he opens it on

his desk. Joanna Christina Sheedy—street name Jaycee. Lankford nods, looking at her mug shot and remembering is visit with the little blonde girl at Kline High School, when he told her to stop hanging out with Wendy Wiseman.

Our meeting was unsuccessful. Why won't people take me as seriously as I would like?

In the file is a description of something called Fresh Start. This kid Jaycee was very lucky to be selected for a cushy halfway house like that. She was dumb to risk her new life over someone like Wendy. Is Jaycee a lesbian or something? Is Wendy? Well, at that age, they probably don't know who they are or what turns them on.

In the file, Lankford also finds a photo of Allison Sullings, who runs Fresh Start. *Why does she look so familiar to me? Do I know her from somewhere?*

He looks up at the bulletin board on his wall. At any time there are dozens of John Does and Jane Does in New York City, people—living or dead—whom the city cannot identify.

On his wall, staring right at Lankford, is Allison Sullings, Jane Doe #63624F. He reads the details: *Discovered at All Saints' Hospital in unconscious state. Diagnosis of acute retrograde amnesia. Transferred to New York State Hospital...*

Lankford frowns. He was the main guy who got Wendy Wiseman that volunteer assignment she wanted at the nuthouse.

Wendy, Wendy, Wendy, what are you up to?

He picks up his phone and starts dialing.

The cafeteria is always open for the convenience of

shift workers. As Sullings and Wendy visit over hot chocolate, a weary nurse sits alone, munching on a sandwich.

Wendy keeps looking at the wall clock and squirms as the time gets closer to 9:30.

Sullings asks, "Everything OK?"

The girl nods, taking a sip of her lukewarm beverage. "Sure, fine." Her stomach is so upset that she's afraid of vomiting.

"You work too hard," Sullings tells her. "You need to have more fun. Back at All Saints' Hospital, they used to joke that as a birthday gift they should give you a nursing degree because of all the hours you'd put in."

Move it, move it, move it! Wendy screams in silence as the clock's second hand takes its own sweet time sweeping across the face.

"Hello? Earth to Wendy, do you read me?"

The girl jumps up. "Gotta go."

Sullings frowns. "Where are you going?"

"Not me—us." She hurries over to the woman's side and pulls her to her feet.

"Where are we going? What are we doing?" Sullings wants to know as Wendy half-drags her across the cafeteria and into the kitchen.

"You'll find out."

"Meaning what?"

Cooks and dishwashers look up at them with frowns and arched eyebrows. The exit is just head, past a row of appliances. Wendy tightens her grip on Sullings.

"That's the exit," Sullings mutters. "We can't leave till they let me go."

"Hush." Wendy pushes her knee into the security

bar and the big, heavy door opens.

Standing in the doorway, smiling, is tall, beautiful Santana. "Wassup, Miz Sullings?"

Sullings, her face white and eyes bulging, tries to pull free from Wendy, but Santana reaches out and snatches the woman into an iron grip. "You're not goin' anywhere but home." In a moment, Teri is there, too, and Sullings can do nothing but stay put.

Then an alarm goes off. Wendy and the Fresh Start girls look at each other, then around.

"Gotta split," Santana says.

The two girls physically carry Sullings over to the truck and stuff her into its rear. Wendy gets in, followed by Santana and Teri.

Jaycee drums on the steering wheel as everyone gets settled in. "Did an alarm just go off?"

Sullings says in the darkness, "Is that you, Jaycee?"

Santana checks to see that the door is shut. "The alarm went off. They know something's up. Hurry!"

"Hold on tight!" Jaycee, like a stunt driver, puts the truck into reverse, backs up, then drives straight for the gate. As she gets closer, she sees the guard at the gate, trying to put the padlock back on.

Jaycee doesn't slow down. She blasts the horn. "Better get back, security guy. They don't pay you enough to risk your life."

The guard secures the padlock and jumps out of the way just as Jaycee slams into the gate. She hears the awful racket of shattered wood and twisted metal as she steers the truck onto the street.

"Jaycee!" calls Santana. "I hear sirens! Cops!"

"Well, what of it?"

"Aren't you going to stop?" Wendy asks.

"Negative." She makes a sharp turn onto a sidewalk, then drives across a vacant lot and down the alley to her left. For a moment she thinks she's faked out the cop and is free to drive back into Manhattan. But then she looks in the rearview mirror and sees the cop, a few blocks away, lights flashing, heading her way. Jaycee accelerates as much as she can, which is very little. "Shoulda got a faster ride," she mutters to herself. The police car gains on them, and within moments its lights seem inches away, its wailer deafening.

"Shake him loose!" shouts Santana.

Jaycee looks left and right, totally disoriented. She knows almost nothing about the street layout of Queens, and it's difficult to lose a cop who's probably been driving here all his life. Plus, his car has a big, high-powered engine and her laundry truck is slower than molasses.

It's dark and she's panicked, but at last she sees a possible way out of her predicament: Not far in the distance is what looks like a bridge. Maybe she can drive up to the bridge and then around it, then hide out as the cop drives across the bridge.

But just as she reaches it, she realizes it's not a bridge at all, but a railroad crossing. Suddenly, a big, lurid red light goes on and she hears the roar of a locomotive. Jaycee keeps going, breaking through the wooden barriers and crossing the tracks just a few seconds before the train powers on by.

She stops the truck a dozen or so feet from the rumbling train, which is so noisy that the truck vibrates and its occupants can scarcely hear themselves think.

CHAPTER 30

SANTANA GROPES HER way to Jaycee and shouts into the driver's ear, "What happened? Where are we?"

"We're next to the trains," she shouts back. "They're between us and that cop."

"How come we're not moving?"

"Because I killed the ignition."

"What do we do now?"

"Wait a little while, then go back to Fresh Start."

"Oh."

After ten or fifteen minutes, Jaycee resumes driving. The truck moans and groans but keeps moving. She gets back onto a street and soon finds the street she needs to return to Manhattan.

"I'm still here," Sullings says, "and I would really like for someone to tell me what this adventure is all about."

Santana starts filling her in.

"'Allison Sullings'? Never heard of her. I don't know any of *you*, either."

"We'll work on that," Santana tells her.

Jaycee sits at the wheel in the darkness, grateful that the train didn't plow into the truck and make quadriplegics of them all. She's pretty sure that the cop, separated from them by a dozen or more railway cars, has given up and driven off. But their biggest issues—the stolen laundry truck and abducted mental patient—will await resolutions.

"Too loud in here to do this," Santana shouts over the din of moving trains. "Can't you drive to someplace that's quieter?"

"First chance I get, sweetie," Jaycee shouts back.

By and by the trains disappear into the distance and Jaycee turns the ignition back on. She creeps back over the tracks, gratified to look over and see that the cop is gone. Once back on the roadway, she goes this way and that. Presently she is approaching Manhattan.

"Where do you live?" she asks Wendy.

"Why?"

"Gonna drop you off at home."

"No—I'm staying with you girls till you get this thing settled with Miz Sullings."

"Nix. I wanna keep you out of our trouble."

Wendy laughs. "Uh, I'm already in your trouble. Who do you think sneaked her out of the laughing academy and into the laundry truck?"

"Wendy can stay if she wants," says Santana.

They get onto Second Avenue, which is full of taxicabs, but Jaycee speeds between and around them, missing other vehicles by inches until she reenters her own little part of Manhattan where everything by now has become familiar. Jaycee smiles as she taps on the steering wheel. Mission accomplished—Sullings is back home and so are they. No one has been busted; she will not be handcuffed and sent back to Milgrom.

Jaycee Sheedy, you've done it again. Let's hear it for the girl!

She shifts into reverse and backs the truck into a

parking space as is she'd been doing it all her life. She's parked it directly in favor of a building marked Abe's Laundry Service, about a dozen feet from where they'd borrowed it.

"Perfect," says Santana. "Jaycee, you're the best driver and parker ever!"

Jaycee smirks. "Tell me something I don't already know."

All five of them hurry out of the truck and half-run through the cold, harsh wind.

"Remember anything yet, Miz Sullings?" asks Santana. "We've walked down these streets together a bunch of times. How about that time you juggled for us?"

She just shakes her head, hugging herself against the cold wind as her legs go faster and faster. "Don't remember anything. Just want to get warm."

"We'll be there soon," Jaycee says.

As they climb the steps to the Fresh Start apartment, Sullings asks, "Is this where I live?"

"Yes, ma'am," replies Jaycee.

"Really? It doesn't look so nice."

"You signed the lease," Santana says. "You worked hard to create Fresh Start. You chose the three of us to live with you."

"That so?"

Santana leans against the door as she reaches into her pocket for the key. The door opens.

"Broken lock," she says. "Call maintenance in the morning. The only things worth stealing here are us four lovely ladies. Maybe Donald Trump will come by tonight and take us home with him."

They all traipse in, and that's when the trouble starts.

CHAPTER 31

JAYCEE FEELS A *whoosh* as s blunt object whizzes past her face. Then she feels herself slammed into a wall. Santana lets out a hellish cry.

Then she hears a scream. *Wendy.*

Jaycee throws herself at the unknown assailant, but doubles over in pain as someone's punch explodes in her stomach. She manages to turn on the lights, and finds a pair of girls sitting on Santana, who thrashes about and curses at them through her bloodied mouth. One thug has Sullings in the kitchen, and another stand over Wendy, who is curled up on the floor.

Rubbing her stomach, Jaycee wishes the pain would subside so she could have another go at her enemy. Then she sees LaDonze, who had managed to wrestle Teri into a full Nelson.

"I got a piece, you know," says LaDonze. "You do something stupid, she dies."

Jaycee is amazed at how cool and even the girl's voice is. LaDonze isn't trying to scare anyone—she's just telling it like it is.

LaDonze stands there looking around the apartment. "Who's the lady in the kitchen? Yo' mama? And how 'bout little cutie there? She live here, too?"

"What you want?" Santana says.

"Don't see how it's any of your business," LaDonze tells her as Teri seems to go a bit limp in her arms. "We're takin' your girlfriend here for a business meeting. She already knows what we want. Question is, will she do it?"

Sullings emerges from the kitchen with one of LaDonze's girls behind her. "Wait," the Fresh Start leader says.

"Didn't tell nobody's mama to speak up," LaDonze retorts. Then, "Here's how it's gonna go: One of you is going with us. The rest of you gonna sit on this sofa real nice and quiet till we're gone. You do it that way, everything be cool. You don't do it that way—folks are gonna die."

After some nodding and murmuring, LaDonze's girls start poking at the Fresh Start crew, who crowd onto the sofa. Teri remains in LaDonze's grip. As the two of them inch their way towards the door, Jaycee, from the sofa, spies Sullings' tennis trophy on the TV set.

If you're gonna do it, do it now.

Jaycee gets up, hops over to the TV, grabs the trophy and fires it at LaDonze. It comes apart while airborne and its jagged half strikes LaDonze in her triceps. She screams in agony and releases her hold on Teri, who bolts for the master bedroom—and the fire escape.

For a moment or two, everyone in Fresh Start stands still, looking at each other, trying to figure out what has just happened and what to do now. But then LaDonze grabs her wounded arm and starts wailing like an infant. But she manages to scream, "Get her!"

By the time LaDonze's girls, and the Fresh Start four, get to the fire escape, Teri is already halfway down. Santana shoves LaDonze and her crew away as Jaycee climbs on and Wendy says to Sullings, "You shouldn't do it—you're not strong enough yet."

"My body's fine. It's my brain that's been roughed up a bit." She hustles down the steps, immediately recognizing the sound of rubber soles on old metal. *I've heard that before!*

She looks around, smiling and wide-eyed. *I've seen all this before!*

Sullings stands on the landing, staring ahead as, on the screen behind her eyeballs, a movie begins—*The Allison Sullings Story*—and she knows it by heart.

"Are you all right?" Wendy calls from the window.

"I'm remembering things," Sullings calls back. "It's coming back to me."

At that moment, LaDonze has forgotten her stab wound long enough to drop from the bottom of the fire escape onto Teri. The two punch and kick each other, Teri trying to exacerbate LaDonze's stab wound and LaDonze aiming high kicks at Teri's face. *They fight meaner than guys*, Jaycee thinks as she jumps on LaDonze's back and tries to squeeze the girl's injured shoulder.

Jaycee, however, cannot hold on for long against a bigger, tougher opponent. LaDonze flings her off, then punches her a couple of times before shoving Teri against the wall and kicking her some more.

"No!" screams Santana, coming to Teri's aid. But LaDonze throws a perfectly timed kick at the girl's face, and Santana ends up colliding with Teri, making them both wobble like bowling pins. A couple of

LaDonze's friends get their hands on Jaycee, and it's all over. Sullings' girls have lost the battle against LaDonze's crew.

"Break her neck," LaDonze says. Her voice could not be colder. One of the girls places her palm under the little blonde's chin.

Then they all turn around to look who's there as a powerful light shines on them.

"NYPD. Nobody move."

Lieutenant Jerry Lankford emerges from the unmarked car and looks at all the girls—their bloodied faces, messy hair and torn clothes.

"Only one pig!" shouts LaDonze, and, like sprinters hearing the starting gun, she and her girls take off. But they choose the closest dark alley, and when more cops arrive, the boys in blue cuff the kids and put them into the patrol vehicles."

"All right," says Lankford. "Everyone else—stand side by side in front of the light."

Jaycee, Teri, Santana, Sullings and Wendy all do as told. Wendy waves and says, "Hi, Uncle Jerry!"

"Wendy? Is that you? Have you been harmed?"

"No, I'm fine. These nice ladies have looked out for me."

Lankford shrugs. "The people at New York State Hospital aren't so sure about that. They're not even so sure about *you*." Then, "Who is Allison Sullings?"

The older woman raises her hand. "That's me. These three girls live with me at Fresh Start. Now I can remember everything."

"Can you, now? Who was looking after them while you were locked up?"

Nobody says anything as the police officers drive away with the girl gang.

"It's all worked out well," says Wendy.

"Not hardly," says Lankford.

CHAPTER 32

Lankford drives off, eventually, and the Fresh Start people go back inside.

"I don't care what happens now," says Jaycee. "Miz Sullings is back and OK, and that's the main thing. If I end up back in Milgrom, well, I can cope with that."

"I don't want to go back to Abbotsford," Santana says.

"I totally blame myself for this whole mess," Teri tells them. "It all started because I saw that here at Fresh Start, I would get some degree of freedom. So I was, like, 'I'm gonna do what I wanna do, and if you don't like, too bad.' Deep down, I wanted to screw up, like I always do. I guess I think I just don't deserve to be given a break."

"I'll call my Uncle Jerry," says Wendy. "I'll tell him what's going on and see what he can do for us."

Jaycee laughs. "Oh, I had a meeting with him. He told me, 'I want you to stay away from Wendy,' and I was, like, 'Uh, I don't think so.' So maybe he won't be in the mood for it when you phone him and say, 'Uncle Jerry, I want you to do a big favor for Jaycee and the girls.'"

Just then Lieutenant Jerry Lankford enters the

apartment, scowling at the occupants. "I'm going to ask you what happened, and everybody better be straight with me."

Sullings says, "We're no saints here, but these girls? They're not bad kids."

"I need facts, not heavily biased opinions," Lankford tells her. "Let's start with your injury. How did it come about?"

"My fault," Teri says.

"All three of us are to blame." Santana looks over at Jaycee. "We were all in this together."

"Surprise, surprise," says Lankford.

Santana says, "We were new in town, New York is a big, glamorous place, and we wanted to check things out. Miz Sullings was, like, 'I have to keep you on a tight leash,' so we tried to sneak out while she slept. She woke up and caught us on the fire escape."

"So she just fell?" the lieutenant asks. "Nobody pushed her off the fire escape?"

Santana shakes her head. "Nobody pushed her. We tried to save her from falling. It all happened way too fast for us to react."

"Do you believe her?" Lankford asks Sullings.

Sullings nods. "Every word of it."

"Keep talking," Lankford tells Santana.

The girls tells him of their struggle to keep Fresh Start running as they fretted over Sullings' chances for recovery.

"So you didn't contact the social worker or anyone else and say, 'We're at Fresh Start. We have a big problem and we need your help'?" Lankford throws up his hands, exasperated. "Didn't it occur to you to do any such thing? Those resources are there to help, you know."

"We thought we could work it out ourselves," Teri puts in. "We were sure that if we told Social Services what had happened, we would all be locked up again."

"While Miz Sullings was away," Jaycee says, "we did everything we were supposed to do. We did it very well, in fact."

The cop laughs. "Then you're telling me that while Miz Sullings was is the hospital, you three ran Fresh Start all by yourselves, even though you could have split and disappeared, but you didn't."

Jaycee nods. "We looked after ourselves."

"We looked after ourselves—and each other," adds Teri.

"While Miz Sullings was in All Saints' Hospital," says Jaycee, "I kept visiting her. That's where I met Wendy."

"Uncle Jerry," says Wendy, "you have to give these girls credit for trying to make the best of a very bad situation. The docs kept saying, 'Your memory will return,' so the girls assumed that was true. They knew that if they went to Social Services and said, 'Here's our problem,' the authorities probably would have padlocked Fresh Start the next day."

Santana tells him, "It totally freaked us out that they said to Miz Sullings, 'You're not hurt physically, so you're going to have to complete your recovery in the Queens hoo-hoo hotel.'"

Lankford grins in spite of himself. "That's how it often works—if the patient no longer needs the All Saints' Hospital bed but can't be released yet, they send the patient to New York State Hospital or another psychiatric facility."

"Well, that was bunk," Jaycee tells him. "We were,

like, 'Miz Sullings' stay at the nuthouse will be very short.' So we boosted a laundry truck, and here we are."

"What about those charming young ladies we met while they were kicking and punching you?"

"I know them from school," says Teri. "Their leader? She's LaDonze something. She was slangin' dope in the girls' can. I introduced myself to her and said, 'I want to hang out with you and your girls.' She was, like, 'If you'll light this bag lady on fire and dump her into the East River, you're in.'"

"Doesn't surprise me," Lankford says. "When we ran her name through our car's computer…well, let's just say that LaDonze has a long and distinguished history herself. If she keeps up her current behavior, she'll be dead or in prison before she's twenty-one."

After a long pause, Sullings says, "What now, Lieutenant? As far as I'm concerned, it's business as usual here at Fresh Start. I'm back and totally together mentally. I'm the boss and these are my girls. Is there any way we can say, 'This crisis didn't happen'? Or at least, 'We've resolved this crisis and now everything is OK'?"

"Wow." Lankford blows out a huge breath. "You're asking me, an officer of the law, to pretend that a number of big infractions didn't happen. What happened to that Abe's Laundry truck?"

"We put it back where we found it," Jaycee says.

Lankford nods. "OK, I guess I can do that for you. Now you have to do something for me."

"Name it," Sullings says.

"You"—he points at Jaycee—"and you"—he points at Wendy—"are through. Whatever kind of friendship you've had, it's all over. You can't even be each other's Facebook friend. Understand?"

"Oh, Uncle Jerry—"

"You heard it. I'm not sure that Jaycee is a menace to society, but I'm not sure that she *isn't*, either."

Jaycee fights back tears as she looks at Wendy, who makes an upturned mouth at the Fresh Start girl. Jaycee knows she's received the best possible of breaks, but feels it's horribly wrong that in this free country she's just forbidden to see her favorite person in all the world.

Teri snaps her fingers in Jaycee's face. "Hey! Wake up! The Man wants you to agree to the deal. Nod or say yes or something."

"Lighten up, Teri," Santana says.

"Yes or no?" asks Lankford.

"Yes," Jaycee and Wendy answer in unison.

"And…this…time…it's…for…real." The cop stands. "I've done you all a huge favor by making so much of your trouble go away. If there's any more trouble from here on out, it will be your trouble, not mine." To Wendy he says, "I'll drive you home."

The two of them exit together. Jaycee closes her eyes; it hurts too much to watch her leave.

I took a deep breath and exhaled slowly. If life kept handing you lemons, you needed to have a viable Plan B just to make any sense of it all.

Nevertheless, I thought I'd better get some kind of test reaction and run my Plan B by Shellie before unleashing it on the rest of the unsuspecting world. Shellie wasn't like Ria; she was less pushy and usually more inclined to hear me out; to really listen and to try to be more understanding of my various ideas.

In the meantime, however, I lay back on the sand and let the sun gently warm my skin because life could be very simple if you made the right choices.

I had to wait until the following Tuesday morning after I'd dropped Josh off at school to see Shellie. I knew for a fact that she was working from home today. Surely she could put up with a few moments' intrusion?

Shellie seemed surprised to see me even though I'd texted her that I was on my way. However, I was too excited about sharing my news to focus on that. I made my all-important announcement as soon as I crossed the threshold.

"I'm going to have a baby."

Shellie was looking unimpressed as she closed the door behind me.

"Do you want to come in or are you the new town crier?"

God, this girl was cool. Apart from the obvious rudeness, she was giving very little else away. I could only assume that the cynical look she was giving me was hiding her true respect for my ability to move my life along when I needed to. It might equally have been concealed horror but I preferred to keep things positive.

Impatiently, I followed her into the lounge and a few minutes later, I was curled up on the sofa.

Shellie's apartment was the opposite of Ria's. She was less of a control merchant and it showed. Her home was an eclectic array of interesting furniture and objects that she'd collected from her travels or from auction houses. It was very easy to feel at home in this space.

"Okay, so, tell me what this is all about?" she said giving me her full attention.

I took a deep breath and prepared to launch into my well-rehearsed spiel even though I was fairly sure she'd heard me the first time.

"I'm going to have a baby."

"That's what I thought I heard," Shellie said. "I didn't even know you were dating anyone—at least not seriously enough to be starting a family with them."

"What's that got to do with anything?" I asked. "Besides, I'm not *starting* a family—just adding to my current one."

"Okay, at least that part makes sense. But from what I know about your dating life, I can only assume that you've decided to use a sperm bank or you're the victim of a one-night stand!"

"You know I'm not the one-night stand type!"

I tried to main good eye contact, because not so very long ago I had been sorely tempted down there by the Lakeshore.

"So, you *are* using a sperm bank!"

"No, I'm not! There are other choices besides desperately sleeping around or using a sperm bank if you want to have a baby. You do remember all that stuff about women's liberation, don't you?"

"Okay, so if you're not going the DIY route and if it's not a hit and run job, then I'm all out of ideas—unless, oh God—please tell me it's not Todd!"

I suddenly felt a little less sure that I wanted to discuss things with Shellie after all.

"What do you mean?" I said carefully.

"You can't have forgotten that mighty moron that you insist on calling a boyfriend. You know, Todd the odd bod."

"I wish you wouldn't call Todd names; he isn't all that bad and yes, you are quite right, as it happens. I have decided that Todd's the man for the job."

Shellie groaned, but I continued regardless, "You're supposed to be my best friend, remember? I thought I could count on your unwavering support, at least."

Actually, I really did need Shellie to lose the uncharacteristic melodrama. The sooner she came to terms with my decision, the sooner I could sign her up to be godmother.

Shellie was still mumbling unutterable little grunts in between shaking her head in despair. Clearly, my news had knocked her off her perch. When she did find her voice, I was surprised at her reaction.

"Are you insane? Didn't you tell me that that guy doesn't know the first thing about women?"

I decided to ignore her outburst because I could feel a little twitch developing near my left eye. I tried to ignore that as well. It might not have been smart to have told her what I really thought about Todd in the past. But the damage was done now and my hastily spoken words could not be taken back.

"I don't know what you mean. Sure, Todd has his issues but at least I know him and, as I've dated him in the past, it won't be adding yet another notch to my bedpost."

"I thought you hated Todd."

"No—*you* hate Todd! *I* just hate sleeping with him; it's not quite the same thing."

Shelly tossed her head back dismissively, "I don't hate that fool. I'm just not understanding how you allowed him to get you pregnant if you hate sleeping with him that much."

I stared at Shellie; really this girl could be totally obtuse when she wanted to be.

"Shellie, darling, I am *not* pregnant."

"But you just said you're having a baby! I totally give up; This is way too complicated."

I shifted so that I was facing Shellie more directly and tried to straighten up because my right leg had gone to sleep.

"You're the one making things complicated! What I *said* was that I am *going to* have a baby, get it? '*Going to*', as in the future. I have not, as yet, done the deed."

"Phew! Shellie breathed an exaggerated sigh of relief. "That, at least, is good news."

"Thanks a lot for the support!" I said sarcastically.

To tell the truth, I was getting a bit cheesed off with her attitude. Why did it matter who I chose as the father—wasn't that my business? Her job was to sound enthusiastic and offer support to her best friend.

"Why would you even consider having a baby with Todd?" Shellie asked. "Come to think of it, why are we even having this conversation?"

This wasn't going to be as easy as I'd thought it would be. I, apparently, had not quite understood the level of antagonism Shellie felt towards Todd. Surely he wasn't all that bad?

"Well, I just think it's a good time. With all the bad stuff that's happened over the last year, I'd like some happiness. Right now all I have to show for my life is a credit card bill."

"What about Josh?"

The thought of my son brought an immediate smile to my face.

"The fact that Josh is the center of my life is understood. You know he's my everything, but he's not a baby. He's going to grow up and go to university, or college, or get married and leave me."

"I think he might be a bit young for all that activity," Shellie said dryly. "Besides, I think you'll find that the same fate will befall the new baby; he, or she, will also grow up at some point."

"Stop being difficult, Shellie. You know what I mean."

"I'm not sure that I do know what you mean by all this."

She furrowed her brows as if deep in thought before looking up suddenly as if she'd suddenly seen the light.

"This is about Nicole, isn't it?"

I drew in a sharp breath.

Nicole.

Yeah—there was a good reason why Shellie was my best friend. She totally got me. She was probably one of the few people who understood how my mind worked. She alone had understood just how much of an impact the death of one of our dearest friends had made on me personally.

I tried to meet her gaze casually but it wasn't working. I could feel the twitch beside my eye kicking in again.

"Maybe," I said in a low voice.

And maybe...just maybe, it was time to deal with some of my demons.

CHAPTER SIX

Up until last year, I'd always thought of Shellie, Nicole and myself as the fearless three. Although Ria would join in our escapades from time to time, she was more of the loner type, whereas the three of us had moved in a pack. That was until Nicole had become unwell.

I could remember her nonchalantly going off for her initial tests when it had all started. No one had thought, even for a moment, that it was anything too serious. But the results of those tests had dealt us all a severe blow when they had come back positive for cancer.

Nicole hadn't really looked that sick for a long while. In fact, with all the weight she'd lost she'd looked pretty good once she'd got past the surgery and chemo. So, it had been pretty hard to accept that she had been in fact fighting for her life.

Before we had even had time to properly register the strange turn of events, Nicole had succumbed to the disease. Just like that, she was gone. And here we were, discussing her in the past tense as if that was normal. I was beginning to understand though, just how fleeting life could be.

"Maybe, it is about Nicole a little," I admitted quietly, "But it is also a lot about me too. My life has been pretty challenging over the last two years. Nicole's death was devastating but it made me realize that if you want to achieve anything, you've got to just do it."

"Yeah, I guess I understand where you're coming from," said Shellie. "I do get that you were badly shaken up about Nicole, we all were. But I'm just not getting how you're planning to cope with having a baby right now."

"It's what I want to do," I said stubbornly.

"All I'm really trying to say is don't rush into anything. As you said yourself, life's been a bit tough over the last little while. You need to give yourself time to heal. Mourn the past before you embrace the future."

"You might be right. I don't know what's good and what's not good anymore. Every week I have a new idea, each one a little more fantastic than the last. But I'm really hooked on this idea of having a baby. I think it's what I need."

"Okay, but if you're not prepared to give up the baby idea, perhaps you should think about the whole Todd thing; I know that I'd sure hate to meet my Mr. Right if I was pregnant with a baby for someone else."

"I'm not like you, Shellie. I've been in a committed relationship remember? Okay, so we didn't quite make it to the altar, but we were close enough and trust me, it was an eye-opener. I think that one experience was enough for me, but I do think I could manage with another child by myself once I've sorted out my work situation."

"Maybe we're more alike than you think," said Shellie with a sudden grin. "It's just that I've gone past the ideas stage of life; these days I don't get the great ideas or anything like that; I just go straight to the *screw-up* stage. That's me—just a long line of screw-ups."

I giggled, "I definitely think I'm ahead of you when it comes to being the screw-up queen; I just prefer to give everyone around me a bit of notice, that's all."

"For which we are all truly grateful," Shellie said solemnly before joining in the laughter.

"We could both just be a bit down in the dumps. It'll pass," I said hopefully because I wasn't used to Shellie being on a downer.

"I agree," Shellie said, "I think maybe we're just making some natural adjustments to some rather dynamic changes in our lives."

"When did we become such losers?" I asked. "Weren't we going to grab life by the balls and make names for ourselves?"

"Shit happens."

"Yeah, but so much of it? I feel like I'm drowning in all this stuff." I shifted position again trying to get comfortable, "Oh, and while I'm having a good old moan—when, exactly, are you going to get a decent sofa like normal people?"

"It's a perfectly good sofa. I paid a full hundred bucks for it at the Value Village. I don't see the point of adding to the landfill crisis if I can reuse a pre-owned sofa. I saved money as well as doing my bit for the environment; it's a win-win. I might get it reupholstered though because it is a nice old piece."

"Old being the operative word! Maybe next time, get one that's not so close to the ground, we're not getting younger."

"Speak for yourself; I'm still young and extraordinarily hot."

I grinned at Shellie, "Well, right now I feel ancient. I also feel panicked, you know, like if I don't get laid, or have a baby, or something, then I'm going to be old and lonely and all shriveled up."

"You can always get laid if you're prepared to lower your standards and, if you use a good moisturizer, there's absolutely no need for you to be shriveled up at all. So right there we've just solved two-thirds of your problems."

"Apparently you're in a flippant mood and I need some real advice."

Shellie glanced over at the large silver clock adorning one of the walls, "Sorry darling, I do sympathize. You know I do—I just think we're all still getting over losing Nicole. But life does go on, surprisingly. We can't let the past destroy us—no matter what it is that we're dealing with. As it stands, I'm currently dealing with a lot of my own crap with work so I'd best be getting on with my current task."

"What's wrong?" I was immediately concerned because I too had experienced the joys of working for idiots.

"I'll tell you about it another time. Maybe I'll even come over for a drink this evening but, right now, I have to make a few calls. My boss is chomping at the bits for my latest report so I have to kick you out."

"I hope they pay you extra for working so hard."

"They pay me enough, I guess."

"Yeah, but you always seem to be working so hard these days. All work and no play makes Shellie a boring old fart."

"Go away, Shaniah."

"Ok, I'm leaving you to make mad passionate love to whatever the hell you're working on. Don't take *too* much crap from that boss of yours. You should get him to join assholes anonymous."

"Bye, Shaniah."

I hugged Shellie briefly, "Be happy for me!"

"Oh yeah, the baby thing. I'm so frigging happy for you right now that I can hardly contain myself."

I ignored the sarcasm and grabbed my purse, "Thanks for listening; I know you're stressed out with work so I'll leave you to it."

"No problem. But I want you to chill out a bit and I'm going to assume that this latest great idea of yours shall fall by the wayside," Shellie said looking at me hopefully.

"I can see I'm going to have a hard time convincing you to take this seriously but it's what I really want to do."

"I'm taking this so seriously that I'm even going to make you an offer. If Todd can't get it up, let me know and I'll pop into that little adult store downtown and buy you some goodies to tide you over. I don't want my best friend to die of sexual frustration."

"Oh, right, well thanks for nothing."

"Don't be mad at me; I do want to support you. I just think you need to take some time out before making too many life-changing decisions."

The last thing I needed at that moment was the voice of reason screwing up my plans.

"I'm not mad and I hear you. You've got a lot on your plate right now and I'm going through a mega crisis. Don't worry though, I'll catch up with you later when you're in a more receptive mood."

Shellie snorted and I knew it was time to leave. It was time to find more sympathetic ears. I would just have to consult with Ria. She was perhaps even less suited to the task than Shellie but she would have to do; these were desperate times and beggars didn't get to be choosers.

CHAPTER SEVEN

I caught up with Ria on the weekend, while Josh was at his martial arts class.

She answered the door in a white toweling bathrobe, matching fluffy slippers and dorky black reading glasses perched at the end of her nose. She looked like a million dollars.

"Hey, Sis," she said, "You're lucky to catch me in. How come you didn't call?"

"I did, several times, but you're not answering your phone."

"Oh crap, the battery probably died. I'd better put it to charge."

I threw my purse on the white leather sofa and tucked my feet up. This was more the business—this sofa was the epitome of comfort.

"Do you need some wine?" Ria asked.

"It's only 11.30."

"Vodka, then?"

"I'll have some herbal tea; I don't need to add liver cirrhosis to my other problems."

"Killjoy!" said Ria.

I considered my position. If I went ahead with my baby-making plans, I would have to completely give up alcohol for the duration, so it was probably a good idea to exploit every opportunity to drink while I still could.

"Okay, forget the tea, I'll go with something white and dry."

"That's more like it." Ria poured the wine and handed the glass to me, before walking off towards her bedroom.

"Keep talking," she yelled. "I've got to find an outfit for a super-hot date tonight."

"Oh, I was hoping I could pick your brain for a minute."

"Come in here then, unless you enjoy shouting."

I followed her voice through to the bedroom.

"Who's the date?" I asked.

"I met this new guy on one of those '*NSA*' type websites."

"What does that mean?"

"No strings attached. Well, it's not strictly NSA, but not far off. I don't know if I can go ahead with the whole *sex with a stranger* thing though."

"Jesus Christ, Ria! You're kidding right?"

"Okay, if it makes you sleep better, I'm kidding."

"Mom would have a blue fit if she knew you were prowling the internet looking for sex."

"It's not exactly like that—give me some credit. I just want an arrangement with one guy. I'm over the whole marriage thing—you should understand that. But a girl's gotta do what a girl's gotta do. Besides, I've got some flavored condoms I'm dying to try."

"Okay, that is way too much information and I'm still not feeling it for this new strategy of yours," I said.

Ria peered at me over the glasses, "I'm doing this by choice. I'm not leaving my happiness to a husband who's too busy looking for a younger model to invest time in me."

I guessed she was referring to her husband who had departed the marital home by way of gross infidelity.

I held up my hands in mock surrender, "Hey, you're an adult."

Ria gave me a surprised look as if she couldn't believe I was giving up the discussion so easily.

"Damn right," she said before holding up yet another outfit, "How does this look?"

I shrugged, "You look good in anything. Maybe you should be focusing on packing a sawn-off shotgun if you're intent on meeting complete strangers for intimacy."

"Don't get too excited. I'm just meeting him for coffee, or maybe cocktails, then dinner—kind of like your own internet date. After that, it's back home, alone—at least for the first date. I've decided to play hard to get; no sex before date number two."

I stared at Ria. I didn't know whether to laugh or not because I wasn't sure if she was being serious. Had she changed or had I? Had she always been this blunt?

Lately, there seemed to be a bit of a hard edge to her. I wasn't sure I liked it. True, she had always been a bit of a tough cookie but this new approach to her love life was on another level. That was, of course, unless she was indeed joking.

"What about the site you recommended to me?" I asked. "How come you told me about it but you're not using it?"

"We have different goals," she said simply. "With this particular NSA site, you can pick someone who's professional, has a clean bill of health and is ready to go. It's kind of like an exclusive speed dating club really. We know what we want upfront. No bullshit. If I don't like the looks of him, it's hello and goodbye. If I like him, then we'll meet again and, at any point when I'm comfortable, I can jump on his bones."

I still didn't like the sound of what Ria was proposing, but I was hardly in a position to judge her because she could have been describing my own recent experience with Jared to some extent. Maybe all dating sites were pretty much the same!

"I still think you deserve more than just some guy looking for sex online."

"Oh, I know that. You're quite right—I do deserve the best of the best, but, as I said, while I'm waiting for him to show up at my door, I'm gonna get me some action with a like-minded Adonis."

"I just assumed that as you work in quite a large firm, you could find at least one decent guy there to date. I, on the other hand, only meet weirdos at the grocery store—although I guess there's always the postman."

"Isn't he about a hundred years old?"

"At least."

Ria giggled, "And I guess I could always resort to dating one of the criminals I'm supposed to be defending."

"You know what I mean. You also meet other professionals. Maybe you could come to an arrangement with one of your colleagues—sort of like a friend with benefits arrangement. At least you wouldn't be putting your trust in a stranger."

"I don't intend to put my trust in anyone ever again and I don't believe in random acts of desperation. Dating a colleague would be even more dangerous than my current plans."

I was beginning to feel a rising panic. Ria was making sense. Of course she was right—it was always going to be a bad idea to do anything out of desperation. Was I desperate? Were my decisions based on all the negativity of the past year, compounded by my disappointment with Jared and the whole online dating saga?

Shellie's words rang in my memory *'I'd sure hate to meet Mr. Right if I was pregnant with someone else's baby.'*

Did I really want to commit to my Plan B? Was it the hare-brained scheme that Shellie thought it was? Maybe it was time to shift the focus away from my plans.

Secretly, I was beginning to agree with Ria and Shellie that I perhaps needed to find a new love interest. It didn't mean that I was ready to relinquish my plans completely just yet; maybe I just needed to think about finding a new potential baby-daddy just in case things didn't work out with Todd.

"I guess I'll just have to leave you to go after one of those online guys," I said. "Maybe you'll have better luck than I had."

"And unfortunately I have to leave you to go after Todd."

"So, should I assume that now isn't the best time to tell you that I'm going to have a baby?"

Ria didn't even bat an eyelid.

"Do you think this skirt looks good with this top?" She held the proposed outfit against her body and did a semi-twirl in front of the mirror that dominated much of one bedroom wall.

Man, this girl was an even cooler piece of work than Shellie.

"Did you hear what I said?"

"Yeah, I heard. I could have sworn you mentioned the 'B' word."

"That is correct. I'm not doing much else with my life right now. My career seems to have tanked and I'm thinking of a career switch, so why not now?"

Ria was still silent.

"Well, haven't you got anything to say?"

"I have plenty to say." She held up a white silk blouse, "Maybe this would work better..."

"Oh my God, just put on with whatever with the damned skirt!"

"Chill out, baby sister!" Ria placed the silk blouse and the itsy-bitsy skirt back on the bed and took my arm.

"Come through to the lounge and have another drink. Then, you can tell me what's going on in that pretty little head of yours. I can see you need intervention from your big sister before you completely wreck your entire life."

Hello. Grown woman in the house here! Less of the condescension please—my name is Shaniah, not Josh.

Of course, I didn't dare say what I was thinking out aloud because I didn't want to totally piss her off. Ria didn't have the most tolerant of personalities and I wanted feedback without the attitude.

"I can look after myself, thanks. You're becoming more like Mom every day," I snapped.

"Ouch! That's a bit of a low blow."

I grinned at her, "It was a bit, sorry!"

I sat on the leather sofa facing her. If anything, Ria was probably worse than Mom because she knew more of my secrets and she would not hesitate in using that knowledge.

"What's all this nonsense about being pregnant and who's the dad?"

"I'm not sure."

"And you're shocked when I tell you my plans for getting some long overdue action in the sex department?"

"Okay, so chill. I'm not actually pregnant, yet. But I think that if I'm ever going to have another child, I need to do something about it before I get too old. As for the dad, I'm thinking of jumping on Todd's bones and letting him do the honors."

"Bad idea!"

"Okay..."

"Find someone with money. How are you going to manage to look after another kid by yourself if the dad is a poverty-stricken, dickhead?"

"I think I'd better go," I said because I wasn't faring any better here with Ria than I had with Shellie.

"Oh, don't be upset. I'm just asking you to face facts about lover boy," Ria said.

"I'm not in the mood, Ria. I'll catch you later."

"Okay. I'm sorry for upsetting you," she said. She actually managed to look contrite for a change because she knew that once I'd got an idea in my head, it was pretty much fixed in there with cement.

"Yeah, you should be."

Really, so far, all I'd actually achieved was to confirm that best friends and sisters were unsympathetic at best and at their very worst, they could be annoying in the extreme.

"Look, Shannie" Ria's voice took on a softer tone, "You should think hard about this; it is possible that in the history of bad ideas, yours is far more up there than mine. You already have one child who's a bit of a handful."

"Josh is not a handful!" I was immediately defensive.

"Okay. He needs a lot of attention then, and you are a single parent."

"I'm managing."

"Yes, that's my point. You deserve more than just managing. You deserve to have a supportive spouse and enough resources to care for you and your children so that you can have a good quality of life."

"I do okay," was all I could think of saying because this was not what I had come to hear. I needed encouragement because my decision was not about to be changed.

"Okay," said Ria, "But do me one favor?"

"What's that?"

"Don't tell Mom just yet."

"Now that's the first sensible thing you've said since I got here."

CHAPTER EIGHT

I was probably about ninety-five percent sure that my current love interest, Todd, wasn't *the one,* but hey, how do you know if someone's the right one?

I had clearly developed a knack for picking the *wrong* one. My own engagement to Josh's father had ended abruptly when, on returning home from work early one afternoon, I'd discovered him ass up with a neighbor.

I hadn't been too surprised because I'd been feeling for some time that he'd been a bit off. My psychic senses had been running riot but I'd been in total denial. What I'd actually found out was that, despite our upcoming marriage, Mark had been sleeping with another woman for the better part of six months. Much later, I found out that he'd apparently had an internet account on a dating site for people wanting to commit adultery—and he hadn't even been married yet! He had clearly believed in starting as he meant to continue.

Obviously, I'd been keen to ditch him once the ugly truth was out but it had damaged me enormously.

Since that colossal failure, I'd had a few brief relationships if you could even call them that— maybe they were more like dating episodes. I'd even had a couple of engagement which I'd broken off because getting married to avoid being alone was such a dumb idea.

Mostly, though, I was now alone because I'd become a bit of a commitment-phobe with trust issues. Still, I was a healthy girl with libidinal urges that needed attention. So, what was a girl to do? It wasn't like I had a string of 'eligibles' lining up outside my door on any given day.

Of this one thing I was now certain however, I could not afford to make too many more mistakes. Nor could I afford to dawdle—I didn't want to hang around until my reproductive eggs were totally fried!

The way things were looking, I'd just have to settle for Todd—at least just for now; just until I'd got past this obsession with having another baby. Once I had the baby, I planned on shutting up shop—no more relationships—just my kids and me. I didn't need a man in my life on a permanent basis to validate my existence.

Todd had managed to father two kids previously so at least he wasn't firing blanks. I tried not to think about the part where most of his salary probably had to go towards child support payments.

I figured Todd had to be as safe a bet as any other man I was prepared to take the risk with and try to conceive. He was the condom king of the Greater Toronto Area—well, as far as I was concerned anyway. My biggest job would be to get him to lose the condom at the right time of the month, then BAM—baby mama on the way! At least, that was the theory.

In practice, Todd didn't really want any more kids. But that was okay too because, the last time I checked, he didn't have a womb so I couldn't figure out what he was bitching about.

I wanted kids—well, maybe just the one more and, in order to achieve that, I didn't exactly need to hold out for the love of a good man or, with my luck, a bad man. It didn't take a genius to figure this stuff out and I didn't need to be in love for this to work; I just needed the baby-making goodies.

According to the websites I'd been reading lately, the average man emits somewhere between forty million to two-hundred-and-fifty million sperm in any one session. So, the way I saw it, although Todd was not the most memorable lover I'd ever had, surely even he should be able to produce one good sperm? I mean, that's all you really need to make a baby—one out of forty million. In the greater scheme of things, that's really not a lot to ask for. Anyway, he owed me big time for putting up with all that crappy sex over the past three years.

However, I would have to think about the baby-making problem later because it was time to pick Josh up from school. Although Josh was quite able to walk home by himself, I just knew that even a small amount of sunshine would aggravate his eczema and he'd end up scratching all night.

I grabbed my keys and headed out

The first thing Josh said when he saw me was, "Why do I have to go to school, Mom?"

That's it? That's all my child has to say to me after not seeing me all day?

I stared at Josh as I tried to think of an answer.

73

Really, I wanted to tell him that he had to go to school because it made for a great babysitting service while parents worked to pay taxes that in turn paid the teachers. I wanted to tell him that once you grow up, there were all these unpaid bills waiting for you and schools were there to help to prepare you for the shock. I wanted to tell him that when your parents got too old to pay bills and taxes, it was your turn, and kids needed to be prepared for that second shock. I wanted to tell my son that school would prepare him for the long haul, the relentless day-in, day-out drudgery of life.

I didn't tell him any of those things because, really, how the hell was I supposed to know why kids had to go to school? Maybe I needed to think about that for a while—you know, maybe I could get back to him in a day or so...

Hey son, don't call me, I'll call you!

In the meantime, my immediate situation was that I was no longer allowed to kiss Josh in public, and most definitely not in front of his school-mates. So, I kind of threw him a weary smile and said, "Hello Josh, darling. It's so good to see you too. I missed you today. Did you have a nice day? I know I didn't, but thank you very much for not asking—oh and I love you too."

Josh stared at me pitifully through his glasses which always seemed to be on the verge of sliding off his nose.

"Mom, you're being weird; people are gonna hear you."

I looked around at the other equally stressed-out parents.

"Call it light entertainment," I said.

"Can we just go home, Mom?" He wasn't sounding too happy.

"Sure thing," I said.

"You didn't answer my question," Josh said as I settled into the driver's seat.

"What question was that, love?"

"Why do I have to go to school? Why can't I just get home-schooled?"

I tried to conceal my horror at his suggestion. Some days, my only relief from dealing with a kid with very specific needs was when he left for school and I could get some personal space. I saw school days as a bit of respite They gave me chance to recharge my battery and get things done. I banished the guilt I felt for thinking that because, although I loved Josh more than life itself, even I had to admit that sometimes he was kind of hard work.

I glanced at him as I turned the key in the ignition and the engine roared to life.

"You need a good education to get a good job," I said. "Besides, I'm not a teacher, so I couldn't really teach you all that wonderful stuff you learn at school."

"I hate school." He said the last bit with such feeling that I felt a wave of pity for all of about two seconds.

"Okay, then, you'd miss your friends," I was starting to feel desperate.

"I can make it without them," he said soberly.

I choked back the laughter that threatened to erupt and quickly put on my serious parent face.

"That's too bad darling, because you've got about another eight years at school, and at least two in college after that, so you've got to find a way to start liking it."

He lapsed into a silent sulk.

"Okay, Josh, so are you going to tell me what happened today?"

"I hate Miss Josephs. She always picks on me. Today all the other children got to watch a movie and I had to put my head down."

Aha! So now we were getting to the real problem.

"What d'you mean you had to put your head down?"

"She said I couldn't watch the movie because I was talking in class, but I wasn't, Mom. Ethan and Luke were making fun of me and I told them to shut up, and she only shouted at *me*. I hate school, I'm never going back and you can't make me!"

I looked over at my son and tried to keep the despair out of my voice.

"You'll feel better tomorrow, sweetheart."

Silence.

I tried again, "Do you need a hug?"

Nothing.

He'd dried up. Not even a few crocodile tears.

We drove home in the silence. Every so often I sent my son a little glance. He was looking out of the window as if he had developed a deep bond with his environment.

Thank God it was Friday, and he was doing a sleepover with his best friend, Noah.

Once we got home, dinner and Scooby on Netflix seemed to cheer Josh up and I breathed a sigh of relief. His current behavior was possibly the only thing that could derail my baby-making plans. I mean, did I really want two Joshes stressing me out on a daily basis?

After dinner, I finally managed to get Josh to do some of his homework and sorted out his gear. The sleepover was a fairly regular thing so there weren't too many instructions to be issued once I'd dropped Josh off. For my own good parental behavior, I was actually allowed to hug and kiss him goodbye.

"Text me later," I instructed in between squeezing in a second hug as he shouldered the backpack that contained his overnight gear.

"Okay, Mom, I've gotta go. I love you."

There they were. Those three words that you need to hear at least once a day. In my case, I was hearing it from my number one son and I was a happy girl. I was going to be okay. My son loved me and he loved the job I was doing raising him.

On returning home, I was thinking that apart from the fact that I really hated being in the house by myself, I would truly miss Josh. We were a team and it always felt weird when he was out.

The upside, of course, was that the evening was mine. I was young-ish, free-ish and single-ish—so I called Todd.

"I'll come over in an hour or so," he said.

Great! That meant we'd watch TV until a respectable time and then we'd go to bed.

On average, sex with Todd was usually like a military operation; in and out before anyone could notice—quick and painful with someone getting hurt—oh yeah, and that someone was usually me.

So the next logical question would be why settle for him? This in itself was not a bad question but it wasn't one that I felt any obligation to answer. I mean, it wasn't as if I needed a psychotherapist or anything; I was sure I had good reasons. For starters, there was the whole trying-to-have-a-baby plan and I had long since figured out that one loser was as good as another.

kids. This was supposed to guarantee glazed over eyes...eye.

It was also supposed to cause a hasty retreat on the guy's part.

David had apparently not read the articles.

"Well, I'm not averse to having kids," he said still looking hopeful as if anticipating the kid making activity.

It was enough.

"The thing is, David," I said, "I don't think I'm your type."

Shit! Shit! I'd meant to say 'you're definitely not my type'.

"Of course you're my type," he reassured me.

"How do you know?"

"Well, I liked your profile..."

"You didn't actually believe that pile of crap I wrote?" I said. I was taking a leaf out of Jared's book as I remembered the feeling of disappointment I'd experienced when I'd realized that I'd been conned.

David was undeterred. Jeez, it was really super hard to get rid of this guy. I figured if I showed him how vulgar I could be, he'd back off. All the magazine articles I'd ever read had also stated that men hate women who swear. Old David saw it as one of my more redeeming features.

"Well, yes, I took it quite seriously." He sounded genuinely offended. My one thought was, '*Finally, some negative emotions.*' I was relieved because I needed to fall off the pedestal that he clearly had me on. The truth is that I'd actually put a lot of thought into my profile but it had apparently been very effective in snaring a range of undesirables. I hadn't exactly forgotten Jared.

"Look," I said, "This was a bad idea. You really don't want to get mixed up with me; I'm really kinda high maintenance."

He looked confused and hurt and I felt kind of bad for that. But you know, even with my low self-esteem, I could tell we weren't going to be an item, so I really needed to start getting through to him via his crocodile hide.

"I think you're painting yourself out to be much worse than you really are," he said smiling indulgently at me.

"No, trust me, I'm not."

Man, this guy was really into me! I was desperate and desperate times called for desperate action. So how did I leave politely?

"Sorry, but I have to go," I said.

"I was just beginning to enjoy our date," David said.

He sounded really disappointed. However, in real life, all good things come to an end. This date had not been good but it too had come to its natural end.

I used my index finger and thumb to pinch the bridge of my nose, specifically the point between my eyes.

Get the message first time, dude—I don't have time to waste. And next time don't Photoshop out your dodgy eye(s); it is very disheartening to spend the evening with someone who has misrepresented his features. A gal can only take so much.

Then I felt like shit for thinking that—I mean, he couldn't really help the way he was born, could be?

The thought occurred to me that maybe he could be good in bed. You know, if you have challenges looks-wise, you had to have something else going for you! Then I thought about what the poor kid would look like if he actually got me pregnant and the moment passed.

In the end, I figured that if I just got up and left, then he'd have to get the message.

"Goodbye, David," I said and I grabbed my purse and headed for the door. David took the cue and followed me.

"Can we do this again real soon?"

I reached the car, opened the door and turned to face him.

"Look, I'm really sorry, David, but the thing is, I'm on some pretty strong meds right now, so I'm kinda getting a bit twitchy. If I don't take them in the next half hour or so, I'm gonna be really screwed up for the rest of the month and then they'll make me go back to that place; all that therapy and shit. No way am I going through that again."

"You didn't tell me you were on medication," he said and took a step backwards.

"Yeah, I'm sorry about that; maybe I should have told you. I'm a bad person," I said softly borrowing a line from '*Kill Bill*'.

It had been my experience that men respond to crazy women in one of two ways; they either marry them or they try their damnedest to escape their clutches. Normal females like me tend to mostly get overlooked.

Now safely in the car, I checked my rear view mirror. David was watching with what could have been disappointment. It was kind of difficult to read his facial expression because it always came back to the eye situation. But the thing is that he made no attempt to stop my progress once he'd thought I was a possible refugee from the local nut house. I was lucky to escape in one piece!

I went home and felt like a real bitch for treating David so badly but pretty soon I got over that too.

So, I could safely say that I was beginning to have second thoughts or maybe even third thoughts about online dating. I was now officially disillusioned. How did people ever hook up seriously like this? All I'd encountered online were a bunch of weird looking guys worthy of only one date; oh and I mustn't forget about Jared whom I'd counted worthy of more than just the one but who still had not measured up.

How many dates had I been on so far? I had to be near, if not past, my quota of *'no more than ten'* by now. I was far from being impressed.

I switched on my laptop and pulled up my dating profile. With one click it was gone—deleted! I'd had enough; it was time to give the dating game a complete break.

CHAPTER SIXTEEN

"I need to get out of here."

Shellie's words jolted me out of my reverie.

I looked around at her.

"Yeah," I nodded, "let's say our goodbyes."

We were seated in Nicole's parents' living room trying to process the fact that today was the anniversary of the day that we had buried a good friend, someone's daughter, sister, wife and mother.

I hadn't quite dealt with the fact that Nicole, Shellie and I were not going to grow old together. Some friendships formed in the innocent years of childhood were eternal, or so it had seemed. Now, we'd come together to remember Nicole and to release pink and white balloons into the sky.

I imagined that they would connect with her spirit somehow; take our love to her.

I hugged Nicole's mom and dad and held it together for their sake. I'd always loved the Lawsons but now I felt awkward; kind of guilty that I was here and Nicole was long gone.

I smiled feebly at Nicole's husband and at their daughter and said a few words of comfort, or at least I hoped they were.

We'd stayed long enough to sample the buffet but it was time to leave before my emotions overcame me.

"Do you want to come back with me for a drink or whatever?"

"Thanks, Shellie, but if it's all the same with you, I'm going to collect Josh from Mom. She's been doing an awful lot of babysitting for me lately and I think they freak each other out after a couple of hours."

Shellie giggled.

"Your mom probably means well but her bible bashing might be a bit much for an eight-year-old."

"Yeah, and her arthritis was acting up today so she's probably visiting divine retribution on a poor sinner like Josh."

"Don't be too hard on her. She's loyal and she does really love you guys even though she might not always show it in an obvious way. Plus, as you said, she never says no to baby-sitting."

Shellie was right. I thought of Mom who'd sacrificed her life for us since dad had died. Mom wasn't actually that old! Sixty-seven was the new forty, apparently; she just needed to get with the program a bit. Lighten up on her nearest and dearest ones—lose the bible!"

I'd been making a huge effort to be nicer to her lately. Humans are extremely fragile. I needed to value her while I still had a mother. Losing Nicole was like receiving a license to live because life was apparently a very fleeting thing. If we could bury Nicole, anything could happen. All that remained of her were grieving family members and memories. I sighed wearily.

"That poor child has to grow up without a mother," I said thinking of the daughter Nicole had tried so hard to conceive.

"I know, eh! At least Nicole had the opportunity to experience true love. I never did meet anyone I could even consider marrying. Right now I can't even find a regular boyfriend."

I stared at Shellie. She was extremely attractive in a punkish, healthy-looking way. If any of our old gang would be likely to live to a hundred, my bets were on Shellie.

"I hear you," I said, "But you meet your fair share of guys."

"I know, but do I want to marry any of the ones I'm meeting? Not really!"

"Yeah, it's tough getting married these days," I said.

"At least you've nearly been married," said Shellie. "Okay, so it didn't work out, but you know at least you could have had the experience and you have Josh. What about me?"

"You were always the sensible one," I said. "You knew you didn't want to compromise and you didn't. I almost married an idiot and a cheat; it kind of cancels out the whole experience."

Shellie giggled. "I think we need to shake things up a bit," she said, "We're in danger of getting old and boring, not to mentioned becoming mentally damaged."

"Yeah, I hear you."

Once Shellie had dropped me off home, I headed out to get Josh.

"It gets better with time," Mom said when I told her that the memorial service had been difficult.

She was a devout stoic and I wasn't about to try to shift her perspective on life, so I nodded and agreed with her.

Josh hurled himself at me, "Hi, Mom. Grandma wouldn't let me watch TV. She tried to make me read a story about the end of the world! Are we all gonna die, Mom?"

I stared at mom, horrified.

"You know that kind of stuff gives him nightmares, Mom."

"I just got him to read the bible portion for the day. It won't hurt him one bit. It was only about Jonah and the Wale."

Mom blamed God for everything, good and bad. I wasn't sure if she saw it as a positive thing either. It was just the way things were, as far as she was concerned, and there was no reasoning with her about it.

"I'd better get on home, Mom. It's been a long day. Thanks for babysitting."

Josh gave her a tight hug. I also gave her a quick hug. Mom had never been given to displays of affection when we were kids and it was hard to adopt new habits. However, I needed to make the effort because there was Josh to think about.

We left the house and ran to the car because it had started to drizzle.

Once home, Josh settled in front of the TV to compensate for the hours of deprivation he'd just experienced.

It had been a hard day and I felt like it had aged me somehow. I stared at my reflection in the bathroom mirror.

I accepted that I was still struggling with the fact that Nicole was lying out at Pine Ridge Cemetery. I also accepted the fact that I was likely suffering from stress because of not having really grieved for her properly.

Everyone had seemed so calm, so accepting, so objective—even Shellie seemed to have healed. I seemed to be the only one who was not able to process and accept this new status quo. Oh sure, academically, I knew it was a fact but I was still confused and angry. Maybe I just had problems letting go of things and people. I was not forgetting how long it had taken me to say goodbye to Todd.

I stared at the hint of a wrinkle around my eye. Surely it hadn't been there yesterday?

When had life become so scary?

Losing Nicole had really been screwing with my mind anyway. She hadn't been given the chance to age at all. It had been a wake-up call that had forced some of us to face our own mortality.

I knew there had to be some changes. Shellie had been right about that, at least. Things could not just drag on as they had been doing for the last year or two. I needed a workable plan to shake things up and ensure I would achieve my life's goals.

Surely there had to be some purpose to my daily existence? Sure I was raising Josh and that was my reason for existing at the moment. Yes, I wanted to have more kids—but my plans were being thwarted by my lack of a consistent man and I wasn't inspired by the whole sperm bank option at this stage.

It dawned on me, then, that I might be a little depressed. Maybe until I fixed what was wrong with me, no man, and definitely no baby, was going to make me happy. I was always going to have this hollow feeling inside.

I wasn't completely abandoning the baby idea for good. I thought of the pleasure I got from raising Josh. Could you imagine if I had two kids? That would mean twice the love.

Right then I just knew that at some point the baby would have to take center stage again but maybe this wasn't the ideal time.

I tried to smile at my reflection, but the smile never quite reached my eyes. Still, it was an attempt to smile and I preferred working on my smile than crying. Maybe I'd take Josh for ice-cream. Screw the diet—you had to live a little.

CHAPTER SEVENTEEN

"Oh for the love of God," said Shellie, "Are you a man or a mouse? Just call him already!"

"I'm a mouse," I said shrinking lower into my chair.

Shellie groaned, "Look, if you don't call him, I'll be truly mad at you and I'll refuse to listen to another word you have to say about him or any other man, ever."

"Alright, alright, jeez," I said. "Just give me a chance."

"There's no time like the present. If you can go out with David in public, you can surely call Jared. At least he looks fairly normal—way better than normal."

I had been wondering how long it would take for her to remind me of my latest bad date.

"Do I really have to call him?"

"Yes, you do. I think you'll regret it if you don't. And don't forget to call me right back to let me know how it goes."

I took a deep breath.

"Okay, wish me luck."

Once I'd ended the call with Shellie, I considered my position for a few minutes. On the one hand, it had been a grueling week and I could use the distraction. On the other hand, did I really want to start up with the raised expectations with Jared again? But hadn't I discovered from my date with

David that it wasn't so easy to meet a normal looking man? If I didn't at least follow through with Jared, would I come to regret it?

The internal battle was raging.

What if Jared was busy? What if he was away again? Then I would have got my hopes up for nothing. But there was Shellie in the background to think about. She'd be unbearable at least at my lack of a backbone. I sighed heavily and grabbed the phone.

"Don't think, Shaniah, just do this," I mumbled as I scrolled down my contacts list and selected his name.

"Well, this is a lovely surprise."

I swallowed hard; I really hadn't expected him to answer so quickly.

"I just thought I'd touch base and see how you're doing." My voice sounded high pitched and strained.

Jared didn't seem to notice, "I'm doing great," he said, "just sitting here enjoying some rare down time with a glass of wine."

"Oh," I said.

I didn't think that Jared was the type to take too much time out, so now I felt bad, "I'm sorry if I'm disturbing you."

"No, not at all, don't be silly. Of course, it would all be much better if I had some company."

I smiled at the phone suddenly confident, "Is that an invitation?"

"Most definitely. Would you like me to come and get you?"

That was Jared—chivalrous to the end.

"No, I think my car is up to the journey. If it acts up, I'll abandon it somewhere and get a taxi."

"Okay. But it would be no problem at all for me to drive over to you."

"Seriously, I can make my way over, I assume you're at the same location."

"Yes, I am, so feel free to come whenever you like; I'll be here."

Gosh, that was simple!

My body was beginning to come to life with desire. I needed to calm down though and take things easy. I breathed deeply and tried to relax.

Once I'd ended the call, I hurried to run a bath. All I needed to do after that was to make baby-sitting arrangements and I would be on my way.

I dressed carefully and didn't even bother to give myself the usual pep talk about being good. Who was I trying to kid? I was going over to visit a good looking man that I had the hots for; the last thing I had on my mind was being good.

In the end I got a taxi because, in reality, I didn't fancy abandoning my car by the wayside should it fail to get me to my destination.

Jared buzzed me in and I tried to gain my composure as I made the long journey in the escalator up to his apartment. He met me at the door and I barely had time to say hello before I was swooped up in a hug and a rather passionate kiss.

Oh my...if he kept that up, I was definitely not going to last very long, especially as I hadn't made any particular resolve to abide by.

The kiss set me alight with desire and I moved back from Jared and looked around the room, just to buy some time.

"It's still the same room that you saw last time you were here. I haven't touched it in any way," he said wryly.

I turned back towards him. Maybe I'd bought enough time. I hadn't come over to inspect his property. This girl had needs and time was a wasting.

"Yeah, it still looks good," I said staring at his lips.

I leaned forward and tugged at the front of his shirt and uttered a seductive little sound of desire as he leaned towards me and into the kiss that I was so eager to share with him.

I opened my mouth widely as his tongue stroked the inside of my mouth. I felt a familiar tightening in my pelvic area.

Yeah—so this was it—time to check out my level of self-control. The tightening continued as I caught my breath in anticipation.

Jared clearly read my response as a signal because he reached behind me to fiddle with the zipper of my dress and I leaned forward to make things easier for him. I could feel the zipper sliding down and then he gently pushed the upper part of the dress off my shoulders. I moved my shoulders to facilitate its removal.

The dress shifted and slid co-operatively down to my waist. I released my arms and reached over to pull Jared towards me. He was single-mindedly fiddling with my bra and I was refusing to relinquish the feel of his lips against mine.

I pressed my body against the smooth cotton of his shirt as he dropped kisses on my neck, my shoulders, my collar-bone and finally shifted down to my breast to take a nipple into his mouth.

"Oh God, you feel so good...taste so good," he said.

I kissed him back, equally hungrily.

"Here, let me help you," said Jared, as he relinquished my lips finally and stood up, pulling me up with him.

He gently eased the dress down a little further and I obediently stepped out of it.

Freedom!

I stood in front of him in what remained of my undergarments and watched as he started to undo the buttons of his shirt. I silently took over and undid the rest. He slowly cupped one of my breasts before bending his lips to suck a nipple and then pulled me against him as he trailed kisses up my neck, then up the side of my face and finally claiming my lips again in a hungry kiss.

I clung to him for dear life as wave after wave of desire flowed through me, drawing me into his web, into surrendering to need.

I needed this so badly. I needed to feel alive after such a stressful and depressing week. Being in Jared's arms made me feel like there was some hope. I was being offered healing, in whatever form, and I fully intended to reach out and take it.

We edged towards the sofa and I sat down as he moved in front of me and I boldly undid his belt. He slid the zipper of his pants downwards as he pushed it below his hips and pushed his hip forward. I giggled as I helped him to wriggle out of the excess clothing.

I scarcely had time to think.

We were squashed up on the sofa and I pulled Jared towards me, needing to get as close as I could to make this work.

"I have a perfectly good bed next door," he said nodding towards a huge wooden door.

Right then, the door might as well have been a hundred miles away.

"I'm sure you do," I said relaxing a bit more into the sofa and grinning back at him.

"Ah, she's playing it cool," he said, looking directly into my eyes and before I could stop him, he stood up and swooped down to pick me up. I gasped and then tried not to squeal too loudly, "You're gonna drop me; I weigh a ton."

"You're as light as a feather," he said as he strolled through to the gorgeous bedroom and lowered me gently onto the king-sized bed before becoming rigid in apparent agony.

"Shit, I think I've put my back out," he said groaning, "Just how much did you say you weigh?"

"You didn't!"

I was horrified. Was I really that heavy?

"I'm only a hundred and eighteen pounds."

"Just joking," he said as he reached over to grab my ass and pull me closer to him.

I tried to punch his shoulder. "That's a rotten thing to do to a girl."

'Shh, you're talking too much," he said as his face came closer and his lips claimed mine. I was more than happy to kiss him back.

"Do you want to do the honors," Jared said holding out a condom which I hadn't even been aware he was holding.

Todd had always put on his own condoms and I'd always let him. No one had ever asked me to put on a condom on them before and I'd never volunteered.

I took the package confidently and managed to open it through sheer luck rather than skill. I needed to act the femme fatale and slip the condom expertly over him.

"Er—I don't mean to be critical, but I think you've got it on the wrong way round," he whispered.

There's a wrong side?

"Sorry," I said, trying not to feel like too big a fool.

He took the condom from me and rolled it on in a flash. Yeah, so I was feeling pretty dumb because how had I got to being thirty-two without knowing this stuff?

"There's no obvious reason why you should know that," he said magnanimously.

"Mmm, I'm not sure about that," I said. "Maybe I need to improve on my level of experience."

"Feel free to use me." He said lying back with his hands behind his head looking very much like a close relative of the devil.

"You're too generous," I said giggling, "But now that you've offered, we could start by doing this."

I bent my head.

He seemed to like what I was doing because I wasn't hearing any complaints. So I focused on the task at hand and listened to his sharp intake of breath, his accelerated breathing and his moans of pleasure and took them as an indication that things were going well.

Sometime later, I lay beside Jared, my head resting companionably on his shoulder and he had one arm slung casually around me.

After a while, he got up and brought in the wine and poured wine into two glasses. We lay propped up against each other, sipping the wine while he flicked through some movies.

I was surprised that he hadn't fallen asleep. I shifted to try and cover my boobs as I was starting to get a bit cold.

"How many dates have you been on?" he asked, suddenly grinning at my discomfort.

"You mean, with the online dating thing?"

"Exactly."

"Well, including you, I've had about ten dates."

"Oh—Jeez—wow! Ten dates and counting, eh? I thought you were, well, I mean, I just assumed..."

"Oh, don't get too excited," I said. "First of all, most of those were before I met you. Secondly, it has been almost a whole month since I last saw or heard from you. But if it helps any, so far you're the only person I've been so wild and reckless with. The others have all been one-off coffee dates."

"I'm glad to hear it, but what's with the *so far*? Are you still on the site?"

"After our last encounter, I took a break," I said.

It was technically the truth—I was no longer on the site and I didn't see the point of mentioning the David experience. It wasn't even like Jared and I were dating properly or like he'd care.

"I clearly made an impression then," he said.

"You made an impression alright. Put me clean off men."

He grinned wickedly, "All part of my overall strategy."

"So, how many dates have you been on?" I asked.

"Just the one with you."

"Oh, wow!"

I hadn't been expecting that, and I wasn't sure I believed him.

"I'm sorry our last encounter had such a detrimental effect," he said taking the wine glass out of my hand, "I'll have to see what I can do to repair the damage."

I giggled a little.

"Lie on your stomach," he whispered.

A thrill zinged through me. Heck, I was lying on a bed in a strange apartment in my birthday suit with a potential *Jack-the-lad* I'd picked up online. The least I could do was to oblige him and lie on my stomach, you know, to see what he had in mind.

"Any particular reason?" I asked, also in hushed tones.

"Be patient," he said, "I'll show you."

I concluded that lying on your stomach offered mind-blowing opportunities—especially if you'd been putting up with mediocre sex for some time. I was totally submitted to Jared and the feel of his entire body covering mine sent my mind reeling. As he positioned himself, he took hold of my hands and held them above my head. I took a long, deep breath that completely relaxed me as he took possession of my body.

This was enough. I smiled happily as our bodies moved together as he whispered words that I couldn't really hear because I was so busy just enjoying the moment. He kissed me where he could. We had sex. We made love. I wasn't sure what to call it. He raised my ass to slip a pillow beneath me and I was grateful for the pillow as he moved slowly and purposely and hit what I discovered just had to be my long-lost G-spot.

"Ahh, that feels so good."

I moaned deeply as he continued to hold my hands above my head, moving with growing momentum.

"You like that, eh?"

"Ahh, hmm."

I had clearly moved beyond intelligible speech.

As our movements grew more rapid we linked our fingers together. I squeezed tightly and bit my lips before crying out as waves of pleasure shook my body. Then I felt his release, even though the condom. I sank into the softness of the mattress with my eyes still closed.

"Hmm, how're you doing?"

Was I still alive?

"I'm good," I whispered. I marveled that I hadn't taken the time to worry about making a long wished for baby. I had simply enjoyed an amazing moment with an amazing man without all that pressure.

"That's great," he grunted

I tried to twist my head to see his face and he leaned forward to drop a tender kiss on my cheek.

"Are you okay?" I whispered.

"Never better," he nuzzled against my ears.

I turned to face him properly. I was getting a lot of pleasure from just looking at him. I wanted to remember his face and to treasure this experience, just in case he forgot to call again.

I snuggled up against his firm body, feeling comforted, resplendent, possessed, intoxicated—and strangely happy. If my life had ended at that moment, I would have been okay. You know, I didn't want to die or anything, but the moment was so complete that it was really the first time in a very long while that I just lay there feeling absolutely amazing, just luxuriating in the moment.

We must have dozed a little but after that brief rest, he was pretty much unstoppable.

When I would have slept he roused me and pulled me over onto my back and kissed me gently and firmly before entering me again. In between glasses of wine, gentle banter, a little teasing, and plenty of laughter, we tried out a few new positions and only finally stopped in the early hours of the morning.

I opened my eyes to find Jared propped up on one elbow looking down at me.

"It's rude to watch a girl while she's sleeping," I whispered.

"You look cute when you sleep. Do you know that your chin quivers when you breathe in?"

I wondered if a quivering chin was a good thing.

"Whatever!"

He grinned crookedly, "Very cute," he muttered.

"I should be going home. I've stayed out a lot longer than planned. My babysitter will be wanting to get home."

"Yeah, that was pretty insane," he agreed with me.

"It was actually pretty amazing," I grinned back at him because it had been a while since I'd struck gold in the sex department.

"I think you've worn me out, woman."

"We're crazy people," I said, "You're not on Viagra, are you?"

"I don't know whether to be offended or not by that question."

"No, don't be, I just meant that you never seemed to get tired."

"That was all me," he said grinning and I laughed because now he did look pretty lecherous.

"Has anyone ever told you that you have the makings of a dirty old man?"

He laughed out loud.

"No one has ever dared," he said.

"Well, you do. You know I always thought that once a man had climaxed, he was done for the night."

"Depends on the man," he said staring at me, "And maybe the woman he's with."

Oh yeah, this guy was real smooth. Smooth, but oh so cute.

We held each other until long after my smile had faded and I sobered enough to think that maybe I should be thinking about keeping him around. Maybe anybody who could make me feel so wonderful just needed to be a part of my life. I was too comfortable to shift. I closed my eyes for a few moments and when I opened them Jared was looking at me again.

"You're going to give me a complex if you keep staring at me like that every time I doze off," I said.

"You're really beautiful," he said simply.

"So are you," I said, and he laughed and hugged me.

"Come on," he said. "I need to get you home; I have a very early start in the morning and you should rescue that babysitter of yours."

"It's Sunday tomorrow," I said.

"Which means absolutely nothing when you own your own business as you too will discover," he said.

"I just need a taxi," I said.

"Shaniah, I'm taking you home."

We didn't speak as we dressed, and I took up my purse and we left the apartment. I didn't think there was much to say anyway. Jared seemed happy enough just to walk beside me. We actually held hands as we walked out towards the car—we were still holding hands when he engaged the engine and the car edged out of the parking lot.

"I'll call you," Jared said when he eventually pulled up outside my town house. I smiled back at him because, in the cold light of reality, I remembered that I barely knew him and I knew better than to look too deeply into promises that men made. It was best to just take it for what it was—mind-blowing sex with a drop dead gorgeous guy.

"Yeah, I won't hold my breath."

"Have some faith."

"Bye," I whispered, suddenly feeling a bit emotional because, really, it would have been nice if this was my own man that I could rely on to call me when he said he would.

Jared walked me to the front door and kissed me tenderly on the lips.

"Go get some sleep," he said gently.

"Good night," I said as I closed the door quietly behind me.

CHAPTER EIGHTEEN

"Good morning, sexy."

"Who's this?" I giggled into the phone.

"You'd better be joking," Jared laughed with me.

I was still feeling high from last night and I thought how wonderful it was to have someone think of me first thing in the morning.

We chatted, briefly, because he had to dash to a meeting but just that little gesture was enough.

I also got a text from Jared mid-morning and I texted him right back.

I smiled to myself. It was one of those secret little smiles that women in love often did when they suddenly thought of their lover and when they thought no one was watching. While I wasn't in love by a long stretch of the imagination, my lust was good enough.

Just the thought of our time together gave me a thrill. Just to know that he was somewhere in the city thinking of me was a great turn on. I knew, or at least, I felt that I had a special connection with Jared. I couldn't put my finger on it exactly, but being around him was definitely like coming home. I was suddenly hopeful for the first time in a long while.

I made a mental note to thank Shellie for giving me that push to stop being a *wuss* and go get my man!

Later on that day, Jared called to let me know he had an appointment out of town that evening, but maybe we could do something together later on in the week when he got back.

I was okay with that because honestly, I had a lot of my own stuff going on. I didn't even mind that he was going away again. I was just happy to know that we could be meeting up soon. I could scarcely contain my excitement at the thought of what we could possibly get up to on our next date.

The following day Shellie called.

"I'm coming over," she said, "I have news for you and I need to tell you in person."

"I hate suspense," I said, "Can't you tell me now?"

"No, but don't go out—this stuff cannot keep."

"Okay, I'm waiting."

When she arrived, Shellie threw her purse dramatically onto the sofa and got straight down to business.

"You'll never guess who I saw down in the entertainment district last night?"

"Jeez, Shellie, I'm not psychic and there are over two million people in this city!"

Shellie was undeterred.

"Your new mystery guy," she said.

"What mystery guy?"

"You know, Jared. The one you're so hung up on."

My level of frustration was growing and I was confused.

"How do you know it was him?"

"Don't you remember the picture that you texted me a while back on date number one?"

"Oh, yeah." I'd totally forgotten about sending her that picture. "Are you sure it was him?"

"Of course I'm sure. So, you remember that new guy I've been dating?"

"Bruno?"

"Oh, please, he's history."

"Shellie, can you please just get to the point?" The suspense was starting to get to me.

"I am getting to the point. So I was on date number two last night with my new man—oh my God, he is gorgeous, you won't believe how amazing he is."

"Shellie!"

"Oh, yes, sorry. So we were at that newly refurbished theatre in the entertainment district and that's when I saw him."

"It seems highly unlikely," I said. I was pretty sure that Jared had mentioned being out of town for a couple of days.

"Of course it was him," said Shellie adamantly. "You know I've always had a great memory for faces. Plus, I still have your message so I even checked on my cell; it was him alright. But that's not all—he was with a woman."

"So, he's a free agent," I said but my heart sank a little.

"There's more," said Shellie. Here her voice softened a little in sympathy, "She looked very pregnant!"

This was clearly the punch-line.

As far as punch-lines went, it was fairly effective. The room suddenly felt close and a heat spread across my face. The sinking feeling turned into a deep disappointment.

"Maybe she was his long-lost sister," I said trying to style things out—the last thing I needed was to learn negative stuff about Jared.

"They looked pretty tight," Shellie said.

I sat down on the nearest chair because I was feeling kind of faint and sick at heart.

"How tight?"

"Extremely tight."

"How pregnant was she?" My voice sounded strained, even to myself.

"Like her water could break if she sneezed too hard."

"I'm gonna puke," I said because I felt genuinely sick.

Right then I felt let down—make that devastated: Sure, I hadn't expected much from any man, but this?

"You're not going to faint, are you?" asked Shellie.

"Not the fainting type," I said vaguely. I was wondering how I could have been such a fool. I'd always known that where men were concerned, you never could tell—but Jared and a pregnant wife? Wow! I couldn't even begin to deal with the irony of the whole situation.

"Maybe she's not his wife and she's pregnant for someone else and they're just meeting up, maybe she's a friend."

"He rubbed her belly," said Shellie.

"Bastard," I said. "Like, what a total loser."

I hadn't even noticed that Shellie had gone to the wine fridge and returned with a bottle.

"Do you need a straw or shall I get a glass?" she asked and if my mind hadn't been in such turmoil, I would have laughed.

"That's the last time I take your advice and call up some loser. I can't believe I slept with a married man."

"So you did sleep with him!"

"That's all you care about at this time? Yes, I did go a bit far with him, but that bastard was married all along?"

"Calm down, Shaniah, he's not worth it."

"Oh blast, I swear I'll—I'll –"

"You'll do nothing," said Shellie, "You don't want a permanent man, remember? You just want to get pregnant and get on with it by yourself."

"I know; that's what I said. Oh, I'm so mad at myself because I forgot to keep my eye on the goal. Who does he think he is?"

"He's a guy—an asshole—but still just a guy and one you had no business being with—he was obviously way below your usual standard if he was cheating on his pregnant wife."

Considering that Shellie viewed Todd as my usual standard, and given her low opinion of him, that was not good.

I was very upset. I'd gone against all my principles when I'd pretty much fallen victim to Jared's charms on that first date. And now this! Well, he'd better keep well out of my neighborhood—because, with such provocation, I couldn't swear that I wouldn't attack him if I saw him in the street.

Maybe I'd try to get in touch with him just so that I could plan my revenge.

Shellie stuck around long enough to make sure that I wasn't going to stick my head in the oven the moment she left the house. I was still in turmoil long after she'd left. I was all alone with my wine, and I waited until Josh was in his room to actually cry a bit. God, I hated crying over men; it made me feel so weak.

Finally, I came to my senses. There was no reason for me to be so upset. He hadn't made me any promises apart from saying he'd call. We were just two consenting adults enjoying some great sex— some really great sex as I remembered. He hadn't told me he loved me. He hadn't even told me much about himself. So, he had been a stranger and I was like some stupid moth that had danced too near to the flame.

By the time Jared called later on that evening I was composed.

"Hi, gorgeous," he said.

His voice that had sounded so sexy, so charming, and so beautiful suddenly made me cringe.

How could he? I had heard about men who felt the need to cheat on their pregnant wives. I had just never met one...until now.

"Hi," I said coldly. Let him figure it out. As far as I was concerned I owed him nothing, least of all an explanation.

"Are you okay, Shaniah?" his voice was immediately full of concern.

"I'm fine," I said abruptly.

"You don't sound fine."

"I am totally okay. Can I help you?"

"Okay," said Jared sounding very concerned and very confused.

Well, that would make two of us, I guess.

"You're obviously not in a good mood," he was saying, "Perhaps I should call back tomorrow."

"Actually, I need to talk to you about that. I think we've been a bit hasty with our activities and we need to cool things."

"Look, Shaniah, I understand that you are a bit worried that we don't really know each other that well but we can make this work."

"Actually, I don't think you understand at all," I interrupted him. "I can't deal with this now. I think it's best if we just move on with our respective lives. I can't even say it was nice knowing you."

I could hear his intake of breath, but I was past caring. I was tired of this unpalatable situation. Perhaps he could figure it out while he was in the delivery ward with his wife.

I switched off the phone quickly before the tears began to fall. I didn't want him to know just how much I had been affected by him.

I did, however, allow myself the luxury of wallowing in self-pity for the rest of the night, but not before I'd blocked Jared's number. So I had no way of knowing if he tried to get in touch with me and I had no intentions of unblocking it—ever.

Anyway, life didn't come to a grinding halt because I'd discover that I'd done the deed with a married man and now all my new found hope and happiness were lying in tatters around my feet.

I carried on with my regular activities. I was on autopilot and I'd truly lost whatever little interest I'd had in most things. I worked at launching my business because I had no choice. There was no fairy godmother waiting in the wings to convert my utility bills to dollar bills.

Josh was ever loving and sweet and needed a lot of parenting. Ria was pragmatic and told me there were plenty more fish in the sea, but I was done with fishing.

Shellie phoned to make sure I was doing okay and met me at *Timmies* for coffee and donuts, which was perhaps as good a source of anti-depressant as I could find without being committed to an institution.

When Ria called some days later with details of her firm's charity ball, I wasn't exactly in the mood for something as challenging as an evening of entertainment.

However, I had a choice—I could stay home and keep wallowing, or I could decide to put on my glad rags and some war paint and get on with my life. I opted for the latter and promised that I would be there. The event was a couple of weeks away so I had plenty of time to get over Jared—not that there was really that much to get over. One night of sex was hardly anything to write home about.

Shellie was concerned about me attending the charity event as she imagined I was somehow on the edge. I had a hard time convincing her that I was alright. Apparently, I failed because she insisted on accompanying me and I was unable to get her to budge. Maybe she wanted to be on hand to make sure I didn't fall for any potential Lotharios out there in my current vulnerable state. I checked with Ria that it was okay for her to buy a ticket at the door, and it was a done deal.

So, two weeks later, I was ready for some diversion. I hadn't exactly sat around wallowing in self-pity, but I hadn't exactly been the happiest of souls either. On the night, Shellie decided to drive because her Mercedes convertible had more street cred than my Yaris.

I thought her car was at odds with her 'save the earth mantra' but I didn't say so because in reality, the silver exterior of her sleek car kind of made a nice background for my backless cocktail dress. It also stood a much better chance of getting us there in one piece.

Ria was waiting for us in the foyer of the hotel where the party was being hosted. "You're late," she said, kissing first me and then Shellie briefly on the cheek. "Come check your coats in and then we're going to meet AJ." She winked at Shellie "He's my boss, and I've been trying to hook them up for the longest time."

Apparently, Ria hadn't registered the fact that I was totally off men and I didn't think it was a good time to update her. I shrugged. She could introduce me all she wanted to any number of men but I was a reconfirmed single girl. Seemingly, it was not in my stars to spend my life with anyone so I was happily resigned to my single state.

"Sounds interesting," said Shellie, "No doubt you've heard the news about her latest guy. She definitely needs a new man now; so take us to your leader."

"As I apparently don't get a say in all this, do I have time to get a drink first?" I asked.

"No," said Ria, "I need you to be sober because I think you should definitely get in there before someone else nabs him."

"If he's so nabbable, maybe he isn't for me."

"Don't be silly. Besides, he said he was looking forward to seeing you. I've told him all about you."

"I hope not," I said, thanking God that she didn't quite know all there was to tell. I exchanged an anxious look with Shellie, who just grinned broadly at me.

"Go get him, tiger."

I rolled my eyes at the two of them as we started the walk through the fairly-crowded room which was rocking with waiters carrying trays of drinks and smart-looking people dressed in cocktail attire. In my present mood, the noise was deafening and if I hadn't been flanked by Shellie and Ria, I would have fled.

We moved over towards a group of people and I could spot a tall, dark-haired man who had his back to us. The few people gathered around him seemed to be listening to him with intent. I thought that there was something familiar about the set of his shoulders and the way he held himself.

As we approached, he turned slightly and my heart seemed to lurch with dread. The profile was too familiar. My pace slowed, but Ria grabbed my hand, "I didn't know you were the shy type," she grinned as she nudged me over to the group.

Several pairs of eyes turned to look at us. Ria was obviously very relaxed because these were her colleagues. Shellie was not usually phased by anything and was standing beside me looking on with interest.

"This is AJ, our CEO," said Ria looking pretty pleased with herself.

Shellie stepped forward and shook his hand even though she seemed somewhat hesitant.

I looked into a familiar pair of piercing grey eyes. I couldn't have moved my hands if my life had depended on it.

Jared!

Confusion!

Self-consciousness!

Embarrassment!

I stared back at the man who was smiling at me.

Okay, so surely this type of situation only happens to other people? You know, the type with loose morals. They go out on a blind date, they act like a slut with a guy whose name they obviously don't know, they continue to act like a slut and get up front and personal with him in his temporary apartment even though he hadn't bothered to call that much after the first slut experience. Then one night they find out he's their sister's boss—and clearly he is some kind of internet crawler with an alias. They die of shame on the spot. Or, maybe they don't quite die on the spot—maybe they go home and kill themself.

CHAPTER NINETEEN

"Shaniah?" I could hear Ria's voice breaking through the fog.

"AJ?"

I repeated the name parrot fashion because everyone was looking at me and I needed to say something.

Was I supposed to call him Jared?

He took my limp hand into his own and shook it like we were business partners.

"Hello, Shaniah."

His grin was warm, maybe even welcoming.

Never smile at a crocodile…

I shook my head to clear the words. Why was I thinking of a child's nursery rhyme? Maybe I was having a major breakdown right there and then.

"I'm glad you decided to come."

His grin looked wider and it made him look self-satisfied; overconfident, smug; like he was party to a great joke that only he got. I sure as hell wasn't seeing anything funny in this scenario.

I felt like a ventriloquist's doll as I tried to move my lips. They felt frozen and yet, I heard a pathetic little sound escape.

I tried to retrieve my hand which I couldn't even remember putting in his. It felt dirty and branded, laying there lifelessly in his. He must have felt me tremble because his look suddenly turned to one of concern. I looked around in desperation.

How could *he* be AJ? I felt betrayed for the second time in one week.

Did no one know about his pregnant wife? Ria had said he was divorced. The office grapevine must have failed.

"You're losing your touch, AJ," I heard a male voice joke as I moved quickly, intent on making a dash for the washroom.

I ignored the voice. I needed to think. No way was I brazen enough to handle this crap. I tried to remember where I'd seen a sign for the washroom. It came to me then. There had been a sign pointing to the left as we'd entered the foyer.

"Shaniah?" Ria and Shellie were coming after me but they didn't catch up with me until I was splashing cold water on my face in the washroom.

All that lovely makeup!

"Shaniah, what is your problem?" Ria was looking furious or it could have been concern—I had no way of telling right then.

"I can't tell you," I groaned.

How could I tell anyone?

Could this ever decreasing circle get any smaller? Ria put her hands on my shoulders and shook me, "Stop acting crazy and tell me right away, or I swear..."

"Okay, okay...it's him. It's Jared."

"You're not making sense."

"The guy I told you about; my internet Adonis."

"Holy shit," said Ria, looking a bit strange.

"What...what?" I needed to know what she knew.

"You're the girlfriend?" Ria sounded incredulous, "I had no idea he'd even..."

"No, you idiot, I'm the one-night stand, I think. What do you mean 'the girlfriend'?"

"Hello everybody, remember me?" said Shellie.

We both looked at her, "What?"

"I'm confused," she said, "What's going on?"

"Jared," I said, "Surely you recognize him? He's also Ria's new boss apparently."

"But, I don't think—I mean—" for once Shellie was struggling for words. She seemed genuinely confused. "I think I might have..." she didn't get to finish her statement because right then there was a knock on the washroom door.

We looked at the door in confusion. Who the hell knocks on the door to a public washroom?

"Er—it's open," said Ria.

The door swung inwards and there was Jared—AJ—whatever the hell his current name was—looking like some kind of avenging angel.

"Shaniah, I need to talk to you."

"Well, I don't want to talk to you," I said.

My heart was still racing but the sense of betrayal and weakness was quickly being replaced by blind anger.

"Don't be so melodramatic," he said impatiently moving a little way into the washroom. "If you hadn't been acting like some kind of drama queen for the past two weeks, I would have explained everything to you."

"You had plenty of time to explain your sordid little life the last time we met up." I was speaking through gritted teeth. But immediately I wondered how he would have woven this little bit of information into the evening. We hadn't invested time in having quality conversation. What could he have said? *'Thank you for the sex; my pregnant wife will be grateful to you for keeping her man happy?'*

I glared at him uncompromisingly.

"Er, excuse me," said Ria, trying to sneak out the door.

"Ria, stay!" I said.

Ria stopped moving.

Shellie was just staring at Jared with her brows furrowed.

"Shaniah," she said hesitantly. "I don't think..."

"It's okay, Shellie," I said. "There's no need for you to get involved."

"No, leave us for a minute, please," said Jared, smiling benevolently at Shellie and Ria.

Obviously caring more about her job than her younger sister, Ria shrugged and looked at me sympathetically, "You'll be fine," she said, and she actually smiled at Jared as if they were conspirators. Shellie looked like she was desperate to say something, but she wasn't quite sure what she wanted to say.

"It's okay," I said to them both. "I can deal with this."

It was show-time!

I needed to tell Mr. Sleaze-ball, AJ, Jared, married man, baby-father, exactly what I thought of him.

Jared took up the position that Ria had previously occupied and tried to put a hand on my shoulders.

"Back off," I said.

"We can't stay in the washroom forever," he said gently.

That had better not be laughter I could hear in his voice because pregnant wife to take care of or not, I was tempted to knock him out cold.

I was livid!

Who did he think he was, laughing at me, or maybe he had been laughing for the last few months?

"You need to leave," I said, "I'm not walking out of here with you...you sleaze-ball!"

"I know it might have been a bit of a shock for you, but I've been trying to get in touch with you despite the fact that you've blocked my number."

"Look, Jared, AJ, Jared—Jesus, I don't even know what to call you."

"Take your pick." He actually had the audacity to grin,

"Well, whatever the hell your name is, I'm not interested. You've had your fun, let's just leave it at that, shall we? Oh, and won't your wife be missing you?"

"Wife? What the hell are you talking about?"

"Your pregnant wife!" I snapped.

"You've gone crazy," he said. "And I have no intention of leaving anything. You know how I feel about you. And for the record, my name is Aaron Jared. You saw my driving license. I got the nickname AJ at school and it's stuck ever since. Nobody ever calls me Jared except my mother... and you. I've always used Aaron for business activities."

How the hell was I supposed to remember the details of his driver's license—I'd been too preoccupied with his eyes, his lips, oh God, I'd been too preoccupied with' getting my hands on his body...that first night by the lake...I'd almost got totally carried away with him, and after that...well.

I could feel myself blushing.

"Yes, it must be very convenient to have so many names to switch between," I said.

The door swung open again and two women walked in.

"Oh, sorry," they said, giving each other a knowing look.

"No, we're just leaving," said Jared and grabbing my hands, pretty much yanking me out into the corridor.

"You're coming with me if I have to give you a fireman's lift out of here—the choice is yours."

As I hated any type of public scene, I acknowledged that he was going to win the first round! Besides, I had plenty I wanted to say to him in any event.

But naturally, I was alarmed. What would people think? I couldn't see his wife anywhere, but that didn't mean I wanted everyone to know that I'd been messing about with her husband behind her back.

Oh my God! What about his wife? What would she think of me if she ever found out? I looked around carefully for anyone with a big baby bump. She was absent.

I traipsed after Jared because I had no choice as the pressure of his fingers on my upper arm was noticeable even though he wasn't hurting me.

As we made our way through the crowded room, I was aware of a few eyes on me. I mean, this was AJ, the boss, and who was I? I was an unknown interloper, apparently—a mere marriage-wrecker.

I cringed as I found myself being led towards an elevator.

"Jared, let go of my hand," I hissed.

I was tempted to stomp on his foot with my heels.

"Not until we've had a chat. I'm taking you somewhere private. Or if you really insist, we can have the chat about our previous meetings right here in front of your sister and her colleagues."

I shot him a dirty look.

"Fine, you win," I said through gritted teeth. Really, Todd had been much easier to deal with.

The elevator arrived and Jared pressed the *PH* button. As soon as the door closed, he pulled me against his body and kissed me hard. I tried to resist. Was there no end to his audacity?

His lips were firm, punishing and my lips felt bruised. I was pinned against his chest—a prisoner in the confined cell of the elevator which seemed to be taking forever to make its way to our destination.

My heart was racing again and despite my anger and disgust, a warm need was spreading through my body.

This guy is smooth Shaniah. He's, a traitor, a con artist, an untrustworthy ne'er do well! Every time you meet him, he has a new personality; a new story; a new location; a new wife—a new pile of bullshit.

My outrage would give me the courage to resist that need.

The elevator door opened directly into an apartment—no corridor—just straight into the penthouse. We barely made it inside before I was back in his arms, his lips raining kisses on my face and then my lips as his hands moved down to clutch my ass.

"Look, get off me, you jerk," I said.

This time I was truly furious. It was one thing to have this secret life of crap that no one knew about, but now the game had changed. Ria knew this guy. Oh, God, how was I ever going to live this down— my behavior was hardly going to remain a secret— what had Ria meant by *the girlfriend*? Did everyone know about my role in wrecking his marriage?

"If you think I'm going to let you lay one finger on me, you are sadly mistaken! You have a lot of explaining to do."

"Later," he said, taking hold of my hands and pushing me up against the wall. I could feel his hands reaching up under my clothing, caressing my thighs. I fought him until he realized I was serious.

"Oh God, Shaniah; why do you have to be so difficult?"

"What about your wife, you rotten bastard?" I shouted, hitting out at him. He caught my hand and held it firmly.

"There you go again, accusing me of having a wife."

"Don't lie," I said. "Shellie saw you with her downtown. Jesus, Jared, she's about to give birth at any moment, don't you have any decency, any shame?"

He seemed genuinely confused for a moment and I thought that his acting skills deserved an Oscar. Clearly, he was in the wrong profession.

Suddenly his face broke into a wide grin. "Come with me," he said and pulled me towards a side room that obviously functioned as an office. He went to a desk and picked up one of the pictures.

"Is this my pregnant wife?" he asked.

I stared at the photo. The woman was a petite brunette with the biggest pregnancy bump I'd ever seen. The picture must have been taken at some party recently because there were other people in the background. The woman looked like she was having triplets. My heart sank for a moment until I took a good look at the man standing beside her.

He looked like Jared, but there was a subtle difference. The eyes weren't as forceful and the hair was curlier and maybe even a bit darker.

"I've seen this guy before," I said.

"It's Paul," he said, "my cousin. Remember him from the website? That's his wife, Anna, who's due to have her baby any day now. This picture was taken just a couple of weeks ago. I can assure you that I am not married, nor do I have anyone pregnant in the background."

I was still suspicious. Maybe that had been what Shellie had been trying to tell me in the washroom, I mean, she'd looked a bit confused and I'd just ignored her.

And what about his daughter whom he had mentioned? Wasn't he in some custody battle? This was all too confusing.

It was then that I noticed another picture on the wall. The picture looked familiar—Jared was standing with a group of other business professionals. The picture reminded of the one I'd seen in Ria's office. I remembered now—the picture of his management team.

I stared at it. So that's why he'd seemed so familiar and all the while I'd thought that feeling of familiarity was because we were kindred spirits. I made an unintelligible sound. I could feel my reality beginning to crumble. There was truly no fool like an old fool. None of what I had been experiencing with Jared had been real. I snapped out of my lethargy to register what Jared was saying.

"Jesus, Shaniah, what type of guy would I be, to come after you and drag you through my entire workforce if I had a pregnant wife in the background? At least give me some credit for basic decency."

"I'm sorry," I said, feeling foolish. If he was telling the truth, then there was nothing to stop us getting back together. Okay, hold it right there. I was shocked by that thought. Surely I didn't still want him?

"But the fact still remains that you lied to me," I said.

"How exactly have I lied to you? Well, apart from the bit with Paul's picture. We met under fairly normal circumstances for this day and age. Clearly, we had an amazing chemistry; we made love, a few times. If my memory serves me correctly, I think I even remember you telling me you loved me during our love making."

I cringed, suddenly remembering how I'd beckoned him to come closer and how I'd whispered those words in a moment of passion. Maybe the wine hadn't helped either. He hadn't responded and I hadn't been sure he'd heard. I'd *prayed* he hadn't heard. Now he chose to let me know that he'd registered those words?

"That was the sex and numerous glasses of wine talking," I said, embarrassed.

"That was probably your heart talking," he said, grinning.

"No, it wasn't."

His mouth covered mine before I could say another word. My hands wrapped themselves around his neck. I hated my weakness, my ridiculous body that allowed itself to be played too often like some cheap instrument by this man who seemed to have problems sticking around or using the phone.

But I pretty much knew I didn't really want to resist any longer. I mean, it wasn't like we were complete strangers. I could deal with the self-respect thing later on.

His tongue darted into my open mouth and I knew I was lost. Ah, what the heck, I thought as I could feel his need pressing hard against me as he pinned me up against the wall. Weird really, but that was how it had been that very first time and yet I was still kind of furious with him.

Maybe the sex thing between us was all that we really had. He was acting like nothing had changed; like I hadn't been betrayed; like this was still the Jared of old; like his name wasn't really AJ.

When I was eventually standing again on firm ground again, he smoothed my hair back tenderly.

"You've probably ruined my dress," I said.

He grinned at me, "I'll buy you a new one."

"No thanks," I said.

"Still mad, huh?"

"What do you think? You totally conned me."

"Shaniah, for the love of...stop arguing with me, and if it helps, I think I love you too."

I gawked at him.

"What do you mean you think?"

"I mean just that. I haven't felt this way about anyone for a long time. Look, we have a lot to talk about. Like, you need to know that I had a wife and that she died well over two years ago.

You need to know that after I lost my wife, I kind of went into a decline. I swore I'd never do permanent again. Anyway, my relationship with Liz was different. We didn't have hot steamy all night sex or romps in cars on the beach on our first date. We dated in college; she got pregnant so we got married. Hell, we were way too young. She actually lost that baby but we stayed married – maybe to prove everyone wrong."

"What's with the custody of your kid then?" I asked.

"Liz was diagnosed with cancer four years ago, just after the birth of our daughter. After undergoing chemo they gave her the all-clear. She was okay for a while but then the doctors told us that her cancer had returned. She died three months later."

"Shit," I said. This story was sounding way too familiar. I thought of Nicole.

"Yeah. I suddenly had a baby to care for and a company to run and no motivation to do the latter."

"Where's your daughter now?"

"She's been staying with her grandmother, Liz's mother. When Liz was sick they volunteered to help out as I had the business to run and a new baby to care for. After Liz died, they thought they would try for custody. I don't think they could handle the loss. Anyway, we've been in a battle over custody; it's all a very long and depressing story."

"Is that why you kept disappearing?"

"Partly that, and partly because I was scared to get too attached to you. On top of all that's been going on, I acquired a new company last year and it turned out to be a lot more problematic than I could have imagined. I think that for once I might have bitten off more than I can chew. So, I've been thinking of ways to try to offload it. Otherwise, it's going to take a lot of work to sort out all the unresolved issues."

"Oh my God, is that what you were trying to tell me the other day?"

"Yes," he said hesitantly. "That, and the fact that I saw you once before we met online. You were with your sister—coming out of her office, in fact. I'd just acquired the law firm where your sister works and Paul and I had popped in to meet the existing management team. I was floored when I saw you. I knew straight away that I had to meet you. I guess Paul noticed. Hell, I'd scarcely noticed a woman in the past two years, so when he saw my reaction to you, I guess he felt he had to do something to help my case."

I was speechless.

"I think I'm a bit confused," I said.

"Well, when I had finally met with all the attorneys I eventually found an opportunity to pick Ria's brain about you—discreetly of course. I just assumed, in any event, that you worked for the company. Anyway, I now suspect that Paul might have beaten me to it and prepped her because she was very forthcoming with a lot of personal details about you."

"Oh no," I groaned. "Just wait till I get my hands on her!"

"Take it easy on her," said Jared, "both Paul and I are experts at what we do. We manage people very well."

"You mean you play people," I gasped.

"As long as you realize that I always play to win."

"Doesn't Paul's wife mind her husband's picture being on a dating site?"

Jared looked like that had been one aspect they hadn't considered.

"She was good with it," he said. "Besides, we took down the picture once I'd met up with you."

"And when were you going to tell me all this?"

I wasn't sure whether to be mad or not. Should I be flattered that someone had gone to such elaborate lengths to meet me?

"But why didn't you just ask for my number?"

"Because apparently you were 'off men', as Ria put it, and you'd recently launched your internet project, so Paul thought I'd better get in on the act before someone beat me to it. He's a force to be reckoned with."

"I'm glad you thought it was just one big game."

"Calm down," he said pulling me into his arms. "Really, I couldn't just bring it up into the conversation. On the first date, I was just blown away by how truly gorgeous you were close up and things just got out of hand. Then I felt bad that I'd got so touchy feely with you so quickly on that first night. For Christ's sake, I hadn't tried a move like that since I was in my teens."

He grinned wickedly at me.

"And I fell for it," I said.

"I could see your attraction to me," he said. "Once we'd kissed, I knew I had no intention of ever letting you go. Well—at least not for a while! Don't feel too bad about the car thing, I was pretty determined and, as I said, I usually get what I want."

I stared at him incredulously. He sounded like someone—or something—out of the dark ages.

"And what if I hadn't wanted you?"

"I'm an entrepreneur, a company director. I acquire businesses and new people to work for me all the time. Failure is never an option."

I looked at him, feeling unsure about what to say next.

You Tarzan…me Jane!

Except, I wasn't Jane. I was Shaniah, a modern girl with very definite ideas about men. Someone needed to talk to this guy, to let him know that other people's feelings mattered. Anyway, I hadn't got a clue how to handle that yet, so I looked briefly around the penthouse apartment.

"Is this another one of your properties?"

"Another temporary home," he said. "I sold the other place sooner than I thought so I had to move fast. We usually keep this for out of town visitors."

I looked around the penthouse apartment. It seemed like a true bachelor pad.

"Look, Jared, I'm sure that you meant well. I'm not used to all this macho stuff. The truth is, I *am* off men a bit, primarily because they pull funky stunts like this. No, hear me out," I said as he made to interrupt me.

"I am flattered that you went to all this trouble to get together with me, but don't you see, none of this is real. We met and got physical far too quickly. Then there's all this skullduggery and all this wheeling and dealing. Basically, I'm a simple girl. I've been going through a tough time lately and so have you. I don't think either of us is making good decisions right now."

"What are you trying to say?"

"I'm saying that I barely know you and you certainly don't know me, or else you would never have gone about things in this manner."

"Yeah, okay, so I admit it was a bit clichéd, but..."

"There is no but. I'm sorry, Jared. I think you're probably a great guy, but I can't deal with all this at the moment. I've got to get out of here."

"Shaniah, I think you're over-reacting."

"Really? Well, once again we differ. But if I'm over-reacting then I won't stick around to get on your nerves. See you around."

"You're deliberately twisting my words."

"Whatever!" I said as I grabbed my purse. I could feel tears prickling the back of my eyelids. I needed to escape because I didn't need anyone's sympathy.

"How do you get out of here?"

I wasn't sure if there was some special code for a public elevator that allowed direct access to the penthouse. Now I was really fighting back the tears and I needed to escape before they could break free. I didn't want to cry in front of him.

"Press the bottom button," he said softly.

I glared at him.

Yeah, just because I'm attracted to you and I'm a weak-willed idiot, doesn't mean I'm going to be an idiot all my life. I have to show some kind of self-respect at some point!

The elevator came and I got into it. He watched me with the patience of a tolerant father humoring a belligerent child.

I escaped before he could stop me. I wasn't even sure he wanted to.

CHAPTER TWENTY

Once I was back on the party level, I made my way through the crowd. Jared and I had clearly been forgotten as no-one seemed to be paying any attention as I headed towards the cloakroom.

"Shaniah, where have you been?"

I was so furious that I hadn't seen Ria approaching me.

"Penthouse," I mumbled and if I hadn't been so pissed, I would probably have burst out laughing as one of her eyebrows shot dramatically upward.

"Jesus Christ, Shaniah, you've been holding out on me big time."

"Yeah, well, I have a bone to pick with you too," I looked at her solemnly, "I can't believe you'd set me up like that."

"Oh God, he told you?"

"What the hell's the matter with you Ria? I'm your sister! How could you play with my feelings like this?"

"I had your best interest at heart, really, Shannie."

I ignored the endearment. No way was she getting around me by being cute.

"You knew I'd been going through a rough time and to sabotage my one and only attempt at online dating for your boss to get a quick bit of fun. Thanks a lot, sister!"

"Shaniah, it wasn't like that."

"Maybe you could tell me exactly what it was like."

"I knew he wanted to meet you, but you didn't want me to set you up so I just tried to help things along a bit."

"By encouraging me to set up a dating profile on some website where he could find me?"

"You've got it all wrong, Shaniah. I didn't even know he'd gone ahead with it. Look, this isn't the ideal place to talk. I don't want the entire company to hear."

Ria was looking a bit unsure of herself and maybe even a bit upset. This was indeed a rare phenomenon but I was past caring about other people's feelings. My chief concern was to find Shellie because it was high time that I left.

Shellie had approached us silently and I guess she must have overheard my exchange with Ria because she too was looking somewhat uncomfortable.

"Are you coming, Shellie? Because if you're not ready to leave, I'll take a taxi."

She put an arm gently around my shoulders and gave me a comforting hug. I guess it helped me to calm down somewhat as we gathered our belongings and prepared to leave.

Ria knew better than to try to stop us. I would just have to deal with her when I was in the right frame of mind.

Shellie's face was pretty grim as she drove eastwards, out of the city. I was less emotional now. I was feeling more drained than anything and definitely confused.

"I'm sure your sister had your best interest at heart," Shellie finally broke the silence.

"How would you like to be on the receiving end of a scheme by those two control freaks?"

"I'd probably murder them."

"Yeah, well it's looking like a pretty good prospect right now, so we'd best just change the subject and forget that the last few months actually happened."

Shellie glanced at me, "Are you going to be alright?"

"Yeah, why not? He was just another dumb guy aided and abetted by my equally dumb sister. They should do well together. Look, please just drive the car; I don't think I can even bear to talk right now."

I massaged my temples, trying to relieve the mega stress headache that had been brewing since I'd first clapped eyes on Jared surrounded by his employees—all having a merry old time.

I looked out the window at the lights of the city shining against the dark background of the night. I supposed that in a few years' time, none of this would be relevant anyway but right then, I just needed to get home to the security of home and my own bed. I closed my eyes and put my trust in Shellie's driving.

By the time the car pulled up outside the house, I'd calmed down a bit. Shellie, bless her, gave me a huge hug, "Get a good night's sleep. You'll get a better perspective on things in the morning.

"Yeah, maybe by then I'll have come up with a plan on how to get away with a double murder. Thanks for coming along with me tonight and for the support. It was a good thing you came."

"No problem. If you don't have to pick Josh up too early in the morning, you should have a long lie in."

"If Mom has one of her church meetings, I'll probably have to get him early."

"I'll call you tomorrow to check that you're okay," promised Shellie.

I could hardly wait to strip off my clothes and step into the showers. I stayed awake long enough for the water to wash away some of the memories of the evening before sliding gratefully between the cool cotton sheets of my bed.

The following day two bouquets of flowers arrived.

One was from Jared with a card asking me to call when I'd calm down. Right, that could take a while, so while we were both waiting for that to happen, I put the flowers in the garbage.

The second bouquet was from Ria which she followed up with a text apologizing for her part in the whole fiasco.

I dumped Ria's flowers on top of Jared's. There was no forgiving her; she was my sister. She should have known better. Obviously, I was going to have to forgive her, at some point in the future, before we hit ninety or whatever. But that was a long way off and I could foresee a few years of loneliness and no sister to comfort me. It sounded perfect.

Later on, I rescued the flowers because I hated waste. I decided to take them to the local senior's home. Maybe they would brighten up their foyer.

I didn't have a foyer, large enough to stash those marks of Judas.

During the next few weeks, I was determined to refocus.

It was time for me and what I needed—not what other people thought was good for me.

I refused to answer Ria's calls. Jared's number was still blocked, so that made things a lot easier. He knew better than to try my landline.

It was time for business.

My new interior design business was getting pretty close to its launch date and I was determined that it was going to be a success. I had my first project which was staging four new homes for Darren, my real estate connection. I threw myself into the task as I couldn't afford to turn down business just because it didn't fit neatly into my launch date.

I also had to find an office. It was okay working from my home office, but I needed somewhere with space for a showroom of sorts.

Scanning the local paper or even online for commercial premises took up a fair amount of my time. It was early Sunday morning and I was looking in the local freebie for suitable space when Josh tapped on my door.

"Come in, sweetheart."

"Hi, Mom,"

He bounced into the room and rocketed into the bed between the sheets.

"Josh, honey, I'm busy looking for office space."

"But I wanna sleep in your bed."

"Okay, but no snoring."

He rolled into a tight ball and squeezed himself firmly into my side. I tried to move and he moved with me.

"Josh, move. You're hurting me."

Josh groaned. "I'm freezing,"

"You need to eat more. You're too skinny; you need some body-fat to keep you warm."

"That's why I'm snuggling up to your fat, Mom; you're nice and soft and warm.

I often wondered if Josh and my mother were in league with the devil.

"Horrible child," I said, "move away from me; fat is very catching; it's just like a big virus."

Josh squealed, "No it isn't"

"Mine is," I said and pushed the newspaper onto the floor so that I could roll over to tickle him. I stopped when his squealing threatened to wake the entire neighborhood.

CHAPTER TWENTY-ONE

"I just can't understand how you put up with Todd for so long yet you won't speak to AJ," Ria said. "It's not like he did anything really bad."

It was one of those rare days in my unmanageable life when I was actually sitting peacefully in my mother's house talking in an almost polite fashion to Ria. I was sipping a glass of wine which was helping me to deal with our first real face-to-face conversation since the infamous Jared incident. I'd relented and had decided to speak to her but I swear that if it wasn't for the fact that we shared a parent, I'd have been hard pushed to forgive her.

Mom was in the kitchen making lunch and Josh was sitting at the island waiting patiently to sample one of the brownies that she was about to take out of the oven.

Ria was still demonstrating difficulties understanding how the rest of the world operated outside of her tiny little mind and I was no longer in the game of trying to teach anyone, who wasn't a child of mine, anything about life—let her figure it out for her damn self.

I was conflicted about how to actually answer her. I'm not saying that she didn't have a good point about putting up with Todd, because she did. She was right—I'd been in a different state of mind with Todd. He had been a much safer bet. He'd never had that same hold on my heart so he had been the less risky option by far.

But somehow, I just knew I would be on dangerous ground if I started up with discussing Jared again. I was largely avoiding anything to do with Jared because he was a heart breaker for sure, and so far, since my failed relationship with Josh's dad, I had survived largely by avoiding the likes of Jared.

"Don't you even bring up AJ...Jared to me," I said. "But if you really want to know, I liked the idea of having someone stable around," I said at last. "Just look what's happened with Jared. I just don't do well with that type. I guess Todd was the exact opposite of my usual type."

Maybe it wasn't fair to compare Jared and Todd because Todd would never measure up in a competition. It really all came down to what was important to me. Great sex with a man I clearly didn't trust, but one that I clearly had problems resisting, or death by *boredom in the bedroom* with Todd. I knew which I would choose if Jared wasn't so full of all that macho crap.

I shook my head to clear it of such wayward thoughts. Ria was doing a pretty good hatchet job on my emotions without me joining in.

"Well, you haven't done too well with Todd either," she said. "You can't even tell me that you were fond of him."

"Of course I was...still am fond of him, as a person, I could even conceivably have loved him, as a person, but I wasn't in love with him. You know, he didn't make my world spin or anything but he was very reliable. When I first met him, it was important to me. It is still very important to me to have someone reliable around."

"Did he make you laugh?"

"Every time we made love."

Ria squealed, "I can't believe you just said that."

"Don't be dumb, Ria. I know you're not a prude so you surely didn't think I was still *virgo intacta*, did you?"

"I'm not dumb," she said looking annoyed.

My moment of peace with Ria was obviously nearing its end.

"Well, you know what I mean," I said, wishing I could take back my words.

It was always the same. I couldn't be around Ria for long; she really rubbed me up the wrong way. It was best to love and leave where she and Mom were concerned.

"I think it might just be time for me to grab Josh and leave."

"You always run away when you don't want to answer questions," Ria said sounding frustrated.

"It's as good a strategy as any."

"You'll have to stay and have lunch or mom will be furious. Besides, what are you going to spend the afternoon doing?"

"I guess I'll be continuing my search for office space," I said.

"Oh, you're still having no joy with that, eh?"

"Nope!"

"That's probably because you're looking out there in the boonies. You need to edge closer to the downtown area. It would be better for your business and there are some pretty interesting buildings that I'm sure you'd love. I'll email you a link."

I thanked her for the offer but I really wasn't sure that I could ever trust Ria again.

However, I was getting kind of desperate. I'd been approved for a small start-up business loan and it was time-bounded. I needed the space so that I could, at least, put my mark on it and get on with the formal launch.

"No problem, what are big sisters for?

Mom chose that moment to pop her head around the door, "Lunch is ready if you guys want to eat early," she said.

"We do," said Ria.

Surprisingly, Mom had allowed Josh to sample the brownie before his lunch and, in the interest of peace, I didn't think it was wise to interfere.

"You've barely spoken two sentences since you sat at the table and you're picking at your food," Mom said to Ria once we'd all settled down to lunch.

"Maybe you should ask Shaniah. She seems to have the ability to annoy people."

"She was bugging me," I said evenly but I was thinking that she was a fine one to talk about anyone being annoying.

"Now you sound like Josh," said Ria looking at me crossly.

Josh's head snapped to attention. "Mom, Auntie Ria said you sound like me; cool."

I turned to face Ria, "How else should I sound? He is my son!"

"He's eight-years-old; you're supposed to be an adult."

"My mom is an adult," said Josh, not caring that everyone was ignoring him.

"I shouldn't have come," I mumbled.

"I'm glad you're here," said Mom gently.

I made eye contact with her. I knew how much it must have cost her to say that. She rarely gave anything away.

"Thanks, Mom." I looked and smiled gratefully at her. It had been a while since I'd felt particularly close to her.

"Now, you mustn't annoy Ria," she said briskly.

"Could someone pass me the vegetables please," said Josh as politely as he was able—it was hard to imagine that might have been trying to be diplomatic.

"You're going to eat vegetables, Josh?" I was bemused.

"Don't you want me to eat them, Mom? They're good for you, you know."

That boy was playing games with me! I had long since given up the fight over vegetables; I watched as he happily gobbled down the soggy looking carrots and peas.

"Grandma, your cooking's the best."

I felt a twinge of jealousy as Mom preened and tried not to look superior.

"It's nearly as good as my mom's," Josh said.

CHAPTER TWENTY-TWO

So it was back to the same old routine.

The only good thing about routines, however, was that they grounded you in times of trouble.

I ran around taking Josh to his various events and appointments.

I tried to balance my accounts.

I followed the link that Ria sent me and shopped for office space.

The first two sites I viewed were too large, but the third was perfect. It even had a small mezzanine and the resulting cathedral effect appealed to my artistic senses. Later on that week, I signed the lease and it was all systems go.

The whole process and the intensity of getting the business off the ground proved to be a panacea. I knew that I was unhappy, but did not have the time to do anything about it.

Maybe it was the impact of getting a little older, but I no longer believed that hearts really break from a relationship breakup. They got damaged perhaps, truly dented, but humans had the ability to overcome all kinds of adversity. All you needed was time. Time and a whole lot of activity or alcohol!

I had no way of knowing if Jared had been trying to contact me because I hadn't unblocked his number. I'd been tempted. I'd stared at his number on numerous occasions. I thought about him constantly. He'd been right about me being stubborn because I'd walked out of that hotel determined to move on and I had shut out all alternatives.

I had no time to think about having a baby. Actually, I'd pretty much decided to shelve those plans. Look at the mess it had caused. They'd gone on hold, along with every other aspect of my love life. I had bills to pay and a child to take care of. Life for single moms wasn't always easy because you had to be mom and dad and a whole lot more.

Shellie and I painted the interior of my studio in dramatic charcoal grey and splashes of orange before we accessorized it.

Ria came by to lend a hand, but she was pretty much horrified at the thought of painting an entire wall. I guess that I had also still not completely forgiven her for her interference in my dating plans so maybe things were still a bit awkward between us. In any event, I wasn't impressed with her stand-off approach to decorating and after about ten minutes, she left in a bit of a huff!

Yeah, big sister – next time doesn't screw with my life.

It was good to be busy. I had an excuse for not thinking about Jared and there was really no rush to unblock his number either

How times had changed. A few months ago, I had vowed to have a baby and I had been convinced that nothing could shake me from my resolve to find the perfect baby daddy. Now, I fell into bed at the end of each day, too tired to even think about dating or making babies.

Now, instead, I was committed to creating and building my business and to finding resources to support Josh's needs.

About the third week after acquiring my studio, work started on the building next door.

I wasn't impressed. I hadn't paid much attention to the notices, I guess. But I could just imagine potential clients walking through the scaffolding and dust to get to me. I was not happy.

I had no choice but to call the number on the display board to find out how long the interruptions would last.

The receptionist answered the phone, "Turner Enterprises."

My heart sank or flipped over – it was hard to determine which.

I prayed there was another 'Turner Enterprises' in the area other than the one owned by Jared.

I gave my name and, after a few seconds, was put through to what turned out to be Jared's office.

"Shaniah ... good to hear from you. I wondered how long it would take you to call."

"This is all business," I said coldly.

"Yes, I gather you've been making inquiries about the work we're doing in the offices next to your suite."

"News travels fast around here."

"I make it my business to know what's happening with all my tenants."

I held my breath as I considered this new punch line.

Had he just said I was his tenant? That was not possible. It was too surreal.

"I think you might be mistaken," I said. "I signed a lease with The Urban Regeneration Group..." But even as I said the words I knew the score. Hadn't Ria sent me a link to potential companies? I knew for sure that I could be pardoned on grounds of insanity if I went ahead with my previous plan to strangle her and Jared. They were trying to push me completely over the edge.

"That's the project name for the work we're doing in East side of the city. As you can see from the current premises next to yours, we have a number of holding companies."

I swallowed as I tried to clear the lump that came to my throat and was making it difficult for me to say the words that were lodged there. I managed to speak eventually even though my voice sounded weary, "Don't you ever get tired of playing games with people's lives?"

"You keep accusing me of playing games," said Jared. "I'm not now, or have ever been, playing games with you."

"Well, it sure feels like it, Jared. I don't know how you pulled this one off and I don't care, and I really don't want the details. Right now my career is too important to me to have it messed up by your need to control everything and everyone around you. I don't know why I'm even wasting time talking to you."

"Shaniah, please calm down. Look, let me take you to lunch. We can discuss this in a civilized manner.

"I'm not hungry."

He sighed heavily and I hesitated for a second.

Poor Jared. Was he really as bad as I thought he was? He'd certainly been having a bad couple of years and I knew exactly how that could feel. He was trying to do things the only way he knew how. He'd just picked the wrong girl for his underhanded or maybe heavy-handed tactics. Roping Ria in to help only got me more worked up.

"I have to go," I said.

Truly, I needed to go and start looking for new premises. No way did I want Jared Turner as a landlord—not after everything that had happened between us.

I put down the phone with a sense of resignation.

I looked around the studio. It was just beginning to take shape. My creative flair was bringing it to life so it would be a great pity to leave.

However, I would have to start the hunt for new premises another day and I wasn't sure where exactly I would get the energy to do that. But for today, I had pressing ideas I needed to get down on paper and some wallpaper to order for an apartment that needed to be staged for the resale market. This whole new very trying situation with Jared would just have to wait.

But apparently, Jared did not share my opinion about waiting because, just as I was thinking of closing up for the afternoon to go and collect Josh from school, he walked into the reception area.

"What are you doing here?"

The words were out before I could truly acknowledge my reaction to the rugged good looks that had not faded in the weeks since I had last seen him.

"If the mountain won't come to me, then obviously I have to come to the mountain."

He spoke slowly and he had an exaggerated resigned look about him.

I rolled my eyes, although secretly I couldn't deny that my reaction to him was still as alive as it had always been. Perhaps I even longed to be back in those arms. But right then there was still too many unresolved issues between us.

Jared looked around the room silently and I was suddenly nervous.

What if he didn't like what I'd done to the place? My lease hadn't said anything about not changing the décor.

"It's looking good," he said.

"What are you doing here, Jared?"

"Do you need to ask?"

I watched as he took a few steps forward. I moved back nervously.

So this is what it would be like to be possessed I thought as he reached out and took my arm, and slowly pulled me towards him.

"I know you're still mad at Ria and me, but really we didn't mean any harm."

"You know what they say about the way to hell being paved with good intentions."

"Have you been living in hell since we last met?"

"No."

"Well, I have," he said. "At least it sure feels like it. I miss you, Shaniah. I know I'm always going away, but that's just because I of all the issues I told you about the last time we met. I can't even begin to tell you how stressful things have been."

"Any reasonable guy would have at least tried to put me in the picture from the beginning," I mumbled as his lips drew closer to mine.

"I'm not known for my reasonableness." He said as his lips descended.

I sighed as his lips made contact and I reached up to increase the contact because I'd been missing this. Truly, I felt totally alive for the first time in weeks.

"Well, if you keep that up, I might have to consider forgiving you," I said when I finally managed to pull my lips away.

"We have a lot of catching up to do," he said as his lips descended again and I thought of the couch in the consulting room at the back. Now would be as good a time as any to test out just how comfortable it really was.

But I resisted the urge because from now on I was going to play hard to get. Being too free and easy with my favors had meant that I hadn't been to assess the situation properly with Jared. You need a clear head in order to keep your wits about you when you're entering new territory and I had failed to do that.

I'd been too keen to jump on Jared's hot body at the first opportunity. It had been a miracle that I had resisted him as long as I had. The result was that I had come away scorched by the heat of that contact.

This time around, I was going to let him woo me the good old-fashioned way. From now on, Mr. Turner, you could have the immense pleasure of wining and dining me and we could just wait to see where that approach would take us.

CHAPTER TWENTY-THREE

Three weeks later I was still waiting for Jared to call.

I know—I know—some things never change.

But this time, I knew exactly where he was. He'd been updating me daily with calls and face time and although I'd been waiting all day for his call, I was coping with his absence a lot better than I'd thought possible.

Jared was currently in Florida. He'd wanted me to go with him, but Josh had school and I couldn't just pick up and run every time a gorgeous man asked me to go on an all-expense paid trip, could I?

I wasn't sure how I would cope long-term with this *'now you see me now you don't'* type of relationship. However, I was willing to give it a try with Jared.

Josh and I had just settled down to watch TV for the evening when the doorbell rang.

"Josh, look through the window and see who that is love, I'm too tired to get up."

Josh ran to the door and came back excited, "You'd better go see, Mom."

"Well, who is it?"

"Mom, just go."

I was annoyed that I had to relinquish my comfortable spot on the sofa but, as I wasn't in the mood for guessing games, I went.

Jared stood on the doorstep looking as sexy as hell and equally pleased with himself as he was partially hidden behind the largest bouquet of roses I'd ever seen.

"Jared!"

I opened the door and hurled myself at him.

"You're not due back until next week," I said finding his lips despite the flowers.

"I figured you wanted me to come and get you," he grinned at me and kissed me back, hard.

"You could just be right," I said.

I took the flowers and had barely put them on the hall table when he grabbed me and lifted me clean off my feet and continued to drop several kisses on my lips.

"Ew...gross!"

I'd clean forgotten about Josh.

Jared put me down and grinned down at him.

"You must be Josh, I've heard a lot about you."

Josh blinked up at Jared from behind his glasses. He wasn't used to seeing me in any man's arms. Todd had never done public displays of affection.

"Hello," said Josh solemnly,

"This is Jared," I smiled down at Josh. Jared was still holding my hand.

"Are you going to marry my mom?" Josh asked in the same solemn tone.

"That is a distinct possibility," said Jared meeting Josh's formality.

"Can I play on my Play Station, Mom?"

"Of course, darling."

Josh trotted off, apparently unconcerned that he might have just talked himself into a stepdad.

"Well, that was easy," Jared said.

"Don't take too much notice," I said, a bit embarrassed. "He asks everybody that. I think he's just interested in trading me off to the highest bidder!"

"Lucky me," Jared said drily, "Note to self: remember to make an honest woman out of Shaniah before some random stranger beats me to it."

"Don't force yourself."

"It's no problem at all," he grinned. "Of course, while you're waiting for me to dwell on the prospect of marriage, you could always ask me nicely; I might just say yes."

"Well, it all depends on how well we connect physically," I whispered, "I mean, it's been so long that I can't quite remember, and a girl just can't afford to take chances that things won't be great, you know."

Jared grinned and edged me towards the stairs. "Do you think your son will notice if I whisk you off upstairs to remind you?"

"You'll have to control yourself," I said. "I can't just ask him to leave home at the great age of eight so that I can have my wicked way with you."

"Are you sure he isn't ready to go to college yet?"

I giggled, "Good luck with that. I'll be lucky to get him through high school. You'll just have to settle for watching my movie with me."

"Or maybe I can take you and Josh for a nice meal. You can also both come out to meet my daughter real soon," he said, "like maybe tomorrow?"

"She's living with you now?"

"She's coming for a visit and then she'll move back permanently next month."

"That would be really nice," I said. "Josh has been longing for a sibling."

And then I worried about saying that because he hadn't exactly asked me to marry him, had he?

I still hadn't specifically told him how much I'd been longing for a baby, but no doubt Ria had already prepared him somewhat by spilling the beans on my baby-making plans.

I smiled enigmatically at Jared. I decided there and then that I would give him exactly one week to propose properly and if he didn't, then I had no reservation about taking the lead in that regard.

Okay, so I had been a bit of a commitment-phobe in the past but that didn't mean I was a fool. It hadn't exactly been easy to meet a man I actually wanted to date more than once and, having achieved the impossible, I wasn't about to throw it away. I really couldn't even imagine attempting another ten internet dates!

I entwined my fingers with Jared's and led him through to the family room.

Maybe I'd marry him first, or maybe I'd just have the baby—who knew what we'd decide to do! Maybe my thirst for motherhood would be quenched once we got married and we had his daughter to care for.

I leaned forward and kissed Jared tenderly on his lips.

It was really a delicious thought that the possibilities were limitless with this man.

"Have I told you lately that I love you?" I whispered.

"Actually, I think you've been falling down a little in that department," he mumbled against my lips.

I sighed deeply and relaxed into his kiss.

Considering I'd met him on what was probably a dodgy internet site that I'd spent years avoiding, Aaron Jared Turner was more than okay.

ABOUT THE AUTHOR

Leah Holden is a mother, teacher and mentor. She has also been an advocate for many of her students with learning disabilities. Leah began writing at an early age and although she has written many short stories, Ten Dates and Counting is her first full length romance novel. When she isn't teaching or writing, she enjoys gardening and collecting antiques. Leah spends most of her time between Toronto and the UK. She can also be found at www.leahholden.com. She is currently working on her next romance novel.

www.ingramcontent.com/pod-product-compliance
Lightning Source LLC
Chambersburg PA
CBHW050930120626
46552CB00001B/133